Desperate to escape his nearness, his touch, his heat, Jane stepped back until she felt cold glass penetrating the fabric of her gown. Only Seth followed, caging her in.

He slid long fingers over her cheek, sparking a fire in her blood that forced the air from her mouth in a hiss.

The calluses of his palm rasped her skin as he gazed down at her, the dark centers of his eyes glowing. "Are you real? Or some enchantress?"

His hot look robbed her of breath.

"Why do you look at me so?" His hoarse voice scraped over her nerves.

Hysteria bubbled up inside her. *Because I loved you. Once. When I knew you. When you knew me.*

She didn't know what undid her more, the heat of his gaze or the way his touch made her come alive after years of living numb.

Other **AVON ROMANCES**

Coming Soon

And Don't Miss These
ROMANTIC TREASURES
from Avon Books

SOPHIE JORDAN

One Night With You

AVON
An Imprint of HarperCollinsPublishers

This is a work of fiction. Names, characters, places, and incidents are products of the author's imagination or are used fictitiously and are not to be construed as real. Any resemblance to actual events, locales, organizations, or persons, living or dead, is entirely coincidental.

AVON BOOKS
An Imprint of HarperCollins*Publishers*
10 East 53rd Street
New York, New York 10022-5299

Copyright © 2008 by Sharie Kohler
ISBN: 978-0-06-133926-4
www.avonromance.com

First Avon Books paperback printing: January 2008

Avon Trademark Reg. U.S. Pat. Off. and in Other Countries, Marca Registrada, Hecho en U.S.A.
HarperCollins® is a registered trademark of HarperCollins Publishers.

Printed in the U.S.A.

10 9 8 7 6 5 4 3 2 1

In loving memory of Sara Jane Israel.

Acknowledgments

To my critique partners: Ane, Christy, Robyn, and Tera. Thank you for your patience and support . . . to say nothing of your efforts in helping me polish this book into shining condition.

And to Maura and May: thank you for your unflagging enthusiasm and belief in me. I've learned so much from both of you.

My soul thirsteth for thee,
my flesh longeth for thee
in a dry and thirsty land,
where no water is.

—Psalms 63:1

One Night With You

Chapter 1

Lady Jane Guthrie stared out her bedchamber window, her gaze following a lone carriage as it rattled down the dark and silent street. A great lumbering beast, it crawled through the night fog, its inhabitants unknown, its destination unknown, yet she wished she were aboard it, sheltered within its depths.

The evening wind tossed the curtains at the carriage window in a taunting farewell. She splayed her hand over the glass, cool and lifeless against her palm, watching as the carriage turned the square and disappeared from sight. Her stomach churned as the fading clatter of hooves echoed dully in the night.

Gradually, she exerted more pressure, pressing harder, as if she could break through the glass and transport herself away, outside—far from Desmond and Chloris and her three fractious nieces who delighted in heaping abuse upon her.

A shaky laugh spilled from her lips, filling the silence. Unreasonable expectations. A year well past mourning yet here she was, a glorified servant in the home she had once managed.

The door opened behind her with a soft creak. She jerked back from the window and spun around, fearing her thoughts had conjured forth demons to stop her night's plans, to put her in place—in her cage. Her pulse beat furiously at her throat and her hand flew to her neck as if she might still the clamoring beat.

Anna stepped inside the room, her middle-aged face wreathed in a broad smile. Jane dropped her hand and drew a calming breath, the thud of her heart quieting in her ears.

"Mr. Billings has left for his club and Mrs. Billings retired to her rooms for the evening." Anna paused, her great bosom lifting with excited breath. "It's time."

Jane nodded, her heart loosening inside her chest with the knowledge that Desmond had gone, that the same roof did not cover their heads. No risk of running into him in the corridor, of suffering his lecherous, insolent stare.

Nothing would stop her. Nothing barred her

from seizing an evening out, a night of freedom. Tonight belonged to her. Even if the rest of her life did not.

Jane pressed a hand to her stomach to still the dance of butterflies there. "Heavens," she breathed, "you would think I've never attended a ball before."

"Well. It has been an age," Anna rejoined with a wry twist to her lips.

Jane turned to the cheval mirror to inspect her appearance one final time. The pale blue gown had been buried in the back of her wardrobe behind all the mourning rags. She hardly recognized herself in anything save dismal black crepe and paramatta.

"It's good to see you in color again." Anna stroked her chin thoughtfully. "But something is missing."

Jane lifted an eyebrow in question.

Anna opened a small lacquered chest sitting on top of Jane's dressing table. Few items filled it. Her husband had not been one to lavish her with jewelry. At least not for her.

She possessed only one item of value. This, Anna pulled from a black velvet pouch, the stones sparkling as though lit from a light within. "Here you are."

Jane brushed her fingers over the necklace, smiling in fond memory at the grandmother who had left it to her. Her fingers caressed the lustrous stones. If possible, they seemed brighter than she recalled. The canary diamonds felt warm, almost electric. Their age-worn surface glided seductively against her palm and the gold chain winked in the light. As a girl, she had believed any woman wearing it could only look beautiful.

"Very well." Turning, she lifted her hair, the tendrils silky smooth. Anna had pulled back the heavy mass with two jet-studded combs and arranged it to trail down her back. Usually coarse as a horse's mane and wound tightly into a knot, her hair felt like it belonged to another woman.

"There now." Her maid stepped back to survey her handiwork. "You don't look the crow anymore."

Jane eyed herself in the mirror, stroking the diamonds weighing heavily at her throat. Her fingers moved from the necklace to the blue sleeve of her dress, rubbing the satin between her fingers. "For one night at least."

"You'll wear color again," Anna vowed in a voice hard with resolve, her dark eyes glinting beneath thick gray brows.

Jane forced herself to nod. Desmond's leering

4

face flashed across her mind and her stomach dipped. If her brother-in-law had his way, she would never wear color again, nor would she rejoin Society.

A deep sigh welled up from her chest. One year, four months, and ten days had passed since Marcus's death, but Desmond remained as determined as ever to sequester her from Society, to keep her dancing attendance to the demanding needs of his daughters . . . and staring at her with what she had come to consider *the look*.

The look reminded her of a gorilla she'd once seen at a zoological exhibition. The beast had swayed behind its bars, his eyes liquid pools of yearning, eager to break loose and devour her.

Anna interrupted her musings. "Come now. Your friends are waiting, and you've an evening of dancing ahead."

Dancing. Jane wondered if she remembered how. She had not been much of a dancer when Marcus lived, spending most of her time on the edge of ballrooms with dowagers long resigned to each other, and matrons preferring each other to the husbands they suffered at home.

Shaking off the cheerless realization that her state of widowhood had not greatly altered her social patterns, she moved to the door, determined to thwart her insufferable relations if only in this small act. Tonight was not about dancing or leisure entertainments. Tonight was an exercise in rebellion. To prove, if only to herself, that she was no one's prisoner, that she alone controlled her life.

"Do try and enjoy yourself. Forget about those little monsters down the hall." Anna settled Jane's cloak about her, giving her shoulder an encouraging squeeze. "You deserve some happiness."

Happiness. Jane let the word roll around in her head, testing it. She had ceased hoping for something as elusive as happiness long ago. For now, for tonight, freedom would satisfy her.

The house was silent as she followed Anna down the servants' stairs. Her feet moved swiftly on the creaking steps.

"I'll see that the door remains unlocked. Here, don't forget this." Anna thrust a black domino into her hand as they reached the back door.

On impulse, Jane embraced her old nurse in the shadows. "Thank you," she murmured, wondering what she would have done without at least one friend within these walls. Anna had kept her sane during those miserable days when her marriage first crumbled. Nineteen, new to Town, new to her role as Lady Guthrie, she had been unprepared for the life her husband introduced her to—a world

6

of glittering hypocrisy that slapped down anyone failing to sparkle. Marcus had been the first to deliver that lesson.

Anna tapped her gently on the chin. "No frowns. I expect to hear you danced and flirted with every gentleman in the room."

Before Jane could respond that flirting was the last thing on her mind—especially since she had no clue *how* to flirt—and that tonight was purely an exercise in freedom, Anna pushed her out into the night.

Like a bird thrust from its nest, she blinked against the thick mist and hovered on the back stoop for a moment, staring down the worn stone steps and wondering if she should perhaps return to the safety of her room.

Where you will remain for all the rest of your days.

The bitter thought barely had time to root before she hurried next door to the massive stone edifice. Having no wish to be seen about at such a late hour, she pulled her hood low and burrowed deep into her cloak, hiding from the soft glow emitted from the street's gaslights as she mounted the steps of her friend's mansion.

The front doors flung wide before Jane even lifted her hand to knock. The Duchess of Shillington stood there, limned in the great foyer's chandelier light, the pale strands in her strawberry blond hair glinting like gold ingots. "I was beginning to fear you changed your mind," Lucy announced.

Just beyond the duchess, her butler shifted from foot to foot, looking chagrined at her commandeering of his duties.

And beyond him stood the Duchess of Derring, a vague smile that could mean anything at all fixed to her face as she leaned against the marble balustrade.

Squaring her shoulders, Jane lied, "I never considered it."

Lucy ushered her inside, sweeping Jane's cloak back from her shoulders even as the butler melted from the foyer, no doubt sensing activities were afoot that need not bear his witness.

Tapping her lip, Lucy assessed her gown with a martial light in her blue-gray eyes. Turning to the Duchess of Derring, she asked with heavy seriousness, "Astrid? What do you think?"

Astrid shrugged. "She looks like any other matron out for the evening."

"My thoughts precisely." Lucy met Jane's gaze squarely. "You cannot wear this."

"You only said that I should not wear black," Jane reminded, feeling the stirrings of annoyance.

"For the purpose of tonight, you must attire yourself in something more"—Lucy's nose wrinkled—"suitable."

Suitable. Jane strongly suspected that Lucy wanted to use a different word. Gathering a fistful of her pale blue skirts, she asked, "How is this unsuitable?"

"It is not—" Lucy stopped, sighed, then tossed a beseeching look to Astrid.

Astrid flicked her dark gaze over Jane, her face mild and unlined with expression. "You're not sufficiently *risqué.*"

"What would you have me wear?" Jane demanded, then gave her head a small shake. "It's of no account. I cannot risk returning home to change. Bryony is a light sleeper. It's a wonder I did not wake the girl when passing her bedroom."

"A swift bludgeon to the head would take care of that," Astrid suggested, eyes unblinking, expression unflappable as ever.

Lucy shot Astrid a quelling glare and propped her hands on her hips. The act opened her ermine-trimmed cloak wide and Jane gasped at her low-cut scarlet gown. The dress hugged her curves indecently.

She pointed speechlessly to Lucy's gown, then looked at Astrid who, with a shrug, parted her own cloak to reveal a diaphanous apricot-colored gown as equally shocking.

"I understand the hostess's chef makes the most delicious lobster pasties," was all Astrid explained.

Food. As usual, everything came down to food with Astrid. It was the one thing her friend openly enjoyed.

"Fear not," Lucy assured. "I have the perfect dress for you."

Jane looked back and forth between their scandalous attire, wariness creeping over her. "What kind of masquerade ball is this?"

Lucy and Astrid exchanged looks and her uneasiness deepened.

"Who is the hostess?" She stared hard at her two friends, compelling one of them to answer.

Not surprisingly, it was Astrid. She lacked the ability or inclination to prevaricate. "Madame Fleur," she stated.

"Madame Fleur?" Jane was well acquainted with the lady's name. All of Britain knew of the famed courtesan. "Why would we wish to attend such an affair? It's bound to be—" she stopped, groping for the correct words. *Scandalous. Outrageous. Sinful.* A strange little thrill coursed through her at the very idea. Functional-proper-widow-Jane would never dare attend such an affair, an insidious little voice whispered in her head.

"I could learn of only one masquerade tonight," Lucy explained. "Besides, I've always been curious about these legendary masques of Madame Fleur. It's bound to be an experience."

"Yes, Bertram was a patron of hers." Astrid's lips twisted with derision. "Why not see where my devoted husband spent my dowry?"

Jane had no doubt *all* their husbands had patronized Madame Fleur's. That their husbands had been less than faithful—had in fact been renowned libertines before and after taking their vows—bonded them from the start.

"What if we're recognized?

Swinging her silk domino, a flutter of scarlet in the air, Lucy insisted, "No one shall know us. We will simply be three masked women among countless others." Snatching Jane's hand, Lucy dragged her up the carpeted stairs. "You were quite ready for adventure when we discussed this a week ago."

"That was before I knew our destination," Jane grumbled.

"Adventure carries risks." Lucy's gaze skimmed Jane again as she pulled her into her lavish bedchamber. "Now. You will never blend in wearing something so modest."

Jane bit her bottom lip, feeling herself relenting. "I wouldn't want to draw undue attention."

"Can we make haste?" Astrid queried. "It's almost midnight. All the best food will be gone."

Tucking Jane's hand in her elbow, Lucy led Jane into her dressing room. "You shall see. It will be a grand adventure. Who knows? Perhaps some charming gentleman will sweep you off your feet and carry you far away from your wretched relations."

Astrid snorted.

Jane's heart fluttered with panic at the mere idea. She didn't want to marry anyone. Once had been enough. And she wasn't the sort to engage in a casual dalliance. Especially with the type of men likely attending a courtesan's ball.

In fact, she couldn't understand widows who took lovers. She had never found anything particularly exciting about the marriage bed. On the contrary.

And as for love . . .

Well, she had never been that fortunate.

Chapter 2

Seth Rutledge, the Earl of St. Claire, stood rigidly at the edge of the crowded ballroom, hands folded behind his back. His nostrils twitched against the overpowering aroma of perfume, longing for the scent of sea and wind as he watched Madame Fleur approach, hips swaying in a manner that brought to mind rolling waves. Her welcoming smile below her peacock-feathered domino faltered when she caught sight of his face.

She stopped abruptly in the middle of the ballroom, her heavily rouged mouth sagging a bit. Her startled expression, followed quickly by a look of pity, was all too familiar.

Seth growled low in his throat. Bloody hell, how he loathed that look.

For a fleeting moment he wished for a mask of

his own. But he gave the thought only a moment, forbidding it to root in his head, to weaken him. Forcing his chin higher, he better exposed his face to the light.

The courtesan recovered and resumed her smile with a finesse that he would expect from one of her legendary reputation. Stopping before him, she brought with her the sweetly sick bouquet of gardenias, roses, and a dozen other floral fragrances he could not distinguish. Acrid as gunpowder, the scent of her stung the inside of his nose. Yet he was glad to see her. Whores didn't judge.

She pressed close, granting him a view down the stiff brocade of her bodice, revealing that she wore nothing underneath.

"It's been too long, *mon cher*, why have you not come to see me sooner?" she purred in an accent that was decidedly not French. He wasn't certain of Fleur's exact origins, but he would wager Seven Dials.

"I arrived in Town only yesterday."

He had departed his family's estate to accomplish the inevitable. At eight and twenty, he owed it to Julianne to marry and provide an heir. His sister needed family. Someone other than himself.

Ironically enough, he had survived pirates, war, pestilence, disease in foreign lands—survived only to return home and find his brother dead. From an ague, no less. No doubt his father cursed that quirk of fate from the grave.

It had been no secret that Seth's father purchased his commission in the hopes that he would never return. Rotten luck that Albert had died, leaving the wrong son to marry and bear responsibility for the family.

Precautions had to be taken to assure his cousin would not get his claws on St. Claire Priory—or his sister—again. If something befell Seth, the right sort of wife would see to that. The right sort of wife would safeguard his sister against villains like Harold. And the darkness. Seth fought to swallow the sudden sourness coating his mouth. He would protect Julianne from the darkness that engulfed her. The darkness Seth had created. He owed her that much.

He needed a bride unlike the female he had let creep beneath his skin years ago. A female not revolted by the sight of him. If such a lady existed.

Shaking off his musings, he dipped his finger between the swells of Fleur's breasts.

"Hmm, I like this fierce face of yours," she purred. "My very own pirate." She trailed a long nail down the white-ridged scar that slashed across his face and cut into his upper lip.

He shied away, unused to the contact, but bemused that she would think he resembled a pirate when it had very nearly been a pirate to cut his face to ribbons. Half a breath to the left and the Portuguese slave smuggler would have had his eye.

Fleur lifted her brows meaningfully. "I know just the thing to celebrate your return. What I have in mind may take hours. Days. Weeks."

"I'm afraid I cannot linger in Town. I've an errand to dispense and then I'm off." Errand. An adequate description of his task.

"To rusticate in the wilds?" She made a pffting sound. "You mean you're not interested in renewing old friendships?" Her eyes shimmered with a wicked light. Only five years older than himself, she had aged remarkably well. Although her hair was an improbable shade of red, her face and body were as tight and smooth as the first day they met. "I'm confident I can provide you with a reason to linger." Her eyes locked with his, hot with promise, gleaming with a desire that had quite undone him as a lad. Him and Albert both.

And yet little moved him now.

"It's been a long time, *mon cher*," she continued, "and you've grown into quite the man." Her heavy-lidded gaze held his eyes, hot with promise.

"I'm ugly as sin and you know it." If she didn't make her living stroking the egos of gentlemen, she'd react as all other women did and steer clear of his menacing mien.

Her plump, bejeweled hand brushed the front of his trousers, challenging his words.

"What are we waiting for, then?" he asked.

Determination had brought him to her. Determination to feel something, anything. He may want nothing to do with tender sentiments, but sex was something else entirely. Especially with a partner who did not have to close her eyes as he leaned over her.

Sex could make him forget. Make him feel again. Even if only for a short while.

His gaze flicked to the many alcoves surrounding the ballroom. Moans and cries floated from behind the scarlet damask drapes, mingling with the music of the orchestra. He doubted there was a room in the house not already occupied. Even the dancing couples appeared to be more in the midst of fornication than a waltz. Distaste filled him at the dissolute scene, oddly echoing the feelings he had after a battle, standing aboard ship and looking out over the carnage.

"*Mon cher*, give me but a moment." Her eyes raked him hungrily.

Seth's lips twisted in a smile. The scar at his lip tightened and pulled, and he quickly released the smile, letting his mouth fall into a mild line. Grasping her fingers, he raised them to his lips, watching for a sign of revulsion to cross her face. Fleur lifted herself eagerly toward his hand.

"It would be a delight," he murmured, aggravated at the desultory tone of his voice. Here stood a woman ready and willing. Why did he not feel excitement, desire? Something. Anything. Why did he not *feel*?

"You remember the lavender salon? It is for my use alone." Her tongue slowly traced her rouged lips. "I shall be along shortly. A few matters require my attention before I can claim the long, uninterrupted hours I desire with you." Her kohl-lined eyes slid over him in heated perusal.

He kissed the back of her hand. "It will be my pleasure."

Anything to put off returning to the thick silence of his house across Town, to keep from staring into the dark and thinking about the unrelenting night that ruled his sister—the darkness that he had forced on her in the reckless days of his youth. But that was his cross to bear. One of many.

Taking a wife was the least he owed Julianne. And it wasn't as if marriage would affect him to any great degree. It was not as if he were holding out for someone special, someone to love.

He simply required a bride with expectations similar to his.

His hand lifted to stroke the scar splitting his top lip, fingering the skin-puckered tear as he contemplated the nameless, faceless female with a heart as remote as his own.

Chapter 3

The iridescent gold gown was a far cry from the modest blue she had worn at the start of the evening. Jane tugged at the bodice, hoping to pull it higher. Her face burned from the way the men ogled her. Not only her, but every woman in the room. They assessed and surveyed like hawks searching the horizon for the choicest morsel.

Costumed gentlemen lurked everywhere: Cupids, Caesars, pirates. They ogled every woman in attendance as if they had the God-given right, as if every female in the room were present for their pleasure, to be touched and fondled at whim. And perhaps they were. None appeared to be ladies overly concerned with their virtue.

The gold diamonds warmed the flesh of Jane's bosom. Her hand brushed the stones every so often, taking comfort in their presence—the only extravagance, the only item of value someone thought her worthy to possess. They fed her courage in the face of so many wolves. Not for the first time, she wondered if she had made a mistake in coming here.

"Taste this," Astrid said, offering a lobster pasty. "They're divine."

Shaking her head, Jane tugged on the dress again. "It doesn't fit," she grumbled.

"It fits," Astrid announced blithely, chewing with an intense look of appreciation, oblivious to the admiring stares sent her way. With her fair skin and honey hair, she looked like a sun-kissed peach in her apricot gown. Hardly the coldly reserved duchess most of the *ton* knew her to be—that even Jane had first thought her to be.

Astrid held up another pasty. "What about this one?" She squinted at it, her dark brows dipping. "Appears to be stuffed with spinach. And perhaps artichoke, um, no, truffles . . ." Biting into it, she moaned with approval, the uninhibited sound rather odd coming from such an austere woman.

Jane raised her voice to be heard over the din. "No, thank you."

Somewhere on the dance floor, a woman squealed in loud delight. Jane looked up, watching as a gentleman tossed the lady over his shoulder and carried her off into one of the curtained alcoves edging the ballroom.

"Astrid," she began, her gaze darting about the ballroom uneasily, trying to ignore the gentleman not two yards away who leered at her, licking his lips as if she were a bit of dessert he would like to sample. "Where is Lucy?"

"There." Astrid nodded to the dance floor, looking up from her plate briefly.

Jane turned, watching as Lucy whirled past in the arms of a pot-bellied Viking. She frowned at the way the Viking clutched Lucy close, his hand skating down her spine, inching dangerously close to her derrière. With admirable composure, Lucy grasped his hand and lifted it higher on her back.

Jane shook her head. This was scarcely what she had imagined when her friends proposed an evening out. Shaking her head she looked away, catching sight of a gentleman at the other end of the table as he fed a woman a morsel from his plate, thrusting his entire finger into her mouth as he did so.

Heat crawled up her face and neck, burning the tips of her ears as the woman suckled his finger as one would a stick of peppermint. Forcing her gaze away, she muttered, "This is not what I had in mind—"

"I warned Lucy you would be frightened."

Frightened. The heat in her cheeks grew scalding at the thought of her friends discussing her possible unwillingness to remain in such a cesspit as somehow a deficiency—a lack of courage. Jane the mouse, her sister had always called her.

Jane inched closer to Astrid as a man wearing a toga slid past, using his proximity to trail his pudgy fingers down the length of her bare arm. Shivering, she tucked her arm close to her side. "This has nothing to do with fear and everything to do with good sense."

"Hmm," Astrid offered in reply. Jane was uncertain, but the sound may have been in approval of the tea cake she chewed.

Jane propped a hand on her hip and glared at Astrid. "Don't you find this all a little"—she groped for the right word— "unnerving?"

"Unnerving?" Astrid angled her head as if in heavy contemplation. Her dark eyes scanned the crowded ballroom before looking back to Jane. "Is that not a convoluted way of saying frightened?" Shrugging, she took another bite.

"Semantics," Jane snapped, searching again among the throng for a glimpse of Lucy's strawberry blond hair, convinced that talking to her wouldn't be half so vexing.

Her gaze skipped over faces. Then she saw . . . something, someone, a profile of a man—*a ghost.*

Her heart jerked, a painful leap in her chest at the achingly familiar fall of brown hair over a wide brow. Dancers whirled in her line of vision. Gasping, she craned her head, leaned to the side, and tried to catch another glimpse. But he was gone. A name whispered through her head like the flutter of a breeze.

Shaking her head, she shoved the whisper from her head and resumed her search for Lucy, at last spotting her. The Viking trailed his hand down the arch of her neck, catching the fiery curl draped over her shoulder and bringing it to his nose. Even across the ballroom, Lucy's cringe was visible.

Jane felt a pang of guilt knowing that tonight's escapade was for *her* benefit, so that she could experience a bit of freedom. And her friend endured that jackanape's paws all over her. *For her.*

"Enough is enough. We're leaving."

Turning, she set her glass of punch on a nearby table with a decisive thud. Standing on her tiptoes, she craned her neck to signal Lucy.

"Hello, my dears."

Jane swung around and her heart shuddered to a painful stop.

The blood ran cold in her veins. Her mouth went slack as she stared into familiar features—thin lips set in a face bloated and fatigued from a lifetime of overimbibing. Had her thoughts somehow conjured this devil before her?

At his club, indeed. The wretch.

Astrid sputtered on her drink and reached for Jane's arm.

"You all right there?" Desmond asked, patting Astrid's back.

Nodding, Astrid pressed the back of her hand to her mouth, the fingers of her other hand tightening about Jane's arm. Her eyes, wide and shocked in her cream-colored domino, collided with Jane's.

Ever so slowly, Jane inched back a step, then another.

Astrid, as though sensing her intent, released her arm.

"Where are you off to, my dear?" Desmond snatched her hand before she could disappear in the crowd and shoved his face alarmingly close to hers. "Something dashed familiar about you." His fingers stroked the inside of her arm in small circles. "Have we met?"

"No," she rasped, heart thundering against her ribs.

His thin lips stretched into a leer. "Must be my heart recognizing its own match, then."

Jane swallowed the bile that rose in her throat. "F—forgive me, but I was just leaving," she managed to get out, relieved at the strangled, unfamiliar sound of her voice.

"You can't leave without first granting me a dance," he insisted, tucking her against his side.

She opened her mouth to object, and then closed it with a snap, too fearful that he would identify her voice. Stiff and silent, she allowed him to pull her onto the dance floor, trying to shrink into herself and make herself small, unrecognizable.

Through whirling figures, she caught a glimpse of Astrid's dismayed gaze. Lucy soon joined her, and together they watched her with Desmond as though they witnessed some freakish exhibition at a carnival.

Desmond's hand slid lower, urging her closer. Her stomach churned as he rubbed his cheek against hers, his fetid breath hot and moist in her ear.

"You are certain we have not met before?" her brother-in-law asked.

Did he know? Did he toy with her?

She swallowed hard and fast, heart hammering wildly in her chest, a caged bird desperate for escape.

Her voice emerged, strained and hoarse, thankfully still unrecognizable. "One's identity is secret at a masquerade."

"Ah, torment me then," he said in a pouting voice that reminded her very much of any one of his daughters when they did not get their way.

"I'm sure I'll work it out." He maneuvered her more snugly against him, fitting her to him and rocking her against his pelvis, his reed thin legs sliding between hers. She closed her eyes in a long-suffering blink.

The irony of her situation left an acrid taste in her mouth. For over a year, she had managed to stay out of Desmond's clutches, knowing he saw her as some sort of trophy to be won—his late brother's wife to be bedded and conquered. And here she found herself, trapped in his arms at a courtesan's ball. Instead of freedom, she suddenly felt caged.

With surprising nimbleness for a man who spent most of his time at cards and drinking, Desmond swept her from the dance floor and down a long corridor. Her feet slid over the slick marble, unable to gain purchase as he dragged her. She tried to peel his fingers from her wrist, but they clung like a creeping vine.

Her voice squeaked with indignation. "What are you—"

He pushed her against a wall, shocking her into silence. The bulge of his belly crushed her, his skinny knee shoving between her thighs through the many folds of her skirts.

His fingers traced her lips and the stink of fish and onions wafted to her nose. With a cringe, she recalled his penchant for using his hands while eating.

His touch changed, became urgent, fierce. He pinched her mouth, silencing her save for her hiss of pain.

"Enough. No more maidenly protests. Only one kind of woman would come here. I'm not going to do anything that hasn't already been done to you." His lips twisted into a semblance of a grin. "Only I'll likely do it better."

Releasing her face, he grasped her wrists and forced them over her head, thrusting his hips against hers in an emulation of sex.

Tugging fiercely on her hands, she bit out, "Why don't you release me and find someone who appreciates your efforts?"

His features twisted. "You've quite the mouth on you. Perhaps I'll put it to better use."

His hands tightened on her wrists until her hands grew numb and bloodless. She whimpered as he lowered his mouth to hers. Panic rose, swirling hotly in her blood.

Recognizing that her protests weren't getting her anywhere, she decided to try another course. However much it turned her stomach.

Meekly, she submitted to his kiss, suffering his fishy tongue in her mouth, allowing him to think he had won her over. After a moment, she broke free and murmured coyly, "You cannot mean for us to engage in a liaison here in the corridor?"

With a slow satisfied smile, he dragged her down the corridor. "I know a room."

"Why not fetch us drinks?" she coaxed. "A bit of cheese? Fruit?"

He paused, blinking small, feral eyes at her.

"I find"—she swallowed to stop herself from choking on the words—"love play makes me famished." Forcing her voice into a low, seductive pitch, she tempted him further. "And nothing loosens my inhibitions more than spirits."

He stared at her lips for a long moment before blurting, "Rum punch, then?"

"Yes," she agreed, nodding hastily, so relieved that she had convinced him to leave. "I'll wait right here."

With an obliging dip of his head, and one final lascivious look, he spun on his heels.

She was on the verge of moving when he spun back around.

"Don't move from that spot," he admonished. "I shall be watching to see if you return to the ballroom."

Then he was gone, swallowed up by the throng of revelers edging the mouth of the corridor.

She had only a moment. Not enough time to plan a solid escape. With his warning ringing in her ears, she darted into the nearest room as if the soles of her slippers were afire, hoping to find a way out through a terrace door.

Once within the room, she shut the door and leaned against it, inhaling deeply as she attempted to still the wild beating of her heart. The door's firm length at her back—a much-needed barrier to Desmond and the revelry beyond—offered some measure of solace, but she knew she couldn't tarry.

It took a moment for her eyes to adjust to the room's gloom. Once they did, it was to behold a scene primed for seduction.

A fire crackled in the hearth, casting entrancing shadows on the plum papered walls. Pillows were scattered about the room on the chaises and sofas. A great lambskin rug lay invitingly before the hearth. The brilliant fabrics gleamed enticingly in the firelight, the colors more vibrant than anything that decorated her home. *Home.* For all the years she had lived at the Guthrie townhouse, she had never felt she belonged, had never felt permitted to make her own mark.

Shaking off her thoughts, she looked to the far wall—and her heart plummeted. There was no terrace door. A single large window looked out at the dark night.

Hurrying forward she fumbled with the latch, only to find it wouldn't budge. With a small cry, she slapped her palms against the window, pushing against the thick panes of glass as if she could somehow will the night to open to her.

"Blast!" Biting her lip, she considered her options.

If she left the room, she risked running into Desmond. Yet she could not remain here to be discovered. Her gaze landed on a pewter figurine of Lady Godiva riding naked atop a stallion with impossibly large genitalia. She glanced back to the window.

Heat flaming her cheeks, she lifted the figurine off the small lacquered table. With a growl of determination, she clenched her fingers around the cold pewter, its weight a solid comfort in her hand. Hauling back her arm, she sucked in a breath, deciding to smash her way to freedom through the window.

A voice stopped her, rumbling over the air and sliding through her to spiral in her belly like an infusion of spiced rum.

"I happen to know that there is a perfectly good door to this room."

Chapter 4

Whirling around, Jane let the figurine slide through her fingers to thud at her feet. Its heavy fall mimicked the drop of her heart to the soles of her slippers as she gaped at the shadow of the man who shared her sanctuary.

She opened her mouth to tell the stranger exactly what she thought of men who lurked in dark corners and announced themselves in a manner that only produced terror in unsuspecting ladies.

But the words died on her lips as he unfolded his great length from a chair tucked in the room's corner and stepped from the shadows. Her gaze narrowed on his face.

The face of a ghost.

Her hand flew to her mouth, doing a poor job of stifling her gasp. Nerves taut as a harpsichord string, she stared. Not a ghost. A man.

He wore no domino, had donned no disguise. A white scar, stark and livid on his swarthy skin, slashed the left side of his face, cleaving his top lip and disappearing into his mouth.

Even disfigured, his was a face she would never forget.

Her lips moved, but no sound emerged. She watched, horrified—elated—as he advanced on her with slow, measured steps. An invisible hand squeezed her heart at the sight of a face that had once been too beautiful for mortal man, a face left to the realm of poets and dreams. A face her memory had refused to release.

She stared at this new face of his. Scarred, hard-edged, unsmiling. A tremble snaked over her.

His name whispered across her mind again. A name she had not spoken in years. A name she pushed from her thoughts daily, allowing it into her head only at night, in her dreams. *Seth*.

He bent and picked up the figurine she had dropped. Without a word, he set it back on the table, his intense gaze never wavering from her face. The hot look in his deep-set eyes gave her a jolt. He had never looked at her in such a fashion.

Then it struck her that he did not recognize her—not masked—and the tightness in her chest lessened as relief swept through her. Her hand flew to her mask. She drew an even breath at the feel of black silk stretched over stiff brocade. Still there.

Cocking his head, he gestured behind him and repeated, "There is a perfectly good door."

She managed a quick nod, drinking in the sight of him. He was taller than she remembered. His skin darker, his shock of brown hair sun-streaked. There was a hardness to his mouth and eyes that had not been there before. Yet she would remember those molten brown eyes anywhere. The same eyes invaded her dreams to this day.

Broad of shoulder and lean of hip, he towered over the room's dainty furniture, his carriage erect, rigid, as though he stood braced at the helm of a ship. His dark jacket and trousers contrasted sharply to the room's plums and lavenders, heightening his masculinity.

She supposed she should have forgotten him over the years. Should not have followed news of the war in Canton so closely. Should not feel so shaken at the sight of him now.

"Can you not speak?" he inquired, his voice deeper, richer than she remembered.

She nodded, forcing her lips to form a whispered reply. "Yes."

Gazing at him, old feelings stirred to life in the pit of her belly.

Her sister may not have wanted him—at least not within the bounds of matrimony—but Jane had. She had wanted him with every fiber of her being. Had looked at him every day for as long as she could remember and prayed that he would feel for her what he felt for her sister. She would have risked her parents' wrath, risked anything, everything, for him to love her back. Only his love had been reserved for Madeline. Not Jane. Never her.

Not then and certainly not now.

She pressed a hand to her face, her skin disturbingly hot against her palm as she commanded herself to cling to that particular reality and not get swept away by the sight of him, ambrosia to her long-starved heart.

"Yes?" he echoed, his voice low, a drag of velvet against her overheated skin. "Then you merely choose not to?" His gaze prowled her face. "A woman with no wish to speak? How singular."

Her throat constricted as he neared, stepping so close the smell of him filled her nose. Leather and some unidentifiable cologne, earthy and wild, reminding her faintly of nutmeg. Her eyes drifted shut.

A thousand images flashed through her mind. A youth spent with Seth. Riding, swimming, apple picking in the fall, holly gathering in the winter. He had been her life's one pleasure. More constant than the parents who preferred her sister to her—and who reminded her of the fact daily.

The moment everything changed revived itself in her mind, fresh and crisp as yesterday. Over the years she had wondered if she could have done something, anything, to prevent it.

Madeline did not usually accompany them on their jaunts, preferring the indoors, but for some reason she had joined Jane and Seth as they wove through apple trees in full bloom, honeybees zipping amid the white, frothy blossoms, the kiss of spring on the air.

Seth and Madeline had lagged behind and Jane had glanced back, her heart surging to her throat at the sight of Seth climbing an apple tree with exceptional vigor, a foolish grin on his face, her younger sister giggling below.

He dropped down from a branch, landing hard on his feet with a sprig of apple blossoms in his hand. With great care, he secured the delicate bundle over Madeline's ear. The most extraordinary look glowed in his eyes. Tenderness, devotion, and desire. All for Madeline.

Something had died within Jane then, a flame sputtering and extinguishing from that single look—a look she had one day prayed to receive, a look he gave to another, her sister.

A shudder washed through Jane and she pushed the unwanted memory to the shadows of her mind with a small shake of her head. Opening her eyes, she found Seth staring intently at her.

"Where'd you go?" he murmured, his eyes dark and probing.

She sucked in a breath and dipped her head, almost afraid he could read her thoughts, glimpse the dark roads her mind traveled. He placed a finger beneath her chin and forced her gaze back up with a single burning touch.

Unable to resist, she leaned into his touch, wanting to feel more than that one finger on her, hungering for what she had missed, what had never been hers.

Surprise flickered in his eyes. His gaze scanned her face, assessing, inquiring with a lift of his slashing black brows. His fingers slid beneath her chin, skimming the soft line of her jaw. A sigh escaped her.

He swallowed visibly, the tendons along his throat working.

Recalling herself, she pulled back before she did something truly foolish. Like forget herself entirely. With a man who would have nothing to do with her if he knew her identity.

Desperate to escape his nearness, his touch, his heat, she stepped back until she felt cold glass penetrating the fabric of her gown.

Only he followed, caging her in, the muscles along his square jaw knotting, rippling beneath the scar. A feverish gleam entered his eyes. He slid long fingers over her cheek, sparking a fire in her blood that forced the air from her mouth in a hiss.

The calluses of his palm rasped her skin as he gazed down at her, the dark centers of his eyes glowing. "Are you real? Or some enchantress?"

His hot look robbed her of breath, especially when her last memory of him contained no such looks. In fact, he had looked at her very little in the end. In the end, she had simply not existed to him.

"Why do you look at me so?" His hoarse voice scraped over her nerves.

Hysteria bubbled up inside her.

Because I loved you. Once. When I knew you. When you knew me.

She didn't know what undid her more, the heat of his gaze or the way his touch made her come alive after years of living numb.

She didn't know, but she didn't dare let herself find out.

And why not? You're no insipid virgin. Why not

experience everything his hot look promised? Everything you've never had? Everything you ever wanted? Would that not be the ultimate exercise in freedom?

Her gaze dropped to his mouth, the lips wide and sensual despite the scar. She leaned forward, letting her breasts graze his chest, imagining tracing her tongue over that corner of his mouth. Her belly clenched.

He didn't know who hid behind the scrap of satin—that *she* hid.

She could embrace anonymity . . . embrace him. One kiss.

One sample and she could experience what she had missed as a girl. And later as a woman. As Marcus's wife.

A bolt of anticipation shot through her, followed by something else. A cold douse of fear. Fear of discovery, fear of stepping outside herself for even a brief moment and doing something so bold. For daring to make long-held dreams a reality.

Swallowing down the thickness in her throat, she gave herself a hard mental shake and let fear win.

Pulling back her shoulders, she stifled a cringe at the feel of cold glass against her bare shoulders and forced herself to resist the dark pull of his gaze.

In as stern a voice as she could manage, she ordered, "Step aside, sir."

Chapter 5

Seth stared at the woman trapped between his chest and the window, commanding himself to move away, to respect her request. But he could not force himself to budge, relishing the feel of her soft curves far too much.

He had watched her with keen interest from the moment she burst into the room.

How could he not? Even if her odd behavior had not attracted his notice, her appearance would have.

He eyed the length of her now—tall, stately, full-bodied. Bloody hell, the woman had curves. More than enough to fill his hands and mouth. His gut tightened with desire.

In the room's gloom, her hair gleamed dark as the night sea, and her eyes, an indeterminate color in her black domino, burned through him with a ferocity he felt in his blood.

He wanted her. Badly.

Even more astonishing, he felt certain she wanted him. Scar and all. Reason enough to keep her trapped in his arms.

His gaze slid over her, a ray of golden light in his arms. "Aurora."

She blinked long lashes. "That's not my name—"

"No? What is your name?"

Her plump lips compressed.

"Then I shall call you Aurora. Fitting, I think." The Goddess of Dawn herself could not dazzle him more.

She gazed up at him with wide-eyed solemnity.

He had never seen a sadder pair of eyes, eyes that called to him, that seemed to . . . *need him*. Against his will, he felt himself sinking, falling under her spell.

Fired by whatever it was about her that moved him, he took her face in both hands and lowered his head, ready to claim her mouth for himself, to see if she tasted as sweet as he imagined.

Small hands pushed at his chest. He stopped, his lips a hairsbreadth from her own.

"Don't," she pleaded, her breath mingling with his, washing through him and thickening the blood in his veins. "Please."

Stepping back, he dragged a hand through his hair. He didn't know what aggravated him more—his irrational desire for a woman he had just met, a veritable stranger, or the fact that he had convinced himself that she could want him, that she could overlook his fierce countenance.

He gestured for her to pass.

She lowered her eyes and slid past him, the scent of apples rushing up to meet him. *Apples*.

Memories assailed him. Sweet memories. Before Julianne's accident. Before Madeline. This woman smelled of home.

The instinct to stop her, to seize and possess her, warred intensely inside him.

She was halfway across the room when the door flung open. A man ambled into the room with a glass in his hand.

"Ah, there you are, my dear. I have your punch."

She stopped abruptly.

Something dark and possessive coiled in Seth's gut as the fop advanced on her.

She shuffled backward until she collided with Seth's chest. His hands came up to close over the warm flesh of her arms. She glanced over her shoulder, her look one of surprise, as though she had forgotten his presence at the other man's arrival.

Seth eyed the other man, vague recognition stirring in the back of his mind.

The fellow returned his stare. "Rutledge? By God, is that you?"

Seth gave a nod of greeting, recalling the man's name. "Billings."

"Heard you'd taken up the title. Didn't realize you were in Town, though." Billings stepped closer, peering closely at his face. "Ack, get that fighting in Canton, did you? Hard luck, that. You were always a favorite with the ladies."

"Slave smugglers," he replied, the point a matter of distinction for him. Taking a scar to impede the illegal trafficking of slaves was infinitely more honorable than taking a scar to enslave a nation to opium.

Billings nodded briskly. "Suppose I should congratulate you then, *Lord St. Claire.*"

"Congratulate me? On my brother's death?" he bit out, suddenly recollecting what a bloody ass Billings had been. He and Albert had been in the same class at school, but Billings had been sulky, always voicing his discontent over his second son status.

Oblivious to any offense he may have given, Billings continued. "Lost my own brother not long ago."

"Sorry to hear that." Seth looked down at the woman who suddenly grew rigid as wood in his hands.

"I wasn't so lucky as you," Billings droned on. "My brother left an heir. Only one, though, so perhaps I'm not without hope."

Seth stared at the weasel before him. Such jackasses abounded among the *ton*, making him wish he still fought on distant shores.

Billings glanced at the drink in his hand. As though suddenly remembering his purpose, his gaze shot back to Aurora.

"Pardon me, did not mean to detain you with idle chatter. Especially with so much more pleasant activities available." Billings moistened his nearly nonexistent lips. "I'll just collect this little tart and be on my way. We'll find another room."

Aurora drove back another step, heedless that she trod over Seth's foot.

Without thinking, Seth flexed his hand around her arm and announced, "I'm afraid not. The lady is unavailable."

"Now see here, Rutledge," Billings blustered, puffing out his chest. "I found her first."

Seth cocked a brow. "And you've lost her."

With a decided amount of force, Billings set the drink down on a marble-topped end table, sending the contents sloshing over the rim. "Fine. There are plenty of other light-skirts about to frig. No need to get proprietary."

Even as he uttered the words, he scoured Aurora with a hungry leer.

Seth stroked her arm in lazy circles, and she shivered.

Quivering with anger, Billings bit out, "Enjoy yourself, Rutledge. I'm sure I'll get another go at her when you're finished."

She flinched in his arms.

A growl rose up from the back of his throat. "I don't think so," Seth grated, wondering at the sudden and fierce protectiveness that surged through him.

With a flare of his nostrils, Billings stormed from the room. The door slammed shut behind him. And they were alone again.

"I take it he was the reason you were contemplating escape through the window?"

She whirled around, her eyes flashing. "I'm no light-skirt!"

"I never said you were," he countered.

She pressed her lips into a mutinous line. "But I'm here. At this ball." She waved a hand. "I'm sure that's what you judge me to be."

"And why should it matter so much what I think?"

She stared at him for a long moment before a nervous laugh escaped her. It was a wholly un-calculated sound that sent a lick of heat spiraling through his stomach. Which was insanity. He was waiting for Fleur to join him, yet he could not stop himself from thinking of ways to seduce the tanta-lizing creature before him.

"It doesn't, of course." Her chin went up an-other notch.

She edged back another step, reminding him of an exotic bird, ready to take flight. He sensed he had her for only a moment more. And for some reason, he found the notion intolerable.

Stepping forward, he grazed his knuckles over her cheek. Her eyes widened, but she did not pull away.

Watching her closely, gauging her expression in the event distaste should emerge at last, he trailed his fingers down her neck, tracing the delicate line of her collarbone.

Dipping his head, he tasted the warm skin of her throat, his tongue licking at the wildly thrumming pulse point, spicy-sweet rum against his tongue.

Her breathing grew harsh. He pulled back to stare into her masked face again. No distaste there. His stomach knotted at the way her eyes consumed him, as if she could see him and not the scar at all, the real him right down to the marrow of his bones.

Absurd, really. No one knew him. Not a single member of his family, alive or dead. Not a soul existed that he could talk to, share his deepest thoughts. But then, no one had ever fit that description. For a brief moment, a face flashed through his head—a young girl with freckles, scraped knees, and a wild mane of hair never pinned in place. *Jane.* They had been friends. Confidantes. His heart twisted. Time changed all.

Yet this woman, this stranger with her large eyes peering at him so intently, so starkly, made him feel oddly connected to her. She felt . . . familiar. She felt like home.

"Why do you look at me as though you know me?" he demanded. "Do you?"

She blinked those wide eyes of hers. "No. Of course not."

And why, he wondered, should he care if she did? If they had met, it had been long ago. It could matter little now. He should be working at seducing her out of that scandalous gown and burying himself to the hilt in her sweet body, quenching the maddening lust she had roused within him. Once he sampled her charms, he would see she was no different from any other woman.

She gave a small shake, as if caught in some kind of daze and needing to jog sense back into herself. Her gaze drifted beyond him, over his shoulder.

Sensing the moment had arrived when she would take flight, he grasped her arms and pulled her to him. Her eyes flared wide and she trembled against his length.

"You don't have to go," Seth murmured, then, incredibly, added, "Please."

Staring at this creature that had awakened desire in him, he felt unbalanced, as if he hovered along a great precipice, waiting to see whether or not he would drop like a stone through the air.

"I can't," she replied in a ragged voice that ripped through him.

Again, he had asked.

Again, he had been refused.

Some lessons were never learned.

Still, he could not let her go. Not until he knew something about the sadness in her eyes, something about the way she looked at him. His grip tightened on her arms.

Ridiculous as it seemed, he would uncover the mystery of her, would know everything about her before they were finished.

Starting with what she looked like out of her gown.

"Come, this is a masquerade. A place where one can cease to exist." His fingers caught hers gently and twined with the slender digits. "You can do anything you want, be anyone you want to be," he coaxed.

She shook her head stubbornly.

"Then why are you here?" he challenged. "Why don a mask and come here tonight?"

"I can't—" she began, but he silenced her with a finger to her lips. Soft lips. Intent on seduction, he traced her plump bottom lip, learning its texture, its shape.

Her mouth parted and he dipped his thumb within, stroking the moist heat of her mouth, running the pad of his thumb over her tongue.

Her eyes widened.

Unable to stop himself, he lifted his other hand to remove the black fabric covering the top half of her face.

In a flash, she turned wild, struggling like a trapped animal in his arms. He hauled her against him, smothering her mouth with his. Her body stilled in his arms, soft lips frozen beneath his. His kiss gentled, coaxing a reaction.

Her mouth softened, lips parting beneath his with a sweet sigh. She wound her arms around his neck, raising herself on tiptoes, soft curves melting against him.

Groaning into her mouth, he lifted her off the ground, deepening the kiss, drinking from her mouth like a man starved, swallowing her tiny mews as if they were the sweetest sips of wine.

One of her slippers slid along his booted calf and he groaned, wishing it were her bare foot, wishing they were unclothed, flat on a bed. A sudden, burning need to strip off their garments seized him. To see her without the scandalous gold gown, without the black domino, to see her face, her expression in all its passion for him as he sank deep inside her.

Stranger or no, he felt as if he knew her, recognized her on some primal level. Madness, he knew, especially considering he did *not* know her. Not her name, not her face. Still, he wanted this woman, his Aurora.

Startled at the realization, he pulled back and looked at her.

Noses almost touching, their ragged breaths mingled, congesting the air as he gazed into eyes that reflected an astonishment similar to his own. In them, a deep need burned, echoing his own hunger—a fire that he damned well intended to stoke to its highest flame.

Chapter 6

Seth reclaimed her lips, helpless to prevent his desire for this woman from spiraling through him with the speed of a firestorm. She had awakened something within him, ignited a dark burn in his blood he was powerless to resist.

Hands diving through her flowing hair, he angled her head for better invasion and forgot that passion—recklessness—ceased to rule him. Forgot that women had little affect on him. Forgot that he deserved only emptiness in his life.

With a moan of her own, she clenched fistfuls of his jacket, pulling him closer. Growling, he dropped one hand to her backside and pulled her hard against him, grinding himself against the softness of her belly, reveling in the freeing of himself from the fog that gripped him these many years.

Suddenly, the door clicked open behind him.

He tore his lips free as Fleur entered the room.

"Seth." Her eyes raked the woman he held in his arms appraisingly. "I had no idea you were interested in a little *ménage à trois* this evening."

Scowling, he dropped his arms from Aurora, a deep ache filling his chest as she put several feet between them. "You misunderstand the situation."

Toying with the fringe edging her bodice, Fleur's lips twisted in a mocking smile. "Unlikely." Releasing a sigh, she dropped her hand. "I can only blame myself for leaving a morsel like you alone for so long. Forgive me. You wish me to leave you and your friend, *mon cher*?"

"No!" Aurora quickly objected, avoiding his gaze as she moved to the door. "I was leaving."

He watched her, fists clenching at his sides, mixed emotions tumbling through him. He did not want her to go. Exhilaration ripped through him at the taste of her on his lips, the scent of her in the air, the feel of her in his hands.

Obviously she knew he wanted her.

Obviously it failed to matter.

Short of tying her up and tossing her over his shoulder, he could not stop her. And perhaps it was for the best. She made him feel. Too much hunger, too much need, too much . . . *everything*.

Liaisons with women such as Fleur were controlled, safe . . . *enough*.

Without a word, his angel slipped from the room like a fast-fading curl of smoke.

He stared at the doorway, cold regret sweeping through him.

He yearned to give chase. Only he did not *chase* after any woman. Not again. Once was enough. Enough to learn that no woman was worth losing his head over. Or his heart.

As the moments passed, Aurora slipping farther and farther away, his longing deepened, growing into a gnawing ache as he stared at the empty threshold. Every passing moment heightened his anxiety that he would never see her again. It was not to be borne.

"Something tells me you're no longer interested in my company."

"Forgive me?" he asked in a distracted voice, moving toward the door, his strides quick, purposeful.

"Of course, love. My ego won't suffer," Fleur called. "She was interesting. Not the usual fare to frequent one of my fêtes."

Interesting. Yes, she was that. That and more. Her heavily lashed eyes flashed through his mind. He still did not know their color. And yet those eyes had seemed to convey so much. Only he hadn't a clue what.

With a curse, his strides quickened. Letting her get away wouldn't solve the mystery of her. Nor would it douse the fire in his blood.

No doubt about it. Seth wanted her. And suddenly enough wouldn't do.

Jane shoved through the crowd, using her elbows to nudge those who wouldn't move, desperation driving out good manners. In her absence, more guests had arrived, cramming the room tight with bodies. The orchestra played louder, no doubt to compete with the deafening din.

Struggling to still the wild hammering of her heart, to block the sound of blood rushing to her ears, she spied her friends through a part in the crowd. Falling upon them, she gasped, "Let's go. At once."

"Where have you been?" Astrid swept a shrewd gaze over her, then looked beyond her shoulder. "Where is Desmond?"

"Did he harm you?" Lucy grasped one of Jane's trembling hands, her blue-gray gaze searching. "What happened? You look as though you've seen a ghost."

A ghost? She supposed she had.

"We have to go. Now." A shudder racked her body as she glanced over her shoulder, half expecting Seth to materialize behind her, intent on picking up where they left off. The prospect thrilled her as much as it terrified her.

He kissed me. Seth kissed me. And I kissed him back.

Amazing. After all these years, she had finally gotten her dearest wish. Well, at least partly. She had wanted more than a kiss. She had wanted love, marriage, children. She had wanted to wipe her sister from Seth's mind and heart forever.

"My poor dear, you're shaking." Lucy chafed her hand with her warm ones. "Of course we will leave."

Jane sighed with relief. "Thank you."

"They're about to bring out dessert," Astrid grumbled.

"You can gorge yourself when we get home," Lucy muttered. "Cook made blackberry tarts this afternoon. You may even take some home."

"Very well," Astrid consented. She held up both hands in mock surrender. "I am all yours. Take me home and feed me until I burst." As they headed for the door, her dark gaze narrowed on Jane. "Perhaps then you can share all the juicy details of where you've been . . . and with whom. I don't think Desmond put that pretty shade of pink into your cheeks."

Following her friends through the crowd, she debated whether to tell them. Somehow her encounter with Seth felt too personal to share, even with her two closest friends.

At the edge of the ballroom, she stopped. Her scalp tingled as a wave of heat crawled over her. She knew with a certainty that *he* was watching her.

Slowly, she turned, her gaze immediately finding Seth amid the crowd of revelers, a source of heat that drew her like a moth to flame.

He stared at her boldly, without apology, his dark eyes scouring her in a predatory way that made her feel hunted.

"Who is that menacing-looking fellow?" Lucy asked beside her.

Trapped within Seth's gaze, Jane shook her head slightly. "Someone," she paused, moistening her lips, "someone I once knew."

"Indeed," Lucy replied in a bemused voice. "Well, from the looks of him, he wants to become reacquainted."

"No," Jane murmured, finally breaking free of his gaze and hastily turning away. "He does not."

With his hot gaze burning into the back of her

dress, she hastened from the room . . .from him, telling herself that she spoke the truth.

She had to get away. Quickly.

For Seth Rutledge, the new Earl of St. Claire, would never want anything to do with Jane.

Chapter 7

Seth stared out his bedchamber window at the dark garden below, his thoughts on the woman he had held in his arms an hour before, imagining that he could still smell the scent of her—apples on the air. The treetops rustled in the breeze, the only sound save the quiet of his breath.

"Lieutenant," Knightly voiced behind him. "I didn't expect you home this early."

Seth smiled grimly. Nor had he thought to return home this early, his body still unsatisfied. He had left Fleur with little explanation. He had none to give. To her or himself. None that made sense, in any case.

What could he have said? That mere moments alone with a woman whose name and face he did not know had ruined him for anyone else? That she had sparked something deep inside him that he thought forgotten, dead?

"Anything amiss?" Knightly inquired.

He swallowed the lump rising in his throat. Without turning to face his former midshipman, he asked, "Do you ever miss it?"

Knightly understood at once. "No, sir. I never wanted in, but at seventeen it was my only option. I'm simply glad to get out alive."

Seth thought of his father, of the commission purchased for him without his wish or inclination. It had simply been done. At twenty, he had been cast out, the useless son shipped off with no hope of survival, no expectation of returning. And he had deserved no less for what he had done to Julianne.

"For me it was . . . convenient," Seth murmured, nodding. And it had been convenient. Uncomplicated. Safe in an odd sort of way. The navy had been a place to hide, to avoid choices, to forget anything save rigid hierarchy. And war. And blood.

Despite everything, Seth missed it. Strangely, he preferred that existence to this one. Here, he was faced with choices again, with the freedom to make decisions and act on his wishes. The last time he had possessed such freedom he had erred grievously.

He would not err again. Would not risk wanting anything, or anyone, ever again.

Jane paused in the threshold of the dining room. She had hoped at such an early hour she would have the dining room to herself. Chloris, however, sat at the table, the subtle light of morning doing nothing to soften her sister-in-law's harsh features. Blunt-nosed with wide flat cheeks and a brow that tended to wrinkle into folds, her face unfortunately resembled one of the Queen's many pugs.

Jane had spent the few hours left of the night gazing into the dark, the thoughts in her head loud and unrelenting in the oppressive silence as she brushed her fingers over lips that still tingled from Seth's kisses.

When dawn arrived, filling the room with its smoky, unearthly haze, she had finally confronted the ugly truth: she had been a fool to deny herself the chance to experience passion in Seth's arms.

One night could have sustained her through the lonely years ahead. One night would have been more than anything she'd ever had before.

Chloris glanced up, her blue eyes bright beneath tightly drawn brows. "You look pale, Jane. Are you ill?"

Jane did not miss the thread of worry in Chloris's

voice and well knew the reason. If she were unwell, then Chloris would have to manage her daughters herself. That or one of the maids would have to oversee them—a chore that would certainly send the maid packing.

"I'm well," she assured her sister-in-law, not entirely convinced that she wasn't ill.

The memory of last night burned in her mind, churning her stomach into knots. The sight of Seth as she had last seen him, staring across a crowded room as if he wanted nothing more than to devour her whole, made her heart thud faster.

Shaking her head, she banished the image from her mind. She had to forget him. Forget that kiss. A morning of conjugating French verbs with the girls would serve well in that endeavor.

Chloris's harsh features softened, the folds of her forehead relaxing. "Splendid. I had planned on shopping today. I saw a bonnet in the window at . . ." her voice droned on as Jane busied herself lathering her favorite apple jam on her toast, the heavy scent of apples filling her nostrils, reminding her of autumn at home. Which reminded her of Seth. *Blast! Is there no way to put him from my mind?*

Scowling, she took a bite of crisp toast and chewed.

". . . and I promised the girls you would take them to the park today."

As this comment registered, her toast turned to dust on her tongue. Jane glanced at her sister-in-law. "You promised *I* would?"

"They've been pestering me to take them—"

"Then perhaps *you* should take them," Jane suggested. "It would be much more special to them if you were to accompany them."

That much was true. A morning spent with their mother would go a long way in pacifying the unruly girls. Especially as Jane suspected their poor behavior was an attempt to gain the attention of the parents who were always too busy for them.

"Me?" Chloris blinked. "Sadly, no. I've other plans. But you must oblige me on this, Jane. I promised and the girls will be so disappointed."

"Indeed," she murmured. Chloris always had *other* plans. Her daughters never came first. And it fell to Jane to ease the sting of those disappointments.

"Would you not enjoy a ride in the park?" Chloris needled.

A ride in the park. A pleasure she had been denied since Marcus's death and Chloris well knew it. Jane inhaled deeply through her nostrils, striving for patience. As much as a ride in the park tempted her, enduring Dahlia, Bryony, and Iris—who had yet to learn how to conduct themselves in public—produced a shudder. Yet she had little choice. If the girls had been promised the park, they would give her no peace until they got their way.

"Very well," she relented.

A scratching sound filled the air as Chloris scribbled on a sheet of parchment at her right. Jane resumed eating. After several moments, Chloris lifted her head. "I've given some thought to your request to come out of mourning."

Jane paused mid-chew, her teeth grinding. The request had been more a statement of fact and it had been made to Desmond.

"Indeed?" she asked, watching as her sister-in-law perused the sheet of paper in her hand, no doubt the evening's menu.

Chloris had claimed that task for herself shortly after moving in—one of the only household duties to hold her interest. Watching her, Jane loathed that she should sit so haughty and contented in what had once been her chair, performing a duty that had once been *hers*.

"Perhaps a drive in the park today will aid in"—Chloris angled her head to the side as if searching for the word— "easing you back into Society.

Nothing too gauche, that. A drive with your nieces would not be unseemly."

Moistening her lips, Jane pushed further. "And later this week I'll take tea with the Duchess of Shillington." She raised her brows, holding her breath hopefully, thinking how nice it would be to not have to sneak next door.

"Tea?" Chloris blinked. "Oh, I think that is perhaps too ambitious of you. It would not do to appear too eager to end your period of mourning."

"Fifteen months is a seemly amount of time for any widow—"

Chloris held up a hand. "We must heed Desmond's desires in this." Her eyes met Jane's with a solemnity that rankled. "You cannot think he would guide you ill, do you? Desmond is very wise, my dear. And men are so much better equipped to decide these things."

For a brief moment, Jane wished she could shock Chloris by confessing the actions of her saintly husband the night before. But then that would reveal her own activities. Self-preservation held her in check. Until her stepson came of age and sent Desmond packing, she had to bite her tongue.

Forcing a smile that felt brittle as glass, Jane replied, "Very well." Setting her napkin aside, she rose to her feet. "I'll ready the girls and change my clothes."

"Change?" Chloris echoed, her wide eyes skimming over Jane's black bombazine. "Whatever for? What you're wearing is perfectly acceptable."

"I thought to change into something else. Perhaps gray? If I'm to begin easing out of mourning, gray is a suitable color to—"

"A drive in the park should be treat enough for you," Chloris declared, her blue eyes sharp. "Don't tell me you intend to be one of *those* widows who gives the barest due to the passing of a husband." Turning her attention to her plate, she chased a kipper about her plate with her fork. "I would think you owe more to Marcus. After all, you brought nothing to your marriage save a paltry dowry. Your father is a baronet of no repute. If not for your sister's marriage to the Duke of Eldermont, Marcus would never have considered you. And don't forget you didn't even bless the union with offspring."

Mortifying heat swept up her neck. Her barrenness had been only one of the problems riddling her marriage, but it was the one for which she had felt acutely responsible. Having already conceived a child with his first wife, the fault clearly did not rest with Marcus. It didn't take long after their vows for the looks and whispers implying her infertility to begin.

"A woman who cannot provide her husband with children is not a true woman." Chloris puffed out her considerable bosom, seeming to swell with self-importance at her own ability to breed.

Chloris caught her slippery kipper, stabbing at it with vigor. "Ungrateful creature! To even *want* to toss your widow's weeds aside with such quick disregard."

Jane clenched her fists at her sides until they grew numb, bloodless. A thousand angry retorts flashed through her mind. Heat stung her cheeks as she recalled the myriad of indignities she suffered at Marcus's hands. True, she had barred him from her bedchamber, but only after a year of marriage, and only after finding him in her bed with one of the upstairs maids. *Her* bed. The humiliation still burned hot, haunting her even now—a dog forever nipping her heels that she could not outrun.

It was one thing to know your husband conducted affairs all over Town, but quite another to be presented with that fact. She would forever recall the scorn twisting his face, his grating laughter when she demanded he end his indiscretions, end making a fool of her.

Banishing him from her bed only earned her further laughter. His words rang bitterly in her head. *I'll not miss your frigid body. What need do you fill? I already have a son. And there are far better women to warm my bed.*

Pushing that ugly day far from her mind, she rose to her feet. Through cold lips, she declared firmly, "No one would accuse me of being less than circumspect." Striding from the room, she paused briefly at the door to direct Barclay to order a carriage around.

Once inside her chamber, the small bedroom she had been banished to when Desmond and Chloris claimed the master bedchambers for themselves, she stripped off the black bombazine. Flinging open her armoire, she pushed unremitting black aside and removed a gray serge day gown from the far back. With sharp, angry movements, she dressed herself, sick unto death of black and determined to have no more of it. No matter what Desmond or Chloris said.

Ungrateful creature!

With a snort, she yanked the dress into place and turned to inspect herself in the mirror.

Don't tell me you intend to be one of those widows who gives the barest due to the passing of a husband.

Patting her hair in place, she frowned at the gray

serge. Somehow it didn't look much better than the black bombazine. Less severe, but still dismal. Sighing, she turned from the sight of herself and exited the room, taking comfort in this small defiance, a reclaiming of herself . . . if only in small measure.

She advanced down the corridor, intent on waking the girls, hesitating when she spied Chloris leaving what had once been Jane's bedroom. A ridiculous confection of feathers and ribbons sat atop Chloris's head, all the more obtrusive with her blunt, scowling features.

Her pale gaze fell on Jane. "I see you've disregarded my wishes."

Jane lifted her chin.

"I shall take the matter up with Desmond when he returns from his clubs," Chloris threatened, a feather quivering over her nose.

Jane fixed a brittle smile to her face. "No doubt you will have to wait. That could be some time from now. At his clubs again, you say?" She bit her cheek to keep from saying more, from suggesting that he was likely engaged in one of his aberrant pursuits.

"Yes," Chloris sniffed. "A good many connections among gentlemen are made at clubs. Desmond is ever the astute businessman. He's hoping to attain a political appointment in the next year. Perhaps Undersecretary of War."

"Indeed," Jane replied with a deliberately vague air, trying not to grimace at the idea of Desmond in a position of power. Moving to Bryony's door, she grasped the knob. "I'll wake the girls and see that they have their drive."

And try to enjoy myself in the process.

With a quick nod, she ordered herself to forget, to pretend, if only for one afternoon, that her life did not stretch before her in a long row of tiresome days until Matthew reached his majority. That she did not live the life of a servant ordered about and demoralized by her relations . . . with nothing to look forward to. And even less to look back on.

Chapter 8

"**I**sn't this . . . nice?" Seth murmured, forcing a cheerful ring to his voice as he glanced at his sister beside him. Outfitted in sprigged yellow muslin and matching bonnet, Julianne looked like a ray of sunshine—the only light in a gray, sunless day.

As he found himself the subject of fascinated stares, countless activities preferable to a carriage ride along Rotten Row crossed his mind. The speculation had already begun. The wide-eyed, calculating expressions, the heads bent toward one other in rapt discussion.

He took special care not to look at any single individual lest they take that as an invitation to strike up a conversation. Although he had vowed to begin his wife hunt this day, he was not keen on idle chitchat . . . especially when everyone they passed examined his scarred face as if it were some specimen beneath a microscope.

He shifted uneasily, averting his gaze from one apple-cheeked matron who elbowed the girl beside her and jabbed a plump, bejeweled finger in his direction. He could guess at their conjecture. Seth Rutledge, second son, officer, man of little worth was now . . . somebody. A coveted commodity for the mamas of the *ton*.

The image of his golden Aurora rose like a flame in his mind. He had thought about her into the long hours of the night. Had wondered, despite his avowals of indifference, what had possessed him to ever let her go. It had been years since a woman aroused feeling in him. And he had let her get away.

He should have pursued her, claimed her, possibly even set her up as his mistress. He could still taste her kiss, intoxicating and oddly tender, artless for the courtesans and experienced ladies that attended Fleur's galas.

"Nice doesn't describe it, Seth." Julianne's voice pulled him from his thoughts. "I cannot thank you enough for bringing me to Town with you."

He glanced at his sister. She stared straight ahead, eyes empty. Always empty. Her smile, however, eclipsed the glitter of the sun on the Mediterranean. And in that moment, he knew it was all worth it. A carriage ride, a name-only wife. Whatever the cost. He owed it to her.

"No thanks necessary. I've missed you. And how could I even consider choosing a bride without your vital assistance?"

"Oh, Seth." She frowned. Her eyes stared vacantly into the air beyond his shoulder. It was the blankness that got to him, dug a knife in his heart every time. No matter the years that had passed since the accident, he could never evade that particular wound to his heart. Could never view what happened as a mere *accident*. His conscience refused to let him. In the same way that his father had.

"Only you can know whom you should wed. The answer will lie within your heart. Not me."

Seth grimaced. Such sentimentality. His sister was so innocent. Untarnished by the world, the *ton* in particular. It was one of the things he loved most about her. And that sweet innocence was the very thing he intended to protect. His marriage would be the first measure he took in accomplishing that.

"Whom I choose is equally important to both of us."

Julianne laughed dryly, the sound far too old

and wise for her. "I fail to see how. You are the one marrying."

He opened his mouth, then closed it. No sense explaining that *she* motivated his decision to wed. Julianne would not understand. It was enough that he did.

Returning from abroad to discover Albert dead had been bad enough, but to find his sister alone and unprotected with their cousin Harold breathing thickly down her neck still made the blood run cold in his veins. Seth had to wed. Had to marry someone who could look after Julianne in the event of his demise. Someone he respected and trusted with the well-being of his sister. Surely a few women existed to accept a marriage the likes of which he proposed. A marriage based on respect. Duty. A marriage void of love.

He had loved once. And once had been enough. Never again would he be so foolish. Never again would he allow himself to *need* a woman. A loveless marriage founded on respect. He sought no more than that. That, he feared, would be hard enough to find.

"I only hope you're fortunate enough to marry someone you love." Julianne paused, releasing a wistful sigh. "I remember what you were like in love—"

"Don't," he cut in, hands tightening on the traces.

"Still bitter, are you? I had hoped you let all that go."

"I have. But that doesn't mean I'm fool enough to succumb to irrational sentiments again. I'll leave that . . ." Seth froze, his eyes catching sight of a hauntingly familiar face in an approaching carriage.

"Seth? What is it?"

"It's . . ." his voice faded as he examined the woman who wrenched old memories from the arid corners of his soul.

"What?" Julianne prompted.

Jane. She had changed over the years, but he knew her instantly, would know those changeable eyes across any distance.

Her nut brown hair was the same, as was the creaminess of her skin. The angles and hollows of her face were new, reminding him more of her sister. The realization both repelled and intrigued him.

Her body had matured. Full breasts pushed at her snug, high-necked gown, concealing yet displaying enough to make his palms prickle in masculine appreciation.

In his mind, Jane had stayed forever the same.

The wild freckled girl whose infectious laughter had lured a smile from him under any circumstance.

"Seth?" his sister demanded, a plaintive edge to her voice.

"It's Jane Spencer," he drawled, his gaze darting to the three girls crowding her in the carriage. Daughters? The idea of Jane with children and the requisite husband—a man permitted to put his hands and mouth on those luscious breasts any time he wished—settled like a heavy stone in his chest.

On closer inspection, he decided the eldest girl appeared too old to be her daughter. Two years his junior, Jane would be six and twenty now. The girl beside her looked no more than ten and three. The other two not much younger.

"Jane?" Julianne cried happily, reminding Seth how fond his sister had always been of Jane, trailing after her and Seth as they roamed the countryside. Happy days. Before the accident.

"Yes," he replied.

"I heard she married. I believe she's Lady Guthrie now."

Lady Guthrie. Seth grimaced, the stone back in his chest as he looked his fill at the lady that had once been his childhood companion.

Jane Spencer, or whatever her name now, had

grown into a tasty morsel, not beautiful to be sure, but the voluptuous sort of female that made men think of sex. Sweaty, copious amounts of sex. And some bastard was lucky enough to experience it—*her*—firsthand.

Suddenly the way he remembered her—full of life and intensity—took on new possibilities. Possibilities he had never considered. The prospect of stripping her of her matronly frock and giving his hands free rein to explore those curves, to taste and caress her and discover whether the intensity he had appreciated in her as a child had transferred into other arenas, tantalized him.

"Please, let us say hello, Seth."

"I don't think . . ."

But it was too late. Jane had spotted them.

Her eyes flared wide and color flooded her cheeks, no doubt recalling how poorly things had ended between them.

She fidgeted beneath his gaze and said something to the driver, motioning with an elegant wave of her hand that he should turn the carriage around.

Does the sight of my scarred face repulse her that much?

Annoyed that she should seek to flee him, Seth slapped the reins and hastened his phaeton forward, before her driver had time to fully turn their carriage.

"My lady," he greeted with a stiff nod, his voice a crack on the misty air.

She gave a jerky nod. "Lord St. Claire, Lady Julianne," she replied, her voice small and breathless.

Apparently she knew of his return and acquisition of the title. Like her father and sister, titles and rank likely meant everything to her. His lip curled, causing his scar to tighten uncomfortably.

Her hand fluttered to the hand of the youngest girl squirming beside her. Gesturing to each of them, she introduced, "Allow me to present my nieces, Miss Dahlia Billings, Miss Iris Billings, and Miss Bryony Billings.

He nodded in acknowledgment, barely sparing the girls a glance, barely hearing his sister launch into effusive greeting as he focused on Jane.

"A pleasure, my lord," the eldest girl greeted in jarring tones, pulling his attention from Jane. The chit eyed him as boldly as any husband-hungry debutante.

Dismissing her, his gaze returned to Jane, finding her studying Julianne with something akin to pity. He was accustomed to the pitying looks people sent his sister. That much hadn't changed in his absence. Each look served as a further heaping of guilt. But there was something different in Jane's look. Something more. Something heartfelt. Something that he would not allow himself to credit.

"It has been too many years, Julianne." Jane's voice washed over him, throatier than he remembered, warm as the Indian sun. Had her mouth always been so damn inviting? Her bottom lip always so moist? So alluringly full? Like the pink meat of a watermelon he would like nothing more than to taste.

"I don't think I would have recognized you. You've grown into a lovely woman."

Julianne beamed, her vacant eyes seeming to sparkle. "Have I?"

"Indeed," Jane returned. "I often remember you bemoaning your carroty hair as a girl. It has deepened into a handsome auburn now."

Julianne gasped. "Truly? No one has told me that." In her enthusiasm, she turned to her brother, "Do you think so, Seth?"

A strange tightness closed his throat at his sister's delighted expression. Such a small thing to bring about a smile, but he had not thought to comment on what he too had observed. Only another sign that his sister needed a lady's attention in her life. "Indeed, it has."

"Oh, Jane," Julianne chirped. "I've missed you

these years. Now that we've crossed paths, I hope we shall not become strangers again."

Jane darted a nervous look at Seth, her voice a trembling thread on the air as she said, "That would be my wish as well."

Seth swallowed down the sudden sour taste to fill his mouth. His sister and Jane had been close once—almost as close as he and Jane. Until his father cloistered Julianne away, treating her like an invalid.

"Perhaps you could join us for tea?" Julianne suggested.

Jane stared at him, her pretty lips parting but saying nothing.

"Yes," he invited, even as he wondered what possibly motivated him to extend such an offer. "Do call."

He might have put the past behind him, but that did not mean he wanted to revisit friendships best left buried. Especially when the friend in question happened to be a married lady and he could not stop agonizing over her mouth, over those plump lips closing around him, drawing his pleasure deep into her mouth . . .

Locking his jaw, he shoved the coarse thoughts from his mind and reminded himself that his wishes meant nothing. Only his sister's happiness mattered. She'd had very little joy in life. If Jane's company brought pleasure to his sister, then so be it. He would not deny her something so simple. Harmless, really.

"Thank you, but I'm afraid Jane cannot accept," the bold-eyed eldest girl volunteered with decided relish. "She is in mourning, and Papa says she cannot go about."

"Oh, Jane," Julianne murmured. "I had not heard. I'm dreadfully sorry."

Seth looked Jane over, noting the flush of color creeping up her neck to stain her cheeks. Even as he told himself to resist, he evaluated her in new estimation. As a woman unwed. A widow. Widows, he had always considered ripe for dalliance. Only not this one. No matter that the sight of her spiked his desire, filling him with a burning urge to peel off her prim, high-necked gown and discover precisely how far that blush crept.

"Thank you, but it has been over a year now," Jane explained, darting a narrow look to her niece. "I am quite ready to rejoin Society."

Her niece's lips thinned until they all but disappeared.

"Oh," Julianne murmured in a hopeful voice. "Then tea one afternoon this week would not be remiss."

"Tea would be lovely," Jane agreed even as her nieces glowered beside her.

"What about us? What about our lessons?" Bryony, the youngest, demanded in a squeak, her nostrils flaring with indignation.

Seth reassessed the girls in their frilly, beribboned gowns, allowing that although his experience with children was limited, this gaggle of young womanhood reminded him of a motley bunch of pirates he had once faced.

"You'll make do for one afternoon." Jane glared down at the girls as though daring them to object. Her gaze lifted then, locking with his. With her lovely mouth compressing into a tight smile, she stared down the slim line of her nose at him.

"I shall look most forward to it," Julianne trilled.

"As I," Jane murmured.

Seth's gaze raked her, sitting so cool and composed in her carriage, a marble statue, nothing like he remembered. No hint of the exuberant, shrieking wild girl who had swum the lake with him, climbed trees in his family's orchard, and gathered holly at Christmas.

He continued to stare after her as she drove away, deciding that that girl of his youth had gone, disappeared. If she ever existed at all.

Chapter 9

Adjusting her careful grip on a fragile Wedgwood teacup, Jane struggled to follow Lady Julianne's animated chatter.

Murmuring and commenting at appropriate intervals, she struggled to understand why she risked the wrath of her relations to sit in the Earl of St. Claire's townhouse.

If Desmond or Chloris returned home and discovered Anna tending to the girls instead of her, they would have a great deal to say on the matter. Her fingers plucked at the arm of her chair and she shoved the prospect from her mind.

She looked up quickly at the sound of the door opening. A maid entered, bearing another tray of biscuits. Rebecca, Julianne's companion, rose to take the tray.

Sighing, Jane leaned back on the sofa feeling an

odd mixture of relief and disappointment. And she had her answer. The one she had been avoiding.

With a small shake of her head, she took a sip of hot tea. No matter how she hid from it, the truth reared its head. She sat in the St. Claire townhouse because she wished to see Seth again. *Craved* to see him. If only a glimpse. Even if he looked on her as he did in the park. With that same remote stare. As if he stared through her and did not see her at all.

Even so, she still longed for the sight of him, recalling him as he'd been at Madame Fleur's. His eyes had gleamed, burned. Burned for her. Jane gave her head a small shake. Not her. He would never burn for her.

"I'm so glad you saw fit to come today." Julianne leaned forward, her voice gentling as she added, "And I respect your need to properly mourn your husband. Did you love him very much?"

Jane choked on her biscuit. She cleared her throat with a deep drink of tea before answering. "It was a match arranged by my parents. Lord Guthrie and I were not . . . close."

"Oh." Julianne leaned back, her disappointment obvious. And Jane felt that disappointment as keenly as a knife's blade to her flesh. Somehow she felt she had let Julianne down. As girls, they had shared dreams of marrying dashing gentlemen and living happily ever after in neighboring castles.

Naturally, Jane had never told Julianne that her brother was the hero of her fantasies. She had told no one that, had kept that particular secret tied close to her heart.

Eager to change the subject, Jane asked, "How long have you been in Town?"

"Nearly a fortnight." Julianne sighed, an edge of dissatisfaction in the sound. "I've longed to come to Town. Remember how we planned taking our Seasons together?"

A smile tugged Jane's lips. "I recall we were to wear matching gowns of white Charmeuse to Almack's," she murmured. Neither ever had that Season. Jane's parents had arranged her marriage without the need for a Season, using the connections of Madeline's new husband, the ancient Duke of Eldermont.

"Yes!" Julianne laughed, then sighed, the sound tired, defeated. "At least I finally made it to Town. I have Seth to thank for that. Albert would never have brought me." Her expression clouded. "But it's not all I thought it would be. Not that I'm ungrateful to Seth. I'm so happy he's back. He's the only one who has ever taken my wishes into account. But . . ."

"But?" Jane prodded.

"He suffocates me terribly," Julianne confessed. "He insists on limiting me to drives in the parks. He doesn't permit me to accept a single invitation." She crossed her arms rather severely, reminding Jane of a child denied. "Why did he bother to bring me? He might as well have left me at the Priory."

"Don't overset yourself." Julianne's companion glanced up from her knitting. "Give him time. He'll soon see how capable you've grown."

Julianne smiled indulgently. "Rebecca is the eternal optimist."

Jane moved beside Julianne. "I'm sure your brother intends to make the rounds with you once the Season gets in full swing."

A frown flitted about Julianne's mouth. "Seth worries how I will be received."

Jane nodded, well imagining the manner in which the *ton* would regard her. Overly concerned with individual assets—internal or external—they would treat her like damaged goods.

"I've told him I don't care." Julianne's chin lifted. "I'm no fool. I realize many will dismiss me. Heiress or not, I am blind." She paused, moistening her lips. "And yet I still yearn for the chance."

Jane scanned Julianne's earnest expression. "If anyone could open minds, it would be you."

"Hmm." Rebecca nodded in agreement.

"Surely a brave enough gentleman exists to ask me to dance." Julianne angled her face, and it seemed that she turned instinctively to the warm rays of light spilling from the open terrace doors. "It would require a special sort of man to want to dance with me—"

"Not so special," Jane argued. "You're charming. And pretty. Two traits I happen to know attract gentlemen."

"Yes." Julianne's mouth twisted in a manner reminiscent of Seth. The similarity caused a bothersome pang in the region of her heart. She must really put an end to this annoying infatuation. It should have died years ago. With all her other childish dreams. "But sight happens to be another trait gentlemen prefer."

"I've told you already," Rebecca inserted, her hands working with feverish ease as she knitted. "Some fellow with less than refined looks is going to hone in on you like a bee to honey."

Jane and Julianne both burst into laughter.

"And I would welcome his attention," Julianne replied, her laughter subsiding. "Blindness has taught me to value an individual's inner light." She exhaled deeply. "Now if I can just convince Seth to let me out for an evening so that I might stumble upon a gentleman with inner light."

Jane studied Julianne thoughtfully and wondered if she had ever witnessed anyone so determined to make the best of her life, despite all hardships. It made Jane more resolved to seize what happiness she could.

"Seth's venturing to Vauxhall tonight," Julianne volunteered, a plaintive edge to her voice. "Of course he claims it unsuitable for me to join him." She pulled a face, indicating what she thought about that.

"Vauxhall?" Jane murmured, thinking of the recently reopened outdoor theater. A prime place for assignations of a less than respectable nature.

Perhaps the reason Seth wanted to go to Vauxhall without his sister was to engage in one such assignation. No doubt that had been his goal at Madame Fleur's. And perhaps he had done so after she left. Vauxhall with its dimly lit paths was one such setting. Even in large groups with chaperones paying diligent attention, ladies managed to steal away to darkened trails with their young swains.

Unable to stop herself, she inquired, "Is this your brother's first visit to Vauxhall since you've arrived to Town?"

"I believe so. He happened upon an old acquaintance yesterday who invited him. I believe Mr. Manchester has a sister Seth is interested in meeting."

"A sister?" Jane echoed, tearing off a tiny piece of biscuit and stuffing it into her suddenly dry mouth.

"Yes," Julianne released a rather wistful sigh. "Since he intends to take a wife this Season, he's making himself agreeable to Society." Her lips twitched. "Lucky him."

With decided care, Jane set her saucer back down on the service and swallowed her bit of biscuit. She tried to think of an appropriate response to this news, but words failed her. *Seth had come to Town to marry.* It shouldn't come as a shock. Marriage was the natural course for any gentleman of means.

At the stretch of silence, Rebecca looked up from her knitting and studied her with a curious lift of her brows.

Feeling compelled to fill the gap in conversation, Jane opened her mouth to speak. "I—" her voice cracked. Clearing her throat, she tried again. "I am sure he will have no difficulty finding many an agreeable lady. His greatest challenge will be in choosing from the vast number of debutantes out this Season." To say nothing of the ones who had not wed last Season. Or the Season before. Or the many widows about Town looking for a new husband. Her heart sank. Heavens, her competition would be endless.

Competition? The thought brought her to a hard stop. She was *not* in the market for a husband. Especially when her relations kept her hidden from Society under a shroud of mourning, too happy to use her as their drudge. Besides, she had Matthew to consider. Someone needed to be home for him during school holidays.

"I fear he will be beyond selective," Julianne groused. "He has unreasonable expectations."

"Indeed?"

Julianne paused and bit her lip. Releasing it, she confessed, "He expects us to like each other."

"Oh." Jane blinked. "Well, that's considerate of your brother to consider—"

"No, you don't understand. That is quite nearly his *only* qualification. He wishes to wed a lady who *likes me*."

Jane stared in silence at the young woman, feeling decidedly confused. That a gentleman would only require that his bride *like* his sister was decidedly odd.

As though reading her mind, Julianne explained, "I know it's strange, but when Seth returned home it was to find Albert dead and our cousin working to have Seth declared legally dead. We did not even know Seth had been transferred to service in China. I had assumed he was still fighting pirates and slave smugglers on the African coast."

"Tell the all of it. Tell her what that wretch Harold did," Rebecca exclaimed from her chair, working her needles with sudden force, as though the scarf taking shape was the wretch under discussion.

Julianne smoothed a hand over her elegantly arranged coiffure. Only the slight tremble of her hand indicated her next words gave her discomfort. "Harold petitioned to have me committed."

"Committed? In an asylum?" Jane sputtered in outrage.

Julianne nodded, tucking a wispy auburn tendril behind her ear.

"Blindness is not a mental affliction." Jane's hands fisted in her skirts at the injustice done Julianne. By a member of her family, no less.

Julianne shrugged one shoulder. "Harold wanted me out of the way. He probably would have succeeded if Seth had not returned."

"The blackguard!"

"Now you see why my brother is determined to marry someone who likes me."

Frowning, Jane shook her head. "I fail to see the connection—"

"He needs to feel confident that his wife would look out for me and protect me from Harold if something should befall him."

Jane nodded slowly, understanding at once. Seth had no desire to marry. He married for the sake of his sister. No doubt his experience with her family had soured him to the notion of marriage.

She would never forget his face that day, earnest and determined as he stormed into their dining room, bellowing Madeline's name, fists swinging at the footmen who tried to stop him. He had been convinced her sister was restrained somewhere within the house, that some *force*—aside from her own fickleness—kept her from meeting him as promised.

He had been wrong. Nothing had kept Madeline from him save her own ambitions to wed someone titled, someone richer—someone other than a second son destined for the navy. A portside cottage and naval lieutenant's trifling wages could hardly entice Madeline to go against their father and elope with Seth.

Jane did not see the unyielding man from the park succumbing to such sentiment again. His cold gaze and scant civility had chilled her. Softer sentiments were lost on him.

The bronze clock on the mantel suddenly released a bell-like tinkle, alerting the hour. Jane rose. "I must take my leave." Anna no doubt needed relieving from watching the girls.

Julianne grasped a silver-headed cane beside her. "I'm so happy you came today. Meeting you in the park was purely providential."

"Indeed so," Jane replied with a smile, trying not to feel a stab of disappointment at not meeting up with Seth again today.

Julianne stepped forward, lightly knocking her cane about what was clearly still an unfamiliar room. "Allow me to walk you out."

Jane grasped her by the elbow. Rebecca tucked her knitting away into a basket and fell in step behind them. They had just cleared the threshold and entered the corridor when a deep voice reverberated over the air.

"Good afternoon, ladies."

The familiar voice slid through her like warm brandy, melting her insides.

"Seth," Julianne greeted warmly.

Jane tensed, meeting his dark gaze, hoping she appeared more composed than she felt. She had hoped to see him, but to look at him now, standing so rigidly, that cold veil over his eyes, a deep ache filled her chest.

She wanted him to look on her with something in his eyes, anything. Wanted some flicker of emotion to show itself in the hard angles of his face. Emotion that proved a shred of the boy she had known still existed, that the same passion that had sent him crashing into her parents' dining room, fed by his love for a woman who would never have him, still dwelled beneath his hard veneer.

She ached to think that no remnant of that young man existed. That her family had destroyed him.

But nothing showed on his face.

The boy she had found so easy to love was nowhere in evidence. The years had stolen him. He looked on her with eyes flat and cold as he lightly took her fingertips to bow over her hand.

Foolish, she supposed, to hope she would see anything when he looked at her.

Chapter 10

Seth could not tear his gaze from Jane. She was dressed in another dull gray gown, this one possibly even more depressing than the last. And yet he felt just as overcome by the sight of her as he had been in the park.

He could not say what kept him standing before her when he knew he should excuse himself to his study and avoid her as he had vowed to do on any occasion that his sister might entertain her company, unwilling to permit her to rouse his desires anymore than she already had.

Seth needed a wife. An uncomplicated female that did not inspire his passions. Such he would not find in Lady Jane Guthrie.

"Jane came for tea," Julianne volunteered.

Bowed over her hand, he schooled his features into a mask of apathy lest she think he felt anything at all when he looked at her. "Yes. I see that."

Certainly he felt nothing for her. No *tender* feelings, at any rate. Any softer emotion he had felt during their childhood died long ago, the very day her family tossed him from their home as if he were nothing more than a mangy dog.

"Lord St. Claire," Jane inclined her head, her manner tight and overly dignified, her voice rigid and clipped as she tugged her hand free of his. The consummate *ton* matron now. She bore no resemblance to the exuberant girl who had once pounced on his shoulders in his family's lake with an ear-splitting squeal. He stared intently at her face, searching for a glimpse of that girl—strangely disappointed when he did not find her. Tempting morsel she may have grown, but no fire lurked beneath.

"Lady Guthrie. How nice to see you again," he returned politely. "I trust you've had a pleasant afternoon?"

The question was innocent enough, but even he heard the edge to his voice, the suspicion, the compulsion to make certain that her time with Julianne had passed smoothly. That Jane had not treated Julianne like some sublevel human as so many Society ladies did.

"I for one have had a splendid time," Julianne volunteered. "Jane is such a darling. We must never let her slip away again."

He cocked an eyebrow and dragged his gaze over her in slow perusal, lingering on the generous swell of her breasts rising and falling enticingly with her even breaths.

He looked away when he began to swell against his breeches. Staring over her head, he sucked in a steadying breath and renewed his vow to avoid her company. To feel nothing at the sight of her.

"Indeed, we must not," he intoned, the flatness in his voice deliberate as he eyed the length of corridor and contemplated escape.

Jane's smile wobbled in the face of his seeming apathy.

His sister continued, her voice light and airy, a direct contrast to the thick tension swirling in the air. "I must say, Seth, Jane was quite vexed to hear you are not permitting me to join you at Vauxhall this evening."

Jane gasped, color flooding her face.

"Oh?" He leveled Jane a look that had sent many a sailor scurrying to the riggings. *Impudent chit*.

Her chin jerked higher under his glower. Indeed, she had turned into quite the *tonnish* lady. Nose in the air and quick to judge, quick to concern herself with matters out of her sphere and voice unsolicited opinions.

"I do hope he's not scowling at you right now, Jane," Julianne interrupted in aggravatingly cheerful tones. "Don't let him intimidate you."

"I fail to see how our social schedule is any concern of Lady Guthrie's," he cut in, the softness of his voice deceptive, considering the streak of irritation that burned through him.

Jane glared at him, her hazel eyes bright as a moss-laden pond. If not for the trembling of her mouth, he would think her undaunted.

He stared back, trying not to focus too long on that mouth, on that full bottom lip that quivered enticingly. Her family may have tossed him out like a cur come to beg, but no whipped dog stood before her now. He would have her see that, have her know that nothing affected him, nothing would ever touch him again. He would give nothing, or no one, that power.

"Seth, be nice." Julianne swatted a hand in his general direction.

"It grows late," Jane murmured, her gaze darting over his shoulder as if she sought escape.

"Allow me to show you out," he heard himself suggest before he could consider why he would want to. To his sister, he added, "Why don't you freshen up and I'll take you and Rebecca for ices."

"Oh!" Her face brightened with delight. Turning to Jane, she hastily said farewell while eliciting another promise to return from her. He watched as Julianne and Rebecca hurried off, tension forming along his shoulders in knowing that he had suggested taking his sister for an ice in order to steal a moment alone with Jane.

Frowning, he took her arm and escorted her down the long length of corridor, his heels clicking over polished parquet. "So you mean to return, then?"

Stopping in the middle of the corridor, she lifted those damnable hypnotic eyes of hers. "I said as much."

"Forgive me," he murmured. "I find it hard to credit."

"And why is that?" she demanded, her eyes glinting in challenge.

"Ladies of the *ton* strike me as the *busy* sort." Too busy for friends like Julianne at any rate.

"I'm not too busy for Julianne," she assured, adding in a softer voice, "nor am I like most ladies of the *ton*."

"Oh? In what manner?"

Shaking her head, she muttered, "Never mind."

"What?"

Her lips flattened into a line and she shook her head harder.

"I don't remember you being so reticent, Jane."

Her eyes widened and he felt certain it was his use of her name, the first time he had spoken it in many years. It felt good to say it, to hear himself say it. Bloody annoying, that.

"People change," she murmured.

"That they do," he agreed, finding himself staring overly long at her mouth again. At *her*. In so many ways, he felt he was seeing her for the first time.

Her eyes, neither brown nor green but a strange mixture, reminded him of a wooded glen that he had seen outside Macao. He recalled the sunlight reflecting off a nearby waterfall, gilding the rich browns and greens, and the peace that had filled him then.

Without stopping to think, he brushed his thumb over her lips, testing the softness, wondering if they had always felt like satin, wondering why he had never thought to find out before . . . and why he wanted to find out now.

He trailed a path down her throat to the wildly thrumming pulse beating against the almost translucent skin of her neck. He drew a lazy circle over the faint pattern of delicate blue veins there.

"What are you doing?" she whispered, inching

away until the wall at her back stopped her from farther retreat.

He followed, closing in, pressing his hard length against her softer one.

Her curves settled against the hard lines of his body, melting against him like lava sinking into the sea. He bit back a groan at the sensation, longing to sink *all* of himself into her soft heat.

Lowering his head, he pressed his mouth to her throat, where her neck met her shoulder . . . driven, compelled by a feeling he could not name, a madness he could not shake. She need only say the word, give the slightest indication of surrender, and he would take her. With no thought to propriety, to servants that lurked in shadows, he would lift her skirts and put an end to his torment.

A breath shuddered through her, vibrating against his chest as he opened his mouth over her warm skin, savoring the sweetness of her flesh with the rasp of his tongue.

Lifting his mouth, he gazed into her astonished eyes.

A similar astonishment echoed through him, surpassed only by the desire hardening every line of his body.

His gaze dipped to her mouth again, to the pouty lips that obliterated the last of his logic.

* * *

Jane shook her head, fingers moving to lightly graze her neck, her skin moist and cool where he had kissed her.

Did he do this to every woman he encountered? Overwhelm them with his magnetism until the only thought in a woman's head was *him*? His hands on her body? His mouth on her skin? Did others fall victim so weakly? So stupidly? Thinking they were special?

Jealously seized her. For whom, she was not certain. Aurora? Absurd considering she only envied herself.

Mortification spread prickly hot through her chest, rising up her throat to choke her. "I—I should go," she managed to get out as she shoved past him, stumbling for the door.

He snatched hold of her wrist, his fingers a vise about her. His hot look burned with familiar intensity.

"Why so unfriendly, Jane? We were friends once, were we not?"

Friends. Had he never realized that she wanted to be *more*? That *he* had been more to her? Everything, in fact. Her fists clenched. Rot him for not seeing, not knowing . . . for not loving her back.

His fingers tightened and pulled her close. Too close. He stared at her in that consuming way of his, his velvet brown eyes warming her blood. "Have you forgotten?" he demanded.

The mad urge to laugh bubbled up in her throat. *Forgotten*? Swallowing down the thickness in her throat, she replied, grateful for the brusque sound of her voice, "Of course not.

"Good." His touch gentled on her wrist, thumb moving in slow circles over the inside of her wrist. "Because I've thought of you."

She snorted. "Have you?"

He smiled loosely and her belly fluttered. "We had fun together. When I thought of home, yours was the face I saw." His smile faded as though bothered by the realization.

She said nothing, too incredulous to formulate a response. Never had she dreamed to linger in his thoughts. Madeline, yes. Her? Never.

"You've changed," he continued. "You're not the little girl frozen in my mind all these years." His eyes slid over her slowly, the seductive movement of his fingers on her wrist radiating heat up her arm.

"You're different, too," she retorted. "The days of stripping to our unmentionables to swim in the pond have long passed."

Fire flared in his eyes. "Pity."

Heat licked her cheeks and she dipped her gaze.

She had thought of him often during the numbing years of her marriage to Marcus. Wondered where he was, how he occupied himself, if he ever thought of her. She had reminisced on the cheerful days of their youth before Julianne's accident. Before he dropped from an apple tree, his love for Madeline emblazoned across his face.

She had envisioned the future where they might meet again, imagined his varying reactions. From mild enthusiasm to polite indifference. Yet in all the scenarios, he had never looked as he did now, with fire gleaming in his eyes. Fire for *her*.

The same fire—a ruthless voice inserted in her head—he had shown for Aurora.

Confused, she wiggled free of his hold. This time he did not stop her as she stepped past him.

"I shall call on Julianne again," she promised.

He stared at her for a long moment, his eyes fierce and glowing. His fingertips rubbed together idly at his side, almost as if he still caressed her.

"She would like that very much," he replied at last, the muscle feathering along his square jaw belying the mildness of his response.

She glanced away, staring at the cuticles of her neatly trimmed nails.

Nodding, she murmured, "You care for your sister a great deal." Perhaps too much, she silently added. Before she could think better of it, she added, "I understand you're looking for a bride."

"Do you now?" He stepped nearer, an encroaching wall of heat. "What precisely did my sister tell you?"

Her mind thought back to all Julianne had told her, recalling the slump to her shoulders as she had confessed her brother's intention to wed . . . and his sole criteria in selecting a wife.

"She said you're marrying because of her. To see that she is protected." Jane hesitated at sight of his scowl. "Admirable of you, to be certain . . . but such a sacrifice weighs heavily on your sister."

He stepped back, crossing his arms over his chest, all warmth gone from his eyes as he bit out, "You know nothing of what you speak."

"Oh? Then you're not venturing to Vauxhall tonight to take measure of a potential bride?"

"Julianne speaks too freely."

"Your sister has no wish to be the reason for your marrying anyone. It's unfair to place such a burden on her—"

"You presume too much," he ground out, "to think your opinion matters here."

Stung, she swallowed back the sudden lump in

her throat. "Perhaps I spoke out of turn, but I'm only thinking of your sister."

Not myself.

Not the knot of discomfort in my belly at the thought of you marrying.

"You mentioned needing to be off, my lady," Seth said, cold, implacable, a man cut from stone, the thrilling intimacy of moments ago gone. "Do not let me keep you a moment more." He sketched a quick bow.

She watched his rigid back stride away before she moved down the corridor to the entrance hall.

A footman appeared with her cloak, bonnet, and reticule. Accepting her things, she forced herself to walk steadily outside. Inhaling the crisp air, she blinked several times to quell the moisture that gathered in her eyes, reminding herself that she had survived years without Seth's affections. The lack did not matter now. She would not revert to childhood, would not long for what could never be.

And when news reached her that the Earl of St. Claire had married, she would not feel a thing, would not feel that same stab in the region of her heart that she had felt the day in the orchard when she realized Seth would never love her.

It was not until she sat safely in her carriage that she allowed the tears to fall.

Chapter 11

Jane braced herself upon entering the Guthrie townhouse. Holding her breath, she stood in the foyer and listened with her head cocked. Blessed silence. No walls crashing down. No frenzied servants. No girlish screams reaching her ears.

She expelled her breath, feeling some of the tension ebb from her neck. No doubt she would face unpleasantness for leaving her nieces with Anna and daring to partake in a fragment of the social niceties that had once filled her days, but she was glad for the respite and would not regret her time with Seth.

However impossible their flirtation, his attentions, his mouth on her neck, the way his gaze burned through her, would be something she clung to in the years ahead.

A throat cleared behind her and the tension returned, streaking through her shoulders.

Turning, she eyed the butler. A stone-faced sentry, Barclay wore his usual mask of civility. His stare impassive, he intoned, "Mr. Billings awaits you in his study, my lady." She tugged free her gloves, despising the way her hands shook at the mention of Desmond.

His study. Even the butler considered Desmond lord and master now. Forget that she was the viscountess. Forget that Matthew was the true viscount. One widow lacking a jointure and a boy halfway across the country did not command respect.

Jane twisted her gloves in her hands, her mind racing, searching for a way to delay, if not avoid the meeting altogether.

As though reading her mind, Barclay added, "Mr. Billings said I was to direct you there at once. Personally."

Jane dropped her gloves on the hall table and smoothed moist palms over her skirts. "Is Mrs. Billings at home?"

"No, my lady."

She inhaled thinly through her nostrils. With their last encounter fresh in her head, she had no wish to see him alone. True, he did not know she had been the woman he accosted at Madame Fleur's, but she knew. And her skin still crawled at the memory.

"Would you send for Anna?"

"Mr. Billings sent Anna on an errand, my lady."

She narrowed her gaze on the butler. Errand indeed. Since when did Desmond use Anna for errands? The wretch clearly wanted her to himself.

Squaring her shoulders, she advanced to the study, determined to present a brave front. In broad daylight, in a house full of servants, he would surely behave himself.

Stopping before the tall double doors, she rapped twice, waiting for his command to enter, trying not to fidget.

"Come in."

Sucking in a breath, she entered the room, noticing as she did that it smelled of leather and cigars—the smell she still associated with Marcus over a year later.

Desmond reclined in her late husband's chair, feet propped up on the mahogany desk, one of his brother's imported cigars clamped between his teeth.

"Jane, m'dear, I was beginning to worry."

Spine rigid as a slat of wood, she eased into the chair across from the desk, not fooled by his display of solicitousness. "I left word of my whereabouts."

"Yes, you called on Lady Julianne. Blind, isn't she?" He shook off his cigar into an ivory ashtray. "How charitable of you." His gaze grew shifty, speculative as he brought the cigar back to his lips. "Word is her brother's in the market for a wife," he said around the moistened end.

Jane carefully schooled her features to reflect none of her surprise. It appeared Seth's intention to take a bride was already public knowledge.

"I wouldn't know about that," she lied, lacing her fingers together in her lap.

"Ah." Desmond dropped his feet to the floor with a thud, surveying her gray gown until she felt as though he had stripped her of every last stitch of fabric. "Chloris thinks it unseemly for you to engage in Society so soon after Marcus's death, and I must convey my agreement."

"It has been over a year. Enough time—"

"On the contrary. Given the shocking nature of Marcus's death—"

"You mean dying in the bed of his mistress?" Jane lifted her chin, seeing no point in skirting the reality of matters. "Not so shocking, that." Especially considering Marcus had spent most of his time in other women's beds.

Desmond rounded the desk, shaking his head ruefully. "Perhaps not. But an unfortunate bit of scandal, nonetheless. And your insistence at rejoining Society so soon after such scandal has most distressed Chloris. And Chloris unhappy—" He broke off to shake his head. "Well, let us just say that an unhappy Chloris can be a bit of a trial for anyone."

"Then perhaps it would be in everyone's interest if I left," Jane suggested, doing her best to keep the ring of hope from her voice.

Immediately following Marcus's death, she had not pressed the matter of leaving, believing Matthew needed one friendly face around when he came home on holiday, someone to stand as a buffer between him and Desmond's bullying. But Jane had reached a point where her instincts demanded she look to herself.

"Perhaps," he murmured, his gaze trailing over her lazily.

"I can retire to the dower house," she recommended. "As many expected I would following Marcus's death."

"But Jane, dear." He clucked his tongue and reached out to brush his knuckles against her cheek. "I enjoy having you underfoot."

She flinched and pulled away from his touch.

He scowled. "Does my touch repulse you so? I daresay someone in your position should not be so particular."

"My position?"

"You are without funds. And seeing as your family has no interest in claiming you, you are at my mercy. Even the clothes on your back belong to me."

"No," she countered, heat stinging her face. "They don't belong to *you*."

He grimaced and then sniffed, flicking a hand at his lacy cravat. "Yes, well. Your clothes belong to an eleven-year-old boy that I happen to hold dominion over."

"You take perverse pleasure in having me beneath your thumb," she accused, "using me as you would a servant."

"Oh, Jane." His gaze raked her in a way that made her feel soiled and in need of a bath. "I want you beneath more than my thumb."

Quivering with indignation, she pushed to her feet, ready to flee the room. "You're disgusting."

His hands seized her arms. "Jane," he murmured, his gaze prowling her face as though searching for a point of invasion. "You must know I'm mad for you. Since Marcus married you, I've wanted you."

"Let me go or I shall call for help."

He released her, his bottom lip protruding in a sulk that reminded her of his daughters' when denied a treat.

She moved back several paces, putting distance

between them. "If you're so concerned with your wife's happiness, let me assure you that molesting me will not garner her favor."

"I can give you what you want, Jane. A house of your own again. Beautiful dresses. The freedom you crave—"

"As your *mistress*?" She snorted. "That sounds like a prison sentence."

"No one need know. We can be discreet." He paused, motioning to her person. "How long can you live like this? The pathetic relation dressed like an old crow?"

Jane shook her head in disbelief. "You think a few pretty dresses will convince me to become your mistress?"

"We'll see how long it takes you to change your mind." His lip curled back against his teeth. "I'll have you yet."

With as much dignity as she could manage, she turned for the door.

"Oh, I almost neglected to tell you."

Jane glanced over her shoulder, unease trickling down her neck at his strangely amiable tone.

"I've taken the liberty in seeing your wardrobe relieved of anything save black. I've also acquisitioned your jewelry since you have no need of such while in mourning."

Apprehension fluttered low in her belly. Had he found the necklace among her things? She had hid it, but who knew how thorough his search of her room.

"I trust you have no objections." The laughter in his eyes told her exactly what he thought she could do if she did harbor objections. Dark anger bubbled to life in her belly.

Jane pursed her lips with determination. Well, she would do *something*. She would not be controlled so neatly, fenced in and constrained as though she were less than free.

She would most definitely do something.

"Good afternoon, Mr. Knightly."

Gregory whirled around to find Lady Julianne sitting quietly and serenely on a bench beneath a large oak.

"Lady Julianne," he greeted her, executing a neat bow to his employer's sister as he realized she could not see the courtesy. Then, recalling she had addressed him by name, he asked, "How did you know it was me?"

"I smelled you."

"Smelled me?" he queried, moving closer on the garden path and feeling a smile pull at his lips. "Am in need of a bath?"

"Indeed not. You smell rather like lemons. You always do. Most unique."

"A habit I picked up aboard the ship. Chewing lemon drops helped ward off scurvy."

"You were in the Orient with Seth?"

"I traveled as a midshipman with the lieutenant nearly everywhere—India, the African coast, China."

She leaned forward on the bench, the movement pulling her bodice tighter across the swell of her breasts. For a tiny woman, she had generous breasts. They would fill his hands. He grimaced at the inappropriate assessment and rubbed the back of his neck. As a man he could not help but appreciate the sight. Even though he willed himself to be immune, he was not. From the first moment he met Lady Julianne, he had been struck by her prettiness.

"There was much of the war in the papers," Julianne commented. "Hugely unpopular by all accountings."

"Naturally . . . yet no English citizen wants to go without their tea," he muttered. No one wanted the war, but they fully expected access to their beloved tea, an import seriously under threat had England not gone to war with China.

"What was it like?" she asked. "Seth doesn't talk about such things."

"For good cause. War is not a fit topic for a lady's ears. Especially yours."

"Especially mine?" she demanded in affronted tones, rising to her feet in a swift, elegant motion. She stared in his direction, her blank gaze fixed in the vicinity of his cravat. "Don't tell me you're like my brother and think me frail, incapable of wiping my own nose." Her delicate hands fisted at her sides. "If so, I fear I shall scream."

Gregory blinked, taken aback that the seemingly sweet-tempered lady possessed such fire. He had not thought such passion simmered within her.

She was really quite pretty and refreshingly candid. Not at all like other ladies who never spoke their minds because they were too busy saying what they ought to say and not what they wanted. If she were anyone other than Rutledge's sister, he would like to know her better.

Her lips loosened in a rueful smile. "From your silence, I gather I have shocked you. Rebecca often tells me I am too outspoken. You are still here, aren't you? You have not absconded over the nearest hedge?"

"Indeed not," he replied a bit breathlessly.

She released a rich laugh that seemed too hearty for one so slight and delicate. "Splendid, Mr. Knightly. Would you care to escort Rebecca and me to the park this afternoon? I think I should enjoy more of your company."

"I do not think that wise, my lady."

She frowned. "Why not?"

He shook his head, marveling at her obtuseness. "I am in your brother's employ."

"That does not mean we cannot be friends. I find I'm in short supply of friends. Both my father and Albert never let me step foot outside the Priory. And now Seth, it seems, is little better."

"Your brother has brought you to Town," he reminded. "Soon you shall have friends more fit than I." Strangely, that fact troubled him.

Her frown deepened into a scowl. "No good." She tossed her head. "I want *you*."

His blood raced at her declaration. He knew she did not mean her words as they sounded, but simply hearing them come out of that delectable cupid's bow mouth of hers made him harden instantly. Made him realize how long he had gone without a woman.

To have such a reaction for Rutledge's sister, the very man to have saved his life on more than one occasion, shamed him. He shook his head fiercely, forcing his gaze off that luscious mouth, off the enticing curve of her breasts within her bodice. Impossible. He was randy as a sailor fresh to port.

Without a word, he turned and strode from the courtyard, not caring how rude he appeared, only concerned with removing himself from her. At once.

"Mr. Knightly," she called, but he pushed on, rounding a hedge of hawthorn, focusing on the sound of his feet crunching over the path, blocking out the sweet, beguiling tenor of her voice and vowing never to be caught alone or in conversation with the far too tempting woman again.

"Mr. Knightly, where are you going?"

Far from you, Lady Julianne. As far as I can get.

Jane paced the length of her room, her fury rising to choke her every time she glanced at her armoire, now bare of the gowns she had worn previous to Marcus's death, the gowns she had planned on wearing again. Soon.

The indignity of knowing that Desmond had commanded a servant to rifle through her things washed over her in bitter waves. As a girl, she'd never been of particular importance to her parents, more often than not missing their detection altogether. They had invested all their energy in Madeline—the beautiful daughter who would marry well and drag the Spencer family from relative obscurity.

She had been neglected, to be sure, but free. That she had so little control now, less even than when she was a child, burned through her like acid.

She was no better than a prisoner in her own home. It was not to be borne. Her mind worked desperately, struggling to come up with a way to free herself from Desmond's suffocating yoke. After several moments, she sighed, ceased her pacing, and collapsed on the small couch at the foot of her bed.

Her bedchamber door opened. Anna bustled inside. "What did that scoundrel do to you?" she cried. "I knew he was up to no good when he sent me halfway across Town to Leadenhall market for clams we could have purchased from the fishmonger who delivers to our very door!"

Jane shook her head. "I have to get out of here, Anna."

"I know, love, I know." The maid lowered her substantial girth onto the bench beside Jane. Wrapping a soft arm around her shoulders, Anna gave her a squeeze. She worked her hand up and down Jane's arm, the rhythmic motion comforting. "I tried to stop that trollop from coming in here, but Mr. Billings was there. I couldn't—"

"Trollop?"

"Yes." Anna blinked. "I thought you knew Berthe was the one who . . ."

"Went through my things?" Jane finished, surging off the bench. "Oh, I'm sure she took great joy in that!" The little viper already gloated over Jane being relegated to a governess.

Her gaze drifted to her armoire, her stomach rolling at the thought of Berthe, Marcus's *favorite* maid, rummaging through her personal things. It brought to mind the day Jane had caught the maid trying on one of her gowns, twirling before her cheval mirror bold as a peacock. Jane never held hope that the girl would be dismissed, not when she earned her wages in Marcus's bed.

"If I stay in this room a moment longer I shall go mad."

Anna pulled back to look at her. "What are you thinking of?"

Jane lifted her chin. "They don't own me." A fire kindled in her blood, burning a smoldering path up her chest. "They may have confiscated my clothes and jewelry, but I'm not their prisoner. Nor am I a child to be led about. Anna, I'll be venturing out tonight."

"They can prevent you from taking a carriage," Anna pointed out.

Jane paced. "The lack of a carriage did not stop me last time. I have friends. Lucy can loan me a carriage." She glanced down at her gown. "And a dress more suitable for my destination."

"Where are you going?"

It took only a moment for her to answer, and she realized that the answer had been there all along, a shadow hovering in the back of her mind—her goal perhaps from the start.

"Vauxhall."

Chapter 12

People teemed Vauxhall, their voices a heavy thrum that competed with the blare of the orchestra. Even though he stood outdoors, Seth craved air. Air and space.

He had decided almost instantly that Fiona Manchester would never do as his wife. She could not look long upon his face. Not an uncommon reaction, to be sure—especially from a lady. He should have come to expect no less. Call him fool, but he wanted a wife that could at least bear the sight of him.

When he addressed her, she held his gaze only a moment before her eyes trailed the line of his scar, then darted away as skittish as a bird.

And that was another matter. She looked as though she could break beneath the slightest pressure. Indeed, she reminded him of some delicate piece of crystal to be handled with utmost care. Not the kind of woman he wanted in his bed.

The image of a full-bodied woman in a gold dress flashed in his head. Now that was a woman he could handle without fear of hurting. And Jane, a voice whispered, unbidden, across his mind. The voluptuous body that strained against her widow's weeds was made for a lover's hands.

His palms tingled and he closed them into tight fists, cursing himself a fool. Jane was not the sort of female to entertain an illicit affair. For no other reason could he have walked away from her earlier today. Not with desire for her pumping through him, fierce as the tide. However, she was the sort a man took to wife. Only not him. He may have put the past behind him, but he was not fool enough to marry into the Spencer clan.

Whether he wished it or not, Fiona Manchester was the sort he should wed. Theirs would be a marriage of politeness and formality—what he had claimed to want.

The question at hand, he reminded himself, was whether she could be trusted to care for Julianne. That was all that mattered. The only thing to be considered. Not his personal desires.

"Lord St. Claire, are you not enjoying yourself?" Miss Fiona Manchester asked, flicking him with her fan coyly. A forced gesture, to be certain. That she took pains to flirt with him, despite her obvious distaste, marked her every bit the social climber he first judged her.

He opened his mouth to respond, then froze at the sight of another woman, wondering if the vision was real or merely an extension of the dreams he had suffered these last nights. Garbed in the same gown of gold silk, she weaved among the throng of people, dodging the hands that tried to grasp her arm and pull her into their circle.

She walked haltingly, her neck craning as though she searched for someone. As breathtaking as the first time he clapped eyes on her, she wore the black domino again. The golden diamonds at her throat glittered in the lamplight.

Seth shook his head, telling himself she couldn't be real. Couldn't be here.

Still, he felt himself moving, breaking from his group, leaving the startled Miss Manchester in midsentence as he advanced on his mystery woman with steadfast purpose. The blood rushed through his veins, filling his ears with a desperate tempo to rival the beat of the orchestra. As he shoved through the crush, other men stopped to gawk and devour the sight of this lone enchantress, and he knew she was no vision, but real. Flesh and blood woman.

His Aurora, set free to fly the night. Even as he told himself it was insanity to react so strongly to a woman whose face he had yet to see, whose name he had yet to speak, he moved, stalking her like a jungle cat honing in on its prey.

She would not get away this time. He would not be fool enough to let her walk away from him. Not this woman who made the blood burn in his veins, who stared at him without fear or revulsion in her gaze, but something else. Something unidentifiable, something akin to admiration. Here, he thought, was a woman he could have . . . perhaps even keep.

Drinking in the sight of her, he vowed to believe whatever he read in her gaze. If only for tonight. For one night he would allow himself to believe he deserved whatever she would lavish on him with her eyes, and, the devil take him, her body.

Jane felt his presence before she saw him. A heat radiated at her back and the tiny hairs at the nape of her neck tingled in familiar awareness. With a small gasp, her hand flew from the stone railing she clutched and she spun around to find herself face-to-face with Seth. He was alone. No sign of his companions. No sight of the lady he was supposed to evaluate as his bride.

She had imagined finding him ensnared in the spell of another woman. Despite deliberately wearing the gold dress and black domino again, she feared he would be too enthralled to give her notice. Relief pinched at her heart to see his dark gaze fixed on her face with single-minded intensity.

She opened her mouth to say something, to offer up some witty greeting, one of the countless quips she had heard during the years she had propped herself against ballroom walls, watching and listening to coy debutantes.

Before she could utter a syllable, he grabbed hold of her wrist and turned, pulling her away from the courtyard and down one of the many dark winding paths. He avoided the wide lamplit lane where groups and couples strolled, choosing dimmer paths where many a maid or matron had lost her virtue.

Still, Jane found she could not speak, could only bid her feet to keep up with his swift pace, could only pray her pounding heart did not burst from her chest. She had ventured out tonight to prove to herself that no one ruled her—that stealing her clothes and jewelry did not steal her spirit, her will. And, if she were perfectly honest with herself, she had come to immerse her barren heart in what it had long been denied. To finish what they had started today at Seth's townhouse.

They rounded one bend, then another, the hedges seeming to thicken around them. Still, Seth strode ahead, his long strides so purposeful she felt certain he had a destination in mind.

His fingers slid from her wrist to her fingers, twining with them. The intimate hold sent her heart racing even harder, and she recalled the times she had stared at his hands, watched in longing as he took her sister's lily-pale hand in his own when they walked ahead of her. How she had wanted to feel her own entwined with his. To walk through his family's orchard with him at her side. Her chest grew tight at the feel of their palms pressed tightly together.

He stepped off the path and plunged them into the foliage. She tripped over a root. He caught her close to his hard chest, and she imagined she could feel the beat of his heart, as wild as her own, through their clothing. Her free hand came up to grasp a hard bicep and his muscles tensed, bunching beneath her touch.

In one sudden movement, he backed her against a tree, its trunk a wide wall at her back, scratching the delicate fabric of her gown.

"I will not let you go again," his voice scraped the air, hard with resolve.

"I do not want you to," she returned. The truth,

but irrelevant. Because she would go. No matter what she wanted. She would have this time, this moment. And she would go.

She could barely make out the outline of him looming over her. The crowd laughed in the distance and faint applause filled the air.

Almost as if he read her mind, he vowed thickly, "It's going to be good between us." His hand cupped her cheek, the callused pad of his thumb tracing the seam of her lips.

She opened her mouth, but no sound emerged. She had no idea what to say at this point. A coy response felt wrong. Instead she bit the pad of his thumb, then sucked where her teeth had nipped.

He groaned. "I've not stopped thinking of you."

"Me too," she breathed, then flushed with embarrassment. "I m—mean," she stammered, "you . . . I have not stopped thinking of you." *For nearly all my life.*

"There is no escape this time," he announced, his hands coming down on either side of her head, caging her in as he had done earlier today.

Her heart tripped. *I don't want to escape you. I never did. You were the one I wanted to run to.*

Almost as if he heard her words, he answered the call to her parched soul, her deprived body, pressing his solid length against hers so that she felt his every angle, every hollow, right down to the hard bulge prodding her belly.

And then he was kissing her.

Her eyes drifted shut, lost to the joy of it. *Bliss.* Seth. The very one of whom she had spun impossible fantasies. As a girl, she convinced herself that if she wished it enough, if she hoped and prayed hard enough, he would be hers. One day it would happen. Could happen. Eight years had passed since her heart had harbored that foolish dream. Since Seth had disappeared. Since she had wed Marcus. Since she had forgotten how to dream.

But tonight, it seemed, the dream would become reality. Tonight, he would be hers. Or rather Aurora's. For a single night, at least. It would be enough. She would make it so.

Tongue tangling with hers, his fingers slid into her hair, scattering the pins. And with those pins, her inhibitions—if any remained—fled. A lick of heat curled low in her belly, tightening and twisting until she grew wet between the legs. His hands slid lower, seizing her buttocks through the fabric of her gown.

She moaned into his mouth, hating the skirts in her way, barring her from finding relief.

She pressed herself against him, winding her

arms around his neck, wondering at the insistent ache throbbing at her core. She'd never felt anything like it, not at the start of her marriage when Marcus had sought her bed. Those nights, however fleeting, had never been more than . . . nice. Never had she felt this blistering passion. Never had she burned.

Her fingers wove through his hair, luxuriating in the softness, in her freedom to touch the chestnut locks that she had spent many a summer day watching ruffle in the wind.

His hands released her derrière and she fell back, boneless, ready to melt down the tree's rough length. Still, their lips clung, drinking, tasting, devouring each other as his hands moved to her bodice. She gasped into his mouth when he cupped her breasts through her dress.

With a growl, he wrenched his lips from hers, dragging his mouth down the column of her throat as he tugged her dress down, sucking, nipping at the cords along her neck. She heard a tear, but didn't care. She needed his hands on her, skin to skin.

Her head fell back on the tree, a cry rising up in her throat as he clasped her breasts, his touch reverent, too gentle for her tightly wound body that wept for fulfillment. Her head lolled side to side, a hoarse plea on her lips. "Please."

His hold tightened, his rough palms chafing the tender skin. He took her nipples between thumb and forefinger and rolled the pebble-hard peaks until she thought she would fly from her skin. She arched her spine off the tree, closing her eyes as shards of pleasure-pain spiked through her.

His breath fired against her throat. She opened her eyes to his gleaming down at her in the dark, as though lit from within. He lowered himself, crouching at her feet. She felt his hands on the hem of her gown, then at her ankles, then her calves. Up they slid, skimming past her garters with astonishing speed before finding the slit of her drawers.

He stood then, his fingers teasing the inside of her thighs until she instinctively parted her legs wider.

"That's it," he murmured, his fingers slipping higher, stroking her before one finger pushed inside her, easing in with tormenting slowness until she nearly wept from pent-up desire. He used his thumb, rolling it over that little nub in fast circles.

"Ah, you feel so hot. So sweet."

She moaned, shuddered against his hand.

"I wager you taste sweet, too," he breathed thickly in her ear.

Overcome with sensation, her legs gave out.

He caught her then, lifting her up and wrapping

her legs around his hips. She had barely recovered her breath from that assault on her senses when she felt him, large and insistent, pushing at her entrance.

Their eyes locked, his burning brightly in the dark. He stopped, held himself there. His shoulders tensed beneath her hands, restraint humming through the corded muscles under his jacket.

"Please," she choked, her voice not her own, but some other wanton creature born of the night, where dreams hid and she ceased to exist.

Then he moved, shattering everything she thought she knew about herself, about him, in a single thrust, embedding himself deeply inside her, filling her in a way that was more than physical. More than life as she knew it.

He groaned, the sound reverberating from his body and into hers. With one hand on her bottom and the other gripping her thigh, he moved powerfully, stroking in and out of her. Again and again. His fingers dug into her thigh, pulling her leg higher for a deeper penetration, for pleasure so intense it bordered pain. The incredible friction drove her mad. She writhed between his hard body and the tree, desperate, searching for something she didn't know, something elusive, something that seemed both near and far away.

"That's it. Let go," he breathed in her ear, taking the lobe between his teeth and biting down, hard, sending a bolt of need bursting through her.

The ache that had started from the moment their mouths met increased, tightening every nerve in her body until she felt on the verge of snapping, exploding into pieces. His thrusts grew harder, faster, stoking the fire within her until—at last— she exploded, bursting from within, shivering like an apple blossom spinning through the wind.

Her internal quivering gradually ebbed and she fell limp in his arms, her cheek resting on one broad shoulder. He joined her, shuddering against her, grinding her to the tree.

She felt him pulse within her, the slightest movement in the still and sudden aftermath.

She remained just so for several moments, pinned between him and the tree until he removed himself from her with a rustle of clothing and stepped back. Her chest rose and fell with deep breaths. Still, she did not move, too afraid, too worried that her legs would give out beneath her, that she would blink and wake in her small bed. Alone. The same.

Cool air crawled over her. A chill chased over her skin, puckering her nipples, returning her to herself, reminding her to pull her dress back up. Feeling less exposed, she lifted one foot, prepared to step from the tree, but her knees wobbled and her legs quivered. Deciding it best not to collapse in an undignified pile, she leaned back against the tree, giving herself further time to compose herself.

"Aurora," he whispered, and his fingers grazed her cheek. They brushed the stiff edge of her domino and she jerked, her heart lurching painfully. Despite the dark, her hand darted to her face to make certain her disguise was still in place.

"Don't you think it's time you showed me your face?" he asked, the husky murmur of his voice rolling over her. "And perhaps we can even exchange names."

Beneath the teasing ring of his voice, she detected a determination, an edge. Seth had just made love to her in a garden. Against a tree. He would want to see her face, know her name. Curiosity alone demanded it. And damn if a part of her didn't want to reveal herself, didn't want to see the expression on his face when he saw it was she—Jane. But the other part of herself, the voice of logic—the realist—knew his reaction would likely be one she did not want to see.

"Perhaps," she returned, her heart beating harder at that total impossibility. Hoping that he took her vague response for playfulness, she ran her hand over his arm, grasping his fingers and pulling them away from her mask.

Eyes smoldering like embers in the gloom, his voice flowed over her, "Come. Let us finish out the night elsewhere." With a hand on her elbow, he pulled her along, back to the dimly lit path. His fingers burned her flesh, a brand that she would forever bear. One she never wanted to be rid.

Unbelievably, the fire in her blood flickered to life again at his words. A part of her longed to go with him, to continue his sensual onslaught somewhere comfortable and private, where they could devote time and attention to one another, where he could stoke her newfound passions to life again. But that could never be. Her chest constricted and the backs of her eyes burned. This would be all she would ever have from him. One stolen night in a dark garden. She could expect no more. Could risk no more.

She allowed him to lead her from the shadows, her mind working feverishly, wondering how she might escape him before he discovered that it was she who hid behind the mask.

"Come," he murmured near her ear, guiding her back into the crowd of revelers with his hand at the small of her back.

A troupe of performers wove through the crowd, drawing upon them. A pair of jugglers led the way, tossing flaming batons. Dancers in flowing garments whirled around them. The crowd thickened, noisy and lively, jostling Jane as they swarmed for a better look at the performers. Seth tightened his hold on her. Nevertheless, one tug and she knew she could be free.

Pressing herself to him, she crushed her mouth to his in a final searing kiss. For a moment, the noise vanished, the crowd disappeared and it was only her mouth on his—needing, taking, giving. Before she became too lost in the moment, in the kiss, in him, she broke away. Her lips still clinging to his, she stared into his eyes and whispered, "Thank you."

"For what?" His eyes smoldered fire in the dark night.

"One night with you."

Dragging in a deep breath, she wrenched herself free and dove into the crowd.

"Aurora," he called after her, his voice clawing the air, terrible in its anger.

She plunged deeper into the mass of bodies as he again called that name she had come to love. And hate.

Pushing ahead, she forbade herself to look over her shoulder, to see if he followed, too afraid that if she saw his face she would freeze, give in, and run back to his arms.

The sound of his shouts faded, merging with the noise of Vauxhall—the laughing crowd, the cries of the performers, the steady song of the orchestra.

She pushed ahead, down the wide lane crowded with both oncoming and departing revelers, until her lungs threatened to burst.

Faces blurred before her eyes. Wind lashed her face, colder where tears streamed her cheeks, but still she ran. Holding her skirts high, she shoved through bodies with no thought to courtesy, no thought to the burning pain deep in her soul.

A dull pain throbbed behind her breastbone. She pressed a hand to the spot, convinced that the sensation had nothing to do with shortness of breath . . . and everything to do with never having another night with Seth.

Chapter 13

Seth stopped short of shoving a pair of dandies weaving unsteadily before him to the ground. He bounced on the balls of his feet, trying to keep sight of Aurora in the crowd. The throng parted and he pressed forward, scanning the many faces, trying to catch a glimpse of a gold dress, of dark brown hair trailing like a banner in the wind. Only nothing. No sight of her.

He cursed fiercely, earning himself a few glances. Dragging a hand through his hair, he knew, deep in his gut, he would never see her again, that she did not wish for him to find her. That kiss had been the last—her enigmatic words the final good-bye.

For whatever reason, she had sought him out tonight. But tonight it ended. He knew he would never see her again. Just as he knew he would never fully be free of her, that he would look especially hard at every lady to cross his path, measuring the rich brown of her hair, the slope of her throat, the generous swell of her breasts against her bodice . . . hoping against hope that it was his Aurora.

Jane took a deep breath and tried to still her trembling. It did no good. She stretched her hands out before her. They shook like the last leaf of fall.

"Well? What happened?" Lucy demanded.

"Nothing," she lied.

Lucy frowned. "Well, did you see him or not?"

"Lord St. Claire?" she asked with deliberate vagueness, unsure what to say, unsure of her friend's reaction.

"Of course. Who else? Isn't he who you wanted to see?"

Jane nodded jerkily, biting her lip. Lucy had asked nothing. Not when Jane requested to borrow her gold dress a second time. Nor when she asked for use of her carriage and driver. No questions, no judgments. Lucy had simply acquiesced, and Jane knew she deserved some sort of explanation.

"Yes. I found him," she confessed, cheeks stinging at the thought of what had transpired when she had.

"And?"

Jane turned her attention to removing the gown, straining to reach the buttons at the back.

"Here, let me help." Lucy brushed her trembling fingers aside. "You talked to him, I assume," she said, probing further as she attacked the tiny satin-covered buttons. "What did you say? Did you tell him who you—" A sharp gasp ripped from Lucy's throat. "Dear Heavens! Your sleeve's torn, and some of the buttons are missing!"

Jane's face burned even hotter as she recalled the sound of the dress ripping in the garden. And all that had followed.

"Jane?" Lucy demanded, her voice sharp.

Jane squared her shoulders and met Lucy's eyes through the mirror.

"I—" she began, stopping at the weak sound of her voice.

Lucy's eyes rounded. "You didn't!"

Revealing heat swarmed her face.

"You did!"

Jane gave a single, hard nod, all that she could manage.

"Does he know it was you?"

"No." Jane laughed then, a bitter, humorless sound. "Horrible coward, am I not?" She shook her head fiercely. "I couldn't. He would never . . ." Her voice faded and she glanced at Lucy, willing her to understand, willing her to see that she was not some pathetic creature so desperate for the fleeting affections of a man that she had succumbed to a sordid tryst. It had been more than that. *It had been Seth.* Only he could make her toss caution to the wind and lose all morals.

Lucy sighed softly, rubbing her forehead. "I don't want to see you hurt."

Jane opened her mouth to assure her that there was no risk of that, but the words failed her when she realized she couldn't make such a claim. The ache in her chest told her as much. Still, she didn't regret it. She would never regret him. Too much of her life had been spent in a state of longing, wishing, dreaming for the reality of tonight. For Seth.

Well, perhaps she had wished for more. Courtship. Love. Marriage. Children. But she would take what she had been given—the memory of a garden hugged by night. It would be enough. She would make it so.

"I knew what I was doing, Lucy."

With a nod, her friend set to work on the remaining buttons. "I hope so, Jane. You're a good person. You deserve more than what life has handed you."

"So do you."

Lucy smiled, but the smile failed to reach her

eyes. "I had all I ever I wanted once. It was enough, it was . . ." She paused, a faraway look entering her eyes that pinched at Jane's heart because she knew precisely where her friend was, knew who filled her heart, her head, her very soul.

"I had enough joy for a lifetime," Lucy murmured, blinking rapidly before turning her attention back to Jane's buttons. Finished, she helped Jane step from the gown.

A lump formed in Jane's throat at the memory of Lucy's daughter, a sweet-faced little girl that had loved to chatter, loved to laugh . . . loved life. She had only known Lucy six months before she had lost her husband and daughter to fever—about the same time Jane's marriage had begun to crumble.

Lucy lifted her head, her blue-gray eyes shining moistly. "Every day I tell myself that I will see her again. If I didn't believe that, I could never go on."

Jane nodded mutely. She'd known pain, emptiness, but not loss in the way Lucy had. Seth had never been hers to lose. And at least he had not died. At least he lived on, breathing in air, even if not beside her.

"Allow me my concern, Jane. You're not one of those frivolous ladies to engage in affairs. You cannot separate your heart from such business."

Jane snatched her black gown from where she left it on a chaise, telling herself Lucy was wrong. Years ago, she had been infatuated with Seth. Tonight was simply an exercise in freedom, a chance to live the dream of her youth.

"It was one time, Lucy. Once does not constitute an affair."

"Oh." Her friend's lips twisted in derision. "That makes me feel better."

Jane sighed as she stepped into her dress. "You're such a mother hen." She stilled, cringing at her ill-chosen words.

Lucy's face paled.

"Lucy, I didn't mean—"

"I know." She waved a hand and motioned Jane around. With deft movements, she buttoned her up. "You're a grown woman, Jane. Sometimes I forget not everyone needs my advice. I'm sure you know what you're doing."

"I do." She managed to say in a convincing manner.

"I'll only say this—you should let him know it was you tonight. If you feel so strongly about him, perhaps there could be a future—"

"No," she broke in. Seth would never see her as anything other than sister to the woman who broke his heart.

"Hmm," was all Lucy offered.

Turning around, Jane glanced at the discarded gown, the gold a gleaming reminder of all that had occurred. Sadness welled in her chest as she gazed at the borrowed gown, realizing she would never have need of it again.

Seth stormed into his room, wrenching free of his jacket and tearing his cravat from his neck. The scent of her still filled his senses, playing with his mind, his heart. He stopped hard in the middle of the room and looked about him, jerking his head to the left and right, searching for what he didn't know. It wasn't as if Aurora lurked in the shadows of his chamber, yet his gaze flew about the room like a wild zephyr skipping over the seas.

"Lieutenant," Knightly greeted, emerging from the adjoining room. "You've returned early. Was the lady not up to your expectations?"

Seth stared at his former midshipman, thinking only that Aurora had surpassed every expectation . . . and wondering how Knightly knew of her. True, there was little the former midshipman didn't know about him. The two had been together for so long, the men knew each other as well as any two souls could.

Seth hadn't treated Knightly as the other commissioned officers did, as though it were his privilege to shine their boots. And although Seth had never expected anything for such courtesy, Knightly had always looked out for him, teaching him how to fight, and not like a gentleman. Lessons that had saved his life on more than one occasion.

Seth gazed at him now, shaking his head. "How did you know—"

"Colonel Manchester's sister?" Knightly prodded. "Is she as lovely as rumored?"

"Oh, Miss Manchester," he murmured. Of course.

He'd forgotten about Miss Manchester. Forgotten everything save the feel of Aurora in his arms— her taste, her body against his. She kissed him as no woman had, as if she couldn't get enough of him, as if his lips were opium itself.

"Yes," Knightly answered, looking at him strangely, "Miss Manchester."

"No, Miss Manchester did not meet my expectations."

How could she when his masked lady had been within twenty yards?

For some reason, his thoughts turned to Jane just then. The sweet taste of her throat beneath his mouth. True, she was no wild tigress like Aurora, but the tremble of her neck beneath his lips, soft as the flutter of a moth's wings, filled him with a different sort of hunger . . . but no less intoxicating.

Shaking off the unwelcome comparison and wondering if he were mad to still crave after Jane when he had been so thoroughly satisfied with Aurora, he vowed to put Jane from his thoughts and concentrate on finding his masked seductress again. A woman more suitable for him to pursue.

Aurora had come to him. He could only hope she would do so again. After tonight he would never get her out of his blood, much less his thoughts.

"Ah, then you must continue looking."

Seth's head snapped back in Gregory's direction. "Looking?" he echoed, wondering how Knightly had read his thoughts.

"For your bride."

"Oh." Realizing Knightly discussed Miss Manchester, he lowered himself to a chair and tugged off his boots.

"Forgive me, but you seem distracted tonight."

Removing his last boot, Seth fell back into the chair and looked Gregory steadily in the face. "I met someone."

"Did you? Who is she?"

The scent of her swirled around him. Closing his eyes, he inhaled, taking the scent of apples deep within himself.

"I don't know. She did not give her name." *Just her body.*

Knightly's brows rose.

Seth stared broodingly across the room, thumping the arm of the chair lightly with his fist. "I will find her."

Knightly bent to collect his discarded boots. "Generally, people are only found when they wish to be."

"I must see her again."

"Perhaps you should focus on finding a bride you like half as much as this mystery woman. Or have you changed your mind about marrying?"

Seth considered that, wishing he could quit the whole notion of matrimony. But he couldn't. All he had to do was think of his cousin, and the risk he presented to Julianne. Seth had to wed, and hopefully, beget an heir or two to keep Harold well in his place.

"I'll find a bride," he asserted, simultaneously vowing that he would never cease looking for Aurora.

Recalling the way she had moved against him, the way he had felt buried deep inside her, he knew he would never be free of her.

He would have her again.

* * *

After departing Lucy's, Jane crept up the servant's staircase, holding her breath until she reached her bedroom door. Hand on the latch, the tension flowed from her shoulders as she pushed the door in and walked inside. A lamp burned low on the dresser, filling the room with dancing shadows.

"Late night, my dear?"

She spun around, her heart in her throat.

"D—Desmond."

"I warned you, Jane." He advanced on her slowly, the thud of his every step a stab to her heart. "Where have you been?" He slapped his hand against the side of his thigh. "Sneaking off in the middle of the night—"

"I—I was at Lady Shillington's." Not strictly a lie.

"Hmm." He stopped before her, his voice lowering. "Chloris is most displeased. She had to take a tonic to calm her nerves. Put her straight to sleep." She struggled to hold her ground and not shrink away as he brushed her collarbone above the stiff edge of her bodice. "She wouldn't hear a cavalry charge."

Her gaze flitted over her sparsely furnished chamber. "Then perhaps we should wait to discuss this in the morning."

Turning, she grasped the door's latch in her hand

again, determined to usher him from the room. He grabbed her wrist, squeezing the bones until they ached.

"Chloris thinks we should send you away."

She lifted her chin a notch and tried not to wince at his grip on her wrist. "Why don't you?"

"You would like that," he growled. "I told you there's only one way out of this house."

"Never will I accept your disgusting proposition."

His small eyes flashed in his gaunt face. "As I was reflecting upon your defiance this evening and trying to come up with a proper punishment, I realized taking your clothes and jewelry was merely a child's reprimand." He paused, his gaze crawling over her. "You're no child, Jane."

The tiny hairs on the back of her neck began to prickle as he stepped nearer. She held her breath, waiting for his words to fall.

"Your maid," he began. "She has been with you some years now, correct?"

Her chest suddenly grew tight, the ability to draw breath difficult. "Anna?" she asked warily.

"Precisely how long has the old bird been with you?" He stared at her, unblinking, waiting for her answer.

With great reluctance, she replied, "She was my nurse."

"Ah." He nodded, a strange smile curving his thin lips.

"What?" she demanded.

"It's a shame, that is all."

"A shame," she echoed.

"Yes. I fear, you shall miss her," he drawled in tones of false sympathy.

"What do you mean?"

"I've dismissed her. Moments ago, in fact."

"Dismissed her?"

"I say, Jane. You're usually not this slow to grasp matters."

"Where is she?" she demanded, anger churning her stomach.

"I told you. I have released her from my employ."

"You have no right," she cried. Jerking free, she pushed open the door, intent on finding Anna.

He grabbed her by the arm and spun her back around, slamming her back against the door with enough force to rattle her teeth.

"I have every right," he snapped, all pretense at kindness gone. "Until Matthew comes of age, I shall make all decisions regarding this family. Regarding *you*. I warned you not to challenge me."

Desperation, thick and cold, clawed at her heart. She struggled against his hold.

"Please, Desmond. Anna is . . ." she choked on a sob, words woefully inadequate. *Everything. All I have. The only one who has loved me all of my life.*

"Perhaps I'll reconsider." He shrugged, his voice slithering through her like a snake gliding through grass. "Much depends on you. On your cooperation."

"You can't dismiss her! Where will she go?"

"It's not my habit to follow the comings and goings of a servant no longer in my employ."

"You cannot do this," she hissed, hands clenching at her sides. "I've done nothing to warrant—"

"Desmond." A voice rang out from the corridor, sharp and grating. Apparently Chloris's tonic had not been strong enough, after all. "Have you finished with Jane?"

Have you finished with Jane? As if she were some disobedient child that required scolding.

"Yes, Chloris. For now." With a look promising more to come, he released her and slipped from the room.

Alone in her room, she leaned against the hard length of the door, taking comfort in its temporary barrier.

"I trust she apologized," Chloris's voice drifted through the door. "I won't even hazard a guess as to where she's been. Or what she's been doing."

Jane bit the inside of her cheek to stifle the acerbic retort she longed to shout. Turning, she dragged a chair from her desk and propped it against the door. However inadequate, it reassured her. She assessed her small quarters, pacing with long strides, back and forth, back and forth, missing Anna, her comfort, her presence, steady as the tide. Her heart hammered wildly, like a butterfly trapped in her chest, beating about for escape.

Worry for Anna filled her. In the dead of night, with no place to turn, where would she go? Jane shook her head, then drew in a long, steadying breath. Anna was no shrinking flower. She would be fine. She would contact Jane. A sob scalded the back of her throat, scratchy and hot, but she held it in.

"Damn you, Desmond," she swore, her voice small as she sank onto the bed, dropping her head onto the pillow.

Her hand slid beneath the pillow to bring the fresh linen closer to her face and her fingertips met something that crinkled. Sitting up, she pulled back the pillow to stare at a piece of folded parchment. Frowning, she grasped it with greedy fingers and quickly unfolded the small square, hope unfurling in her chest.

A deep sigh escaped her lungs as she scanned

the note from Anna. She pressed the missive to her heart as relief flowed through her. Anna had gone to Lucy's. Jane must have just missed her. She was safe. That was enough. That was all that mattered.

Burying her face in the pillow, she gave in to the tears, unsure why she wept. Because Anna had been taken from her and she was well and truly alone? Or because of Seth? Because tonight had been wonderful, better than the dreams that had followed her these many years . . . and suddenly everything in her life seemed dimmer than ever before?

Chapter 14

Jane stared at the missive, blinking several times before refolding it and slipping it back in its envelope. Stubbornly, she resisted the weakening of her will and carefully smoothed out the envelope's crinkled edges, pretending not to feel the hard, watchful eyes across the table, pretending not to hear the whispers in her head that urged her to accept the invitation, to run, to flee. If only for an afternoon.

It was the third letter from Julianne in the last fortnight—penned in Rebecca's hand. Again, she requested Jane's company. Today the request was for a drive in the park.

The very prospect both tempted and dismayed. Dismay won out . . . as it had in the face of Julianne's previous letters. It was the chance of facing Seth that had her declining Julianne's invitations.

Weeks had passed since Vauxhall, but in no way did she possess the nerve to face Seth again. Not this soon. Perhaps not ever.

"Who is that from?" Chloris demanded.

"Lady Julianne invited me to join her in the park." Jane saw no reason to keep the truth from her. It wasn't as if she would be accepting Julianne's invitation. This day or any other.

"Again?" Chloris muttered, her tone aggrieved as she stirred her tea, the spoon clanking the inside of her cup. "Doesn't she have anything better to do than plague you? Well. . ." Chloris's lips twisted in a semblance of a smile and she answered herself. "Likely not, poor creature."

Jane pushed aside her barely touched food. Her stomach had been off lately, ever since losing Anna, and Chloris's company did nothing if not sour it further. Rising, she dropped her napkin on the table. Even morning lessons with her nieces held greater appeal than a leisurely breakfast with Chloris.

"I promised to take Bryony shopping," Chloris announced. "Her birthday is next week, you know."

Yes, Jane knew. The girl had been working industriously on her wish list for the last several months, to the neglect of her lessons. "I suppose Dahlia and Iris can come, too. Although Iris has the most wretched tendency to fidget." Chloris's nose wrinkled, her discontent clear. "We will need at least three maids to carry parcels. And an extra footman." Chloris wiped the corners of her mouth with a fastidiousness that set Jane's teeth on edge. "See to that, will you?"

She hesitated, feeling suddenly bold. What did she have to lose by asserting herself? Desmond had seen fit to rob her of anything that mattered. "Since you intend to take the girls to Bond Street, I will make free with my morning."

"What?"

"I'm in need of a respite."

"Respite?" Chloris echoed.

Jane turned to leave.

Chloris called after her. "You've become annoyingly contrary of late, Jane."

Contrary. Jane let the word roll around her head, deciding she liked the sound of it.

A glance over her shoulder revealed helpless frustration on Chloris's face. "The sooner you remember your role in this household, the better." Anxiety threaded Chloris's voice, betraying her bluster.

Your role. The words ricocheted through Jane's head, begging to be challenged. Her tone deliberately offhand, she asked, "Better for whom?"

Chloris broke eye contact, ignoring the question entirely. Setting down her cup, her hand trembled. "Take the morning off," Chloris said, as if it were her suggestion. "But see that you're ready for the girls after lunch. I'm certain I'll be weary from shopping."

Fed by the same impulse that had guided her of late, that drove her to be bold, defiant, Jane lingered in the threshold, her fingers curling at her side. "I think I shall catch up on my correspondence to Matthew," she drawled. "I will be sure to let him know you're faring well in Town and enjoying his home and all the marvelous shops on Bond Street."

Color rushed Chloris's face.

Satisfied, Jane turned and left the room.

Contrary, she mused as she made her way up the stairs, letting herself, briefly, consider donning her mask and seeking out Seth again. Then she shook her head. No, that would be something more than contrary. That would be reckless, unwise. No matter how her heart wished it, she could never be Aurora again. Sooner or later he would discover that it was she behind the mask.

A small shiver coursed through her.

But then, perhaps that was what she wanted.

* * *

A week later, Jane found herself frozen in the threshold of her drawing room. Fighting to swallow the lump in her suddenly tight throat, she entered the room, unsure whether to be grateful that Chloris and Desmond were not present to bar her from leaving the schoolroom and receiving callers.

Not that she had been presenting the day's geography lesson with any great expertise. Her gaze continually strayed to the window that faced the gardens, letting the rare sunlight warm her face.

As always, her thoughts lingered on Seth and their one night and how she might learn to accept that nothing as thrilling or wonderful would ever happen to her again.

And now he stood before her. As fiercely handsome as she remembered, even with his menacing scar and eyes that looked on her with no knowledge of the intimacy they had shared. A perplexing annoyance that. To be flooded with titillating sensation just at the sight of him, to recall the fullness of him moving inside, the heated friction of their bodies coming together . . . and know that he recalled none of it when he looked at her.

Julianne sat on a sofa, her brother looming on his feet beside her. Lifting her face in Jane's direction, she apologized, "Forgive us for calling unannounced. I know from your letters you've been busy."

"Yes," Seth drawled. "Our apologies for interrupting your busy day, but my sister has missed your company."

His voice was thick with accusation, justifiably so. Her face burned in shame, recalling her promise to visit Julianne again.

She pasted a brittle smile to her face, hoping it stayed in place as she lowered to a chair. "How kind of you to come, Julianne. Your company is always welcome." She lifted her gaze to Seth. "Would you not care for a seat, my lord?"

He held her gaze for a moment, the anger and accusation still there. Finally, he gave a curt nod and sat beside his sister.

"Today is Rebecca's afternoon off and I convinced Seth to take me out," Julianne volunteered cheerfully.

"Harassed is a more accurate word," Seth supplied, a twist to his mouth that almost resembled a smile.

"Oh, very well, harassed." She waved her hand in the air, unbothered. "It wasn't as if you were doing anything. You've moped about the house now for weeks and been surly as a bear."

Jane cocked an eyebrow. Why would Seth mope about? Certainly it had nothing to do with their tryst at Vauxhall? That would be too much to hope for. True, his furious shouts still echoed in her head at night, but she credited that to male pride and her eluding him, not any true sense of loss.

"We're in Town," Julianne continued. "Might we not actually step outside? Enjoy the Season? Go somewhere exciting?"

Seth's expression grew shuttered. His lips tightened. For some reason, Jane felt the unreasonable need to defend him. "I'm sure your brother experienced quite enough excitement while abroad and desires only a little peace now."

Surprise flickered in his eyes, and she looked away, regretting her impulse to defend him.

"Perhaps," Julianne allowed. "But while he was off playing war I've had enough peace to last a lifetime."

"Did I not relent and bring you here today?" he asked, leaning back and throwing an arm along the back of the sofa.

"Yes, curious that." A teasing smile lifted the corners of Julianne's mouth. "You've denied nearly all my other requests at social outings. I almost suspect you wanted to see Lady Jane."

Heat lit her face.

Seth stared at Jane for a long moment before murmuring, "Perhaps."

Jane wrenched her gaze away. Hoping to detract

from the conversation's embarrassing turn, she motioned to the tea service one of the servants had left. "Would you care for tea? A biscuit?"

"Yes, that would be lovely," Julianne replied.

Jane poured and rose to secure the cup and saucer in Julianne's hands. "I hope it's warm enough. Lord St. Claire?" Turning, she looked down at Seth. Her breath caught to find him evaluating her person. His gaze traveled over her with a thoroughness that heated her face even more.

"Lord St. Claire?" she asked, her voice sharp.

His gaze snapped to hers.

"Tea?"

"Yes. Thank you," he murmured, accepting the cup. His eyes glowed with a mocking light. The wretch. Surely he would not leer at her if his sister could see him.

She sat down hard on her seat, feeling unreasonably angry. Had he forgotten his midnight lover so quickly that he could leer at another lady? Clearly he did not pine for his Aurora. Likely their one time was already forgotten.

He lifted his cup in salute, his expression taunting as she lowered herself back into her chair.

In that moment, she wished she could tell him the truth—that she was Aurora. If for no other reason than to wipe that smug look off his face.

He thought he knew her so well. Thought her just another Spencer, cut from the same cloth as her sister. A lady to mock, to scorn. Simply someone Julianne persisted in calling upon, someone who inconvenienced his life with her unwelcome friendship with his sister.

Would that she could reveal to him she was more than that. A woman who defied convention to seek her own pleasure. Pleasure in the form of him.

Seth felt an odd sense of satisfaction as he watched his hostess sit so indignantly in her chair, the color riding high on her cheeks.

For weeks, he had suffered Julianne's pouts and sighs. Her attachment to Lady Jane ran deep. Damnable bonds of youth. Seth had tried to explain that Jane was a lady of the *ton* now, too busy to concern herself with lapsed friendships.

He had thought she genuinely cared for his sister. She had promised to call, and he had believed her. Believed that she wouldn't hurt his sister. But she had failed. Failed to keep her promise, convincing him that he should never have dropped his guard with her, never considered that she might be different from her family. Better.

Still, he had caved to his sister's demands and permitted her to call on Jane. More than that, he had accompanied her on her call. For the life of him, he could not fathom why.

"So what has kept you so occupied you could not accept a single one of my sister's invitations?" he inquired, his voice surly even to his own ears.

"Seth," Julianne reprimanded.

"It's quite all right," Jane assured Julianne. Such assurance only further rankled him. Crossing his arms, he glared at her. It was not her place to soothe his sister. She had shown how little she cared for Julianne by ignoring her these last weeks.

Jane suffered his glare, her expression cool as frost. She paused to moisten her lips, saying, "I should have made the time. My apologies, Julianne."

Seth studied her in silence, noticing that her bottom lip quivered ever so slightly. The only hint of emotion in her haughty reserve.

Several times over the years, he had stared off the ship's deck at a quiet sea, reflecting over the hoyden that had chased him about the countryside, curious over what had become of her. Now he saw that she had become all that was proper and correct. A boring bit of starch in her widow's weeds. Disappointing.

And yet he devoured the sight of those lips, the full mouth that promised passion even as the rest of her hid behind ladylike diffidence. It was only that expressive mouth which reminded him of the girl he once knew. The girl, he admitted, had grown into a woman he would like to thaw with the heat of his mouth and hands . . . to strip of her mourning rags and spread naked on his bed.

The unwanted thoughts brought an uncomfortable tightness to his breeches. He reached for a biscuit, intent on distraction. Chewing, he forced himself to think about his hunt for a bride. About chits like Fiona Manchester. Prospective wives that would do nothing to ignite his ardor. The sort of ladies whose drawing rooms he ought to be occupying.

At that moment, Billings strode into the room, his skinny legs swaggering like a rooster's.

"Rutledge," Billings exclaimed, tugging the ends of his plum vest over his bulging middle in a self-important air.

They stared at each other for a heavy moment, no doubt recalling their last encounter.

"Billings," he returned, inclining his head, recalling the bastard's attempt to claim Aurora.

"This is unexpected. What are you doing here?"

Jane rose. "Lord St. Claire and Lady Julianne were kind enough to call upon me. If you recall, we grew up together."

"Ah," he murmured, his gaze flicking over Julianne before returning to Seth.

Awkward silence fell.

Jane cleared her throat and motioned to the tea service. "Would you care for refreshments, Desmond?"

With a nod, Billings dropped to the chair next to Jane, his gaze drifting to Julianne, staring overly long at the bodice of her dress. Seth's hands curled into fists at his sides.

Billings leaned forward to select a biscuit. "You must forgive my sister-in-law." The delicate wood frame of his chair creaked as he settled back and popped the biscuit whole into his mouth.

Jane stiffened in her chair but looked resolutely forward, hands clasped tightly in her lap.

Billings glanced sideways at her and smiled, a smug stretch of lips over uneven teeth. "I fear Jane has been remiss. Did she not explain that she is still in mourning?" He stretched an arm along the back of her chair, his fingers a hairsbreadth from her shoulder. "She is not receiving callers."

"Forgive us," Julianne murmured, cheeks pink, her awkwardness apparent as she fumbled for Seth's arm, clearly ready to rise and depart.

Billings's eyes danced. Seth's jaw tensed. The bastard was enjoying their discomfiture.

"No harm," Billings assured breezily, his fingers brushing the top of Jane's shoulder, grazing the crisp fabric of her sleeve. Back and forth, back and forth, his fingers crawled, encroaching like a white moth creeping over the unremitting black of her gown.

Seth watched, a strange tightening in his gut as he considered the slight motion, considered Jane's bent head. In a flash of insight, he knew. Knew that Billings pulled the strings and controlled her as he would a puppet.

Anger flooded him. Where was her backbone? Why did she let this strutting peacock speak for her? Did she not possess a voice, a shred of autonomy?

"Perhaps in another year Jane may entertain once again," Billings mused with an idleness that made Seth's already clenched jaw ache. The bastard lifted both brows, daring him to object.

Clearly Billings thought he was sniffing about his sister-in-law's skirts and needed to be set in his place like some overardent schoolboy. Seth looked Jane over again and immediately felt the stirrings of desire that had plagued him since first seeing her in the park. To be fair, Billings might not be far off in his concern.

Seth could not deny there was something about her. Those changeable eyes, the rich nut brown hair. The hint of a girl he remembered. Even though he longed to deny it, she tugged at some forgotten part of him.

Jane shrugged Desmond's hand off her with a twist of her shoulder. "You're mistaken, Desmond. I am quite able to receive social calls."

Desmond's face reddened. His gaze flicked to Seth, then back to Jane.

"Perhaps you did not realize it has been over a year," she added in a firm voice.

"No," he bit out through compressed teeth. "I did not."

Seth fought a smile, pleased to see that some of her spirit remained intact.

She met his gaze, and a familiar spark in her eyes reminded him of the Jane he had known. The Jane, he admitted to himself, he would like to know again.

Rising, he took Julianne's elbow. With a bow, he murmured farewell, his gaze lingering longer than it should on Jane before turning and leading his sister from the room.

As he departed, he told himself that he would smother his growing fascination and put Jane far from his mind, focusing, instead, on finding a bride. The sort of woman who would not muddle his head and twist him into knots.

Chapter 15

A low hum of conversation, broken only by the occasional rumble of laughter, reached her as she stood in the cavernous foyer of Lucy's mansion. A footman took her cloak and led her toward the music room.

Jane was late, having waited for Desmond and Chloris to leave for the evening before venturing out. Cowardly perhaps, but why suffer a scene? She still achieved her goal in the end. A pleasant evening out among friends. Good company, entertainment. A small exercise in freedom, to be certain, even if less dramatic than her previous forays.

The hum of conversation ebbed as she was led down the portrait-lined corridor. The famous Italian contralto Lucy had engaged for the evening eased her rich voice into song.

Upon reaching the tall double doors, Jane hovered for a moment, eyeing the rows of velvet-backed chairs occupied with two dozen guests.

Astrid sat in the front beside Lucy, a chair vacant beside her, doubtlessly intended for Jane. Not relishing making her way to the front amid the performance, she moved from the threshold to the back of the room and lowered herself to a sofa that had been pushed to the wall to make room for the evening's company.

With a sigh, she closed her eyes and let the lilting chords float over her. Sad, haunting words stretched over the air like slow curls of heat. Jane wished her Italian was better so that she might understand their meaning. No doubt it was some tragic tale of love lost, ideal for her dark mood.

The woman sang with her entire person, the generous curves of her body angled forward, palms lifted in supplication, face tight with emotion that plucked at one's heart. Very affecting. So much so that Jane felt moisture gather at the corners of her eyes.

Fearful that she would turn into a blubbering mess and draw attention to herself, she slipped from the room, deciding her current mood not the most suited for tonight's performance.

The haunting voice followed her and she quickened her pace, turning the corridor in the direction of the gallery. Her slippers moved swiftly and silently over the runner. Wall sconces dimly lit her way, stretching her shadow long before her, eerie and strange, as though it belonged to someone else. Another woman fleeing the memory of a night never to be relived.

The corridor opened up to the gallery—a wide, room with an elaborate mosaic covering the floor. She always felt a bit sacrilegious to walk upon such a beautiful rendition of Madonna and child.

Lucy's late husband had fanatically toured the continent to gather a collection that was the envy of every museum in Town. Jane lingered, drifting among the various pieces, studying the magnificent array as she did on almost every visit, grateful at least that the singing had eased to a soft croon on the air that no longer made her throat thicken.

She stopped before a white marbled bust of the god Anteros, the avenger of unrequited love, and her thoughts drifted to Seth.

She had been a fool to think one taste would be enough. That she could forget Seth and move on now, content with having had her time with him, however brief.

She wanted more. She wanted *him*. Not just once but over and over again. Sighing, she rubbed her fingertips over her forehead. The heart was a greedy beast. Always wanting more than it should.

"No taste for opera?" came a voice behind her.

Jane whirled around, her hip nudging the pedestal upon which the bust sat. Heart in her throat, her hands shot out to steady the piece, her panic subsiding as Anteros stilled.

Chuckling, Seth advanced, his long limbs moving loose and powerful as a jungle cat. "That would have been a mess."

Nodding mutely, she eased her hands from the pedestal and inched back until well clear of it and any other object of value, not trusting herself to be conscious of anything when he was in the vicinity and all her attention centered on him.

"You shouldn't sneak up on people."

He grinned and crossed his arms over his chest in a way that made his shoulders strain against his jacket.

She frowned as realization sunk in. "What are you doing here?"

"I was invited."

"By whom?" she demanded, unable to believe Lucy would have invited him without telling her.

His grin broadened. "Lady Shillington, of course."

Lucy invited him? And forgot to mention it? Suspicion settled along her shoulders.

He continued, "I thought my sister might enjoy a small gathering such as this."

"Your sister is here?"

"Yes. Were you not of the opinion that I should allow my sister out in Society?"

She blinked. "Yes. Only I did not think my opinions bore much weight."

Instead of responding, he glanced about the room, his eyes skimming the various pieces. "Impressive collection."

She nodded.

"Enough to draw someone away from the evening's entertainment, I suppose." His gaze fell on her. "The haste in which you left, one would think you have an aversion to opera, Lady Jane."

"Not at all."

"Hmm." He drew closer, his steps clicking sharply over the mosaic.

She skirted a statue of Aphrodite and he followed, his stride lazy, hands clasped behind his back as though he strolled the park—as though he did not stalk her.

"And what of Billings?" he queried, all mildness. "Did he have no wish to attend tonight?"

"My brother-in-law and his wife had other plans." Not that Lucy would have invited them.

"And they have no objections to your attending?" he pressed, his eyes glinting knowingly. "Billings seemed most determined for you to remain in mourning."

Jane inhaled deeply. "And I am most determined to live my life as I please. I am no green debutante to be led about by my nose. My family does not control my actions. I'm a free woman to come and go as I please. To *do* as I please."

"Indeed," he drawled, sliding to a stop directly before her. Her head fell back to lock with his molten eyes. "And do you?" His voice glided through her like a shot of spiced rum, settling in her belly in a burst of heat. "Do as you please?"

For a moment, the sensation of his hard maleness driving into her washed through her, rippling over her skin and transporting her to a moonlit garden where he breathed Aurora against her ear.

Throat dry, she could only nod.

"Is that so?" he asked, his voice soft and taunting as he encroached closer, forcing her against a tapestry-lined wall. The tapestry felt scratchy at her back.

Even without looking, she knew the scene well, had studied Zeus's ravishment of Leda in secret, rapt fascination. In her mind she could see the swan alighting down from the sky upon Leda, the woman's lovely face an odd mixture of horror and rapture.

A deep tug pulled on her belly as Seth's hands closed on either side of her head. Trapped between his body and the tapestry-covered wall, she stared into his stark gaze, trying to read his thoughts, feeling somewhat like the prey Leda must have felt.

Faintly, the contralto's voice grew, winding its way into the room, vibrating through the heavy silence of the chamber.

Jane succumbed to temptation and brought her hands up to play with the cravat at his neck.

"I'm no schoolroom miss anymore," she murmured, enjoying the words the moment she said them, enjoying *herself* the moment she decided a little bit of wickedness wouldn't hurt. "I do a good many things I shouldn't do . . ."

"You?" he queried.

"You don't believe me?" she asked in offended tones, imagining his reaction if he knew she was the woman he made savage love to against a tree at Vauxhall.

"No," he asserted. "You're much too proper."

Moistening her lips in determination, she commanded, "Close your eyes."

His eyes glowed down at her, wide and unblinking, mouth curving in mockery.

"Close your eyes," she repeated, determined to wipe the mockery from his face.

After a moment's hesitation, he complied.

She closed her fingers around his wrist, removing his hand from the wall near her head. Intent on showing him she could—and did—do as she pleased, she brought that hand to her lips.

Lightly, teasingly, she brushed her mouth over his palm. His skin quivered beneath her lips and she smiled. Opening her mouth, she lavished him with a kiss, trailing her tongue over warm, slightly salty skin.

Pulling back, she blew on the moist flesh. Watching his closed eyes, she sucked a single finger deep into her mouth, running her tongue over his fingertip and nipping the callused pad with her teeth.

With a hissing release of air, his eyes flew open, the centers sparks of light that seared her to the spot. Deep satisfaction gripped her as she slid his finger slowly from her mouth like a sweetmeat long savored.

She smiled saucily. "See."

Dropping his wrist, she attempted to step around him, but his arms came up around her again, bands of steel on either side of her.

"You play a dangerous game," he growled, shoving his face so close she could see herself in the gleaming titian centers of his eyes.

A muscle flexed in his jaw. "Now it's my turn. Close your eyes."

On this beast she freed from its cage? Not a chance. She shook her head.

"Time to play fair," he chided.

Reluctantly, her eyes drifted shut. Blackness engulfed her, every sensation intensified as she waited for his next move.

She did not have long to wait.

Cool air caressed her legs as he lifted her skirts. With a gasp, her hands dove for his, seizing his wrists and forcing them still.

"Let go," he ordered, his voice no less commanding for its quietness.

For whatever reason, she complied, fingers slipping from his wrists. She had permitted this man to do much more than lift her skirts after all. Even if it had been under the guise of Aurora.

His hands caressed their way up her legs, past her stockings and garters to her bare thighs. Her flesh trembled beneath his touch, but she did not move, did not open her eyes. In her mind, she saw Leda, lips a crimson slash in her pale face as her swan lover swooped down upon her.

His fingers slipped within her drawers, sifting through the soft curls with infinite gentleness. Without hesitating, he went directly to the aching spot between her legs. She gasped at the first touch of his thumb there.

"That's it," he whispered, the sound of his voice directly in her ear. "Does *this* please you?" He pushed his thumb against the small nub, exerting enough pressure to make her gasp sharpen and veer into a cry.

Without thinking, she widened her stance.

He added his forefinger and squeezed, rolling the nub in quick, savage circles.

She cried out again, hands clawing the tapestry at her sides as moisture rushed between her legs and sweet release washed over.

Seth's ragged breathing filled her ear. His fingers delved into her wet heat. Parting her folds, he impaled her with one finger. She lurched off the wall, fingers digging into his shoulder as she sobbed her pleasure.

"God, I wager you taste sweet, too."

I wager you taste sweet, too.

Her eyes flew open just as he slipped his hand from between her legs and lowered himself, no doubt intending to find out.

The wretch! The libertine!

Was every woman the same to him? To be bedded and discarded?

To be fed the same whispered words of passion?

A dark fury seized her. A strangled cry on her

lips, she shoved down her skirts and pushed at his shoulder.

Seth staggered to his feet, eyes burning with a desire she now knew to be cheap and common, something he likely dispensed on women with disgusting regularity.

At sight of her face, his brow furrowed. "Jane? What—"

Indignation scalding a bilious trail up her throat, she sent her palm cracking against his face.

He fingered his cheek, the white imprint of her hand quickly appearing on his swarthy flesh.

"Forgive me," he said, the fire in his gaze suddenly dead, buried, banked beneath cool brown again. "I misread the situation. I believed my advances welcome."

"You were mistaken," she lied, heat crawling up her neck and face to think that she had almost been seduced by a man who evidently thought women were as interchangeable as neckcloths.

"It won't happen again," he promised, taking several steps back, putting a respectable distance between them.

No, it would not.

Because she would never be foolish enough to be caught alone with him again.

"I think the performance has ended. I don't hear

singing anymore," she murmured, sweeping past him.

"Nor do I," he drawled, so quiet she barely heard him.

She stopped. "You better wait here for a short while. It won't do for us to be seen returning together."

He gave a stiff nod. "Or course."

With a stiff nod of her own, she turned and left, determined not to look back at the man she was only beginning to see for his true self. Seth was not the loving boy of her youth. The sooner she accepted that, the safer her heart.

Seth watched Jane go, unsure what had just transpired, only knowing that he had gone too far with the proper lady.

He throbbed painfully, his erection pressing at his breeches, aching for her. His cheek ached, too. Only from the sting of her slap.

"Bloody hell."

Shaking his head, he traced the burning imprint of her hand on his face. He should have known better. What was he doing tossing her skirts as if she were some common strumpet? Of course Jane would not be agreeable to such coarse treatment.

His thoughts drifted to Aurora. Jane was not so

impulsive, not a creature ruled by passion. For a moment, he had forgotten, feeling only as he had at Vauxhall, determined to have, to possess the woman for which his blood burned.

He couldn't understand it. Two women. Two desperate hungers. It had been years since he felt this way for one woman. What was he doing feeling this way for two?

Dropping his hand from his face, he vowed that he would leave Jane alone. He would concentrate his efforts on securing his bride . . . and attend every masquerade ball he could in hopes of finding Aurora again—a woman upon whom he could freely unleash his baser passions.

Chapter 16

Jane opened her eyes to bare slits. Morning sunlight stabbed her sensitive eyes and she flung the backs of her hands over her face, blocking the rude intrusion.

Too late. Darkness did nothing to help, did not offer the safe haven she sought. Nausea washed over her in violent waves, forcing her to move. Vaulting from her bed, she lunged for the washbasin. Gripping the sides with her hands, she emptied the contents of her stomach. Shuddering from head to toe, she retched in misery, tears streaming from the corners of her eyes.

Her stomach had been unsettled for days. Since the morning after Lucy's musicale.

"Third morning you woke up puking your guts," Berthe, the maid Desmond had assigned her, spoke from her side, her voice a grating scrape on the morning air.

Jane jerked, startled. She had not heard the maid enter the room. But it had always been that way with Berthe. Ever since Jane had first come into the Guthrie household, the maid had been there, always near, glaring, watching, smirking, letting Jane know that she *knew* Marcus. And even worse, that Marcus *knew* her.

Wiping her mouth with the back of her hand, Jane frowned at the woman Desmond had forced on her, wanting to shout at her to leave the room, the house, her life, once and for all. She had attempted to dismiss her while Marcus lived, but he had put a stop to that, declaring that Berthe served his *needs*. In ways Jane did not.

"Leave me," she commanded in a shaky voice, giving no thought to courtesy when addressing the woman who had sneered at her for so long. "I can dress myself."

"Very well." Berthe nodded and turned for the door. Hand on the latch, she stopped. "You're certain you don't want me to send for the physician?"

"That won't be necessary."

"Perhaps Cook then?" Berthe's eyes glinted with dark humor. "She's a marvel at home remedies . . . especially for what's ailing you."

An icy finger trailed Jane's spine as she shoved away from the basin. "And what might that be, Berthe?"

Blinking in mock innocence, Berthe replied, "Why you're breeding."

Her stomach pitched again, dropping to her bare feet before heaving back up. Pressing a hand to her belly in an attempt to still the violent reaction, she ground out, "That's not possible. You're mistaken."

Berthe cocked her head sideways. "Not about this, I'm not. I was one of thirteen children. I can tell when a woman's breeding." Her dark eyes raked Jane. "I suspected as much, so I questioned the laundress. You're well overdue for your courses."

That Berthe should be the one to reveal something so intimate, something Jane should have realized herself—made her cheeks catch fire. "You're mistaken," she repeated, denial surging to life within her. Her mind worked, feverishly counting the days, grasping that the impossible was suddenly . . . possible.

Berthe shrugged. "Time will tell soon enough."

Head swirling, stomach churning, Jane dove for the basin again as Berthe left the room. Only nothing remained in her stomach. After some moments, she lifted her head, panting, stomach and throat aching from the strain. Unsteady on her feet, she sank to the floor, her nightgown pooling around her like a milky puddle. Wrapping her arms around her knees, she huddled into a small ball, rocking slightly, shaking like a brittle branch in winter's peak.

A child. She carried a child. *Seth's* child. Horror and delight battled within her, churning her stomach into a queasy froth. A child. Someone to love. Someone who could love her back.

For years she had longed for a baby, had thought herself barren. She squeezed herself tighter, elation bubbling inside her chest. Then she remembered herself. She was no well-married lady in a position to bring a child into the world. Once word leaked, she would be ruined. Then what kind of life would her child have?

Berthe knew. As did the laundress. No doubt the servants were whispering about her below stairs even now. Soon Desmond and Chloris would know.

The desperate thoughts brought her to her feet. She dressed herself, barely taking the time to pull her hair into a knot at the base of her head. She must act quickly.

Foolish as it seemed, one face emerged. Seth should not be the visage her heart leapt upon, yet there he was nonetheless. In her mind. In her heart. Shaking her head, she called herself ten kinds of fool.

She had only one destination in mind. Hopefully, a solution would reveal itself with the counsel of her friends.

A chill blew through her heart when she imagined telling Seth the truth. That she was Aurora. That she carried his child. Burning moisture filled her eyes. Impossible. She could never bring herself to do such a thing.

"You know you must tell him."

Jane stared grimly into Lucy's blue-gray eyes. Beside her, Astrid nodded, the motion slight, reluctant, but in agreement nonetheless.

"No," Jane said, her voice trembling on the air. The idea of confronting Seth sent a jolt directly to her heart. She rose from the sofa she had collapsed upon not so long ago and began pacing. "Why must I?" she asked, her steps quick.

"Because he's the father," Astrid responded with her usual equanimity as she added another biscuit from the service to her already overcrowded plate. "It's his responsibility, Jane. You cannot go this alone."

"Is it?" she snapped, her voice brittle as glass. "Is

it his responsibility when he has no clue it was me that he—he—" she stopped abruptly and stalked to the window. Wrapping her arms tightly about herself, she stared out at the street. Dusk settled over the square. Desmond would know by now. And Chloris. Berthe would have seen to that. If she returned home, it would be to face them. The prospect held little more appeal than facing Seth.

Moistening her lips, she struggled for a steady tone. "Is it his responsibility," she asked again, "when I deliberately set out to seduce him? When *I* knew he would have nothing to do with me had he known it was me?" She shook her head fiercely. "It's not fair to him."

"And denying your child a father is fair?" Lucy asked. "Denying your child both parents? A life of privilege free of scorn?"

Jane drew a ragged breath, squeezing her eyes shut as if physically struck. Count on Lucy to consider the child. A mother to the core.

"You cannot rely on Desmond or your parents," Astrid's voice, cool and calm as ever behind her, infused her with spirit. "You needn't feel *wrong* taking the only option left to you."

Jane opened her eyes to observe a nanny pushing a pram across the square in the fading light. The lace fringing the pram's awning fluttered in the breeze. She closed her eyes tightly, the pain in her chest suddenly too much.

Lucy sighed quietly behind her and Jane realized she had moved close. Her hand landed on her shoulder, soft as a butterfly setting down. "Astrid and I will support you in whatever you decide."

Turning, Jane smiled thinly at her friends, the bend of her lips almost painful. "I know. I'm lucky to have you both."

Anna arrived then, bearing a tray of cucumber sandwiches. "Thought you might need replenishing." With a knowing look at Astrid, Anna added three tiny sandwiches to her plate before setting the tray down on the service.

"You're welcome to stay with me," Astrid volunteered, rearranging the food on her plate with strategic care.

Jane smiled, recognizing the true generosity of that offer. Since her husband fled the country over a nasty forgery charge, Astrid barely possessed the means to feed and outfit herself and few remaining servants.

Jane inhaled deeply, letting the breath fill her lungs and fortify her as she strove for some of Astrid's mettle.

"Naturally you can stay with me, too," Lucy added, "if that is your wish." However, her gaze conveyed that she did not think Jane *should* make that decision.

Wish. Jane *wished* to turn back the clock.

Bittersweet memory flashed through her mind. A garden at midnight, a lover's hot hands, burning lips, *him*, Seth, inside her, his hard flesh dragging against hers . . .

Did she really wish that night never happened? Would she take it all back if she could?

Rubbing her temples, Jane willed her head to cease spinning, willed herself to make a decision.

She looked at the three women staring so expectantly at her, waiting for her to say something, to do *something*. She had never anticipated that a single tryst could result in a child. Not after years of believing herself barren. A painful knot formed in her throat. "You know Marcus quit my bed after one year of marriage, claiming it wasn't worth the effort. That I was barren."

"Bloody ass," Anna growled.

"More likely the difficulty rested with him," Astrid muttered.

Jane shook her head. "His first wife conceived on their honeymoon."

"I knew his first wife." Astrid snorted as she lifted a sandwich to her lips. "Her *fruitfulness* may have had more to do with a certain officer that left for India." Her dark eyes glinted meaningfully as she took a sizable bite.

Lucy nodded sagely.

Jane gazed at Astrid and Lucy. It was the first time she had heard such an allegation. It would certainly explain the lack of further offspring in Marcus's first marriage.

With a shrug, she sighed. In any case, it failed to matter now.

For a moment, she considered accepting her friends' offers and residing with one of them. But only for a moment. She could not be that selfish.

Astrid could barely feed and support her household. And Lucy. Well, Jane couldn't bring scandal upon her. She stood as a pillar among the matrons of the *ton*. Jane would not sully her spotless reputation.

Her friends watched her, waiting. She could well imagine what they saw. A bloodless face. Haunted eyes staring into space. Eyes that desperately searched for an answer. Anything that would save her from doing, in her heart, what she knew she must do.

Seth looked up from the papers littering his desk at the knock on his office door and bade entrance.

Leaning back in his chair, he schooled his features to hide his surprise at the sight of his butler leading Jane into the room. He had not thought to see her again. Not after the Dowager Duchess of Shillington's musicale and his imprudent advances had been so ruthlessly rebuffed.

With a quick nod for the butler, they were soon alone, staring silently at one another. Alarm hammered inside his heart at the sight of her. An alarm fed by his realization that he was *glad* to see her. Despite his avowal to leave her be, to forget her.

Why, he suddenly wondered, had Madeline stolen his heart when it had been Jane with whom he spent all his time? They had ridden together, swum, fished, explored the countryside. Yet he had chosen Madeline. He had allowed her beauty and bold gaze to weave a toxic spell around him. Callowness of youth, he supposed.

He took his speculation further, wondering what would have happened if he had fallen in love with Jane. Would she have betrayed him for a man of wealth and influence?

He closed his eyes in a long blink, eliminating such senseless thinking from his mind. One could not undo the past.

"Lady Jane," he greeted, rising to his feet. With a wave of his hand, he indicated she take the seat across from his desk. "This is a surprise."

She settled herself in the chair's depths, a black crow against the blue damask.

"I believe my sister is in the garden with Rebecca," he went on, assuming that would be the only reason she had come.

"Actually I've come to see you." Her voice rushed forth as she tucked her hands within the voluminous folds of her skirts.

"Me?" He lifted a brow. After the musicale, he had thought she would never speak to him again—much less request a private audience. "What is it I can do for you?"

Moistening her lips, her gaze darted about the room, assessing, looking everywhere but at him. He found himself admiring the elegant slope of her nose, wanting to stroke its length with his finger before moving on to test the softness of her luminous cheek.

The impulse jarred him and he gave his head a hard shake. He had done more than enough *touching* of her person.

"I have been less than honest with you," she hedged, voice gossamer soft, as if whispering the words would somehow lessen the impact.

"Have you now?" An icy finger landed at his nape and began a slow descent down his spine.

"Yes." Dipping her gaze, she nodded, staring at

her skirts as if transfixed, spellbound by the sinister-dark fabric.

"Jane?" he prompted after a long moment had passed.

"God," she choked, the single word turning and twisting into a ragged sob. "I can't do this." Surging to her feet, she stumbled for the door in a graceless lurch.

In a flash, he was on his feet and moving. His hands seized her shoulders and forced her around before she was halfway across the room.

Her stricken gaze flitted over his face and he felt transported to an afternoon years ago. A fence with the top rail splintered to shards. Grasses tall and lush around them as they crouched over his sister's still body. Jane's look of horror had echoed deeply inside of him . . . as it did now.

"What is it?" he demanded, panicked in a way he had not felt in years. In a way he had not thought to feel again.

Moisture swelled in her eyes, brimming in the hazel depths. She shook her head fiercely. A lock of nut brown hair fell loose, straggling over her eye, making her look suddenly young and achingly sweet. Tempting as hell.

His hands tightened, flexing on her yielding flesh. He pulled her closer.

A strange little sound escaped her lips. Not quite a cry. More like a moan.

"Sssh," he soothed, dropping his forehead to hers, inhaling her scent, letting it surround him. Apples. Orchard fresh. Autumn on the wind. The scent of home. The scent of Jane. The scent of . . .

He pulled back, his heart jerking violently in his chest as he scanned her face.

Two women that smelled exactly alike. That stirred him in ways long forgotten. That filled him with a desire he had never known. What were the odds?

She watched him, dread crowding the fear that already gleamed in her eyes.

"Aurora," he whispered, uncertain of the wild notion seizing him until her eyes flared wide, dousing him with a cold wave of comprehension. And he knew he was not wrong.

Color drained from her face.

He dropped his hands as if stung, nausea churning his gut.

She staggered backward, colliding into a side table. A vase fell, shattering, matching the noise roaring through his ears.

His hands curled at his sides, the urge to wreck something, to destroy, to shatter another vase overwhelming. Realization washed through him, acrid as gun smoke. The woman he couldn't get out of his mind, the one he had searched for among the crowd at Vauxhall with a desperate fervor, who haunted his dreams . . . she had been under his nose all along. She had been the proper, starchy widow he had agonized over wanting—the *lady* he fought to resist because she was not that *sort* of woman. He shook his head as if he could shake free from the reality, the unwanted truth.

"You must have had a good laugh," he ground out.

"No." She shook her head fiercely, her knuckles whitening where she clutched the table, water running over its surface and dripping to the carpet. "It wasn't like that—"

"Is that how you amuse yourself?" he bit out. "Disguise yourself and bed whomever you like? How many others have there been?"

Fire lit her eyes, flecks of gold in her green gaze. She swiped a hand through the air. "There have been no others."

"Oh, I'm certain," he scoffed, dragging a hand through his hair. "Only *I* inspired you to toss yours skirts to the wind."

Angry color mottled her face, chasing off her pallor. "Stop," she spit out, her lips trembling. "It wasn't like that!"

"Why did you come here?" he demanded, stalking an angry path toward her. "To gloat?"

His eyes raked her, seeing past the ugly black sack she wore to body beneath, the warm flesh that had sheathed him, hugged and milked him, erasing the memory of every other woman that came before.

The memory betrayed him, inflaming him. Unable to stop himself, he hauled her against him, indifferent to her struggles.

He had never thought to see her again. And here she was. Aurora. *Jane.* Anger and desire surged inside him, a drugging poison smoldering through his veins.

"All this time I thought you were so different, so changed." He burrowed his fingers through her hair. The pins dropped free, skimming the tops of his hands on their way to the floor.

"Please," she moaned as her hair flooded past her shoulders in a rich mantle.

"So cold, so proper, all ice in your veins," he snarled against her quivering lips, fingers fisting in the silken tendrils of her hair. "You should have told me you only wanted this."

Crushing his lips to hers, he smothered her cry and plundered her mouth in a brutal kiss. His hands spanned her waist and lifted her onto the wet table in a hard move. Using a knee, he forced her legs apart, settling himself between her thighs.

An erection pushed at his breeches, aching and hungry for her sweetness, for the snug heat of her. Grasping her hand, he forced her to touch him there, groaning at the tremble of her slight fingers against his length. Heaven and hell in one touch. He guided her fingers over him until she moved on her own.

He ravaged her mouth, punishing her.

She submitted, complied, caressed him in feverish strokes. Not a sound escaped her as she took his kiss, suffered the savage invasion of his lips and teeth and tongue on her soft mouth.

Not fighting, but not responding. Not blossoming to life in his arms as she had done at Vauxhall. Or at the musicale . . .before she had slapped his face.

Disgusted, he cursed and broke contact. Chest heaving with serrated breaths, he fought his need for her and demanded, "Why have you come?"

Her fingers traced her lips, wet and swollen from his kiss.

"Why?" he thundered.

She stared, her eyes hunted, wounded. Large and bright in her pale face. Beautiful. Hell's teeth, even now she got beneath his skin.

Bile thick in his throat, he stepped back and swung around, the erotic picture she made with her skirts bunched between her legs atop the table too much to bear.

With the desk between them, he snarled, "Say something, damn you."

"I—I had no choice."

He heard something in her voice then, in her barely audible words that had him looking at her with fresh dread sealing his heart.

The agonized look in her eyes told him her next words would forever change his life.

"I'm with child."

Chapter 17

Jane shoved her skirts down and slid from the table, regretting the decision as soon as her knees gave out. She grasped the edge of the table, barely catching herself from falling to the carpet and shattering into pieces alongside the vase.

Seth made no move. Merely stared at her. Through her. His scar so very stark, lightning-white on his swarthy face. Her stomach heaved, pitched, and for a moment she feared she would be sick all over the fine Persian rug. She clutched a hand over her belly as if she could quell the violent reaction.

His brown gaze darkened, the amber light in the centers vanishing as he followed the movement of her hand. His granite-carved face cracked and emotion bled through. Fury. Astonishment. Shaking his head, his lips peeled back from his teeth in a bitter laugh. "Oh, this is rich."

His laughter carried an edge. Like a finely honed razor, she felt its slice keenly, digging and twisting into her heart. Dropping her hand, she squared her shoulders. "I've come because you have a right to know—"

He laughed harder, the sound slicing through her. "And you're so concerned with what's right, are you?"

Heat swarmed her face.

"You've come only to inform me of this. You want nothing."

She dropped her gaze, studying the swirls in the carpet with rapt attention. "I don't know," she replied, squeezing her eyes in one long blink, mortified at the feebleness of her response.

"You sought me out at Vauxhall," he proclaimed, his eyes narrowing. "Why? Was this your scheme?" His slid his gaze to her stomach again. "Is the child even mine?"

Her hands curled into fists, the nails digging into her tender palms. "I suppose I deserve the question." She wet her dry lips and wondered if she would ever endure something so shaming as this again. "Yes, it's yours. Whether you believe me or not."

He studied her a long moment, his hot gaze roving over her face in searing thoroughness, as if he stripped away flesh and bones to see all she hid within.

"And you're expecting a proposal no doubt?" he demanded, his voice frightening in all its calm. Standing before him, suffering the hot condemnation of his stare, she wished she had not come. Some shame, she decided, was in fact too much to bear.

Spinning about, she headed for the door. "I shouldn't have come. I don't know what I thought to accomplish—"

His hands clamped on her shoulders, whirling her around. "Don't you?" His fingers flexed, burning through the fabric of her dress. "You knew precisely what it was you wanted from me when you walked in here."

She struggled in his arms, furious at his words because she could not deny them. "Release me."

"What's wrong, Jane? Is this any way to treat your husband-to-be?"

She froze, staring at him with wide, aching eyes, certain she had misunderstood.

"Isn't this what you wanted? Can you not find the nerve to admit it?" He jerked her against him. "Ironic, isn't it? Once upon a time I wasn't good enough to marry a Spencer."

Molded so tightly together, she was unsure where

either one of them began or ended. He cupped the side of her face, and the warmth of that large hand, the rasp of his calluses on her skin sparked a response deep within her. She had to stop herself from leaning into his palm like a purring cat.

"Why?" His strained voice sounded almost suffering to her ears—something her conscience could not bear. She had never set out to hurt him. Had only thought to have something for herself at long last. "Just tell me that."

She struggled to swallow past the lump in her throat. "I—I wanted us to be together. Because of what I once felt for you." There. She had said it. Perhaps not the full truth, but close enough.

"If you felt something for me, you have a strange way of showing it." His grip on her face tightened. "Likely all you saw was a plump pigeon, ripe for the plucking. A convenient escape from Billings and the sort of half-life he would have you lead. You'd do anything to be free. Even shackle yourself to me." He set her from him forcefully.

She staggered away, touching her face, still feeling the burning imprint of his hand. His rebuff stung. It had cost her much to say those words, to admit that she had gone to Vauxhall out of the love she once felt for him, mirage that it had been.

A bitter taste filled her mouth. She hadn't changed much over the years. At seventeen, she knew nothing of love. A woman grown, she knew even less.

Gathering the scraps of her pride, she turned for the door. "Think what you like."

She would not suffer another moment convincing him that her foolish heart, and not a cunning scheme, drove her into his arms at Vauxhall.

"Where are you going?"

"Home," she replied, hastening from the room as if the devil himself were after her. And perhaps he was.

"You march in here, announce you're carrying my child, and think to leave," Seth's harsh tones followed her into the foyer, as did the stomping of his boots.

"I owed you the truth," she tossed over her shoulder, releasing a shaky, grateful breath when no butler or footman lurked near. This was difficult enough without an audience.

"Look me in the face and tell me you don't expect me to drop down on bended knee?"

Slowly, Jane faced him, a strange calm settling over her.

She scanned his face, memorizing every stone-carved line, resting briefly on the deep scar slashing his hard mouth. Stark. Bleak. Like blood on new fallen snow.

She envisioned him dropping on one knee to the cold marble floor and asking for her hand in marriage. The vision blurred at the edges, impossible to see distinctly. Even Marcus had not extended the courtesy. Her father had negotiated her marriage in his study, minus her presence. It had been a coldly calculated union from the start. Marriage to Seth, she realized, would be little better. Born of necessity, it would be just as cold. Grow just as empty. She saw that now.

Her calm threatened to snap then, and she knew she had to flee before her composure crumbled and she fell to pieces at his feet. Later, alone, free of him, the fog would lift and her mind would clear. And in the clarity she would see things perfectly— would see a solution with which she could live.

"I expect nothing from you, Seth. Nothing at all." Expectations were for other people. Fresh young girls with their innocence and souls fully intact. It had been years since she had been such a girl. She should not have come. Should not have attempted to rob him of the chance to find such a girl.

But then it had been years since he had been such a boy.

Before she could convince herself that they perhaps deserved each other after all, she marched out the front door, her entire body trembling in fear that he would stop her . . . and in agony when he did not.

Seth stared after her, watching the rigid line of her spine as she ascended her carriage, the black swish of skirts at her ankles a taunting flash.

What game did she play? Surely she did not mean to depart as if matters between them were settled.

His hands curled and uncurled at his sides, his right index finger twitching with the impulse to jump down the steps and yank her into his arms. Whether to hug her or shake her, he did not know. But he resisted. The woman affected him too much, threatened his control. The very control he had sworn to never again surrender.

Standing still as stone, legs braced as though aboard ship, he watched the carriage clatter down the street.

"Seth?" Julianne approached from behind.

Instinctively he turned, shielding her from the brisk afternoon air. Taking her elbow he shut the door and guided her back to his study.

"I thought I heard Jane's voice."

His gut tightened at the hopeful ring in her voice. Julianne liked Jane. There was no getting around that. "Yes, she was here. She left."

Her face fell. "Oh. I see." Julianne sank onto the sofa, her hand sliding along the heavily padded arm as if searching for a handhold, for reassurance. "She did not wish to see me, then."

"We had matters to discuss."

Her brow creased. "What could you have to discuss? I did not think you much liked her."

The memory of Jane's yielding heat surrounding him, binding him like silken chords, tormented him. As it had for nights.

For weeks, his hunger for two different women had confounded him. He had ached to possess both of them. Discovering they were the same woman made sense in an odd sort of way.

Closing his eyes, he imagined he could smell her—apples and country air. His feelings for Jane ran more complicated than like or dislike.

"Julianne," he began carefully, knowing the answer to his question before he even asked. "You care for Jane?"

"Of course," she replied.

Shaking his head, he released a deep sigh and rubbed a hand over his face. "I suppose that will have to be enough," he muttered.

Jane claimed she carried his child. He could not risk doubting her. Would *not* risk his child being raised without him. A child of his own. The prospect meant more than he had ever realized. The chance to be a father—the kind he never had—to do something right filled his chest with an odd tightness . . .stronger than the rage he felt when he considered the feckless female who had duped him.

"How would you feel," he paused to swallow, knowing the moment the words were out there would be no going back, "if I married Jane?"

"Jane?" Julianne exclaimed, bouncing to the edge of the sofa, a radiant light crawling over her cheeks, reminding him of how she had looked before the accident. Happy, carefree. A girl with the world before her. "You want to marry Jane?"

Want. He let the word roll around his head. *Wanting* Jane had nothing to do with it. Obligation drove him, that infernal sense of guilt and responsibility that never ceased to gnaw at his insides, that compelled him to set matters to right.

Not a day passed when he did not feel the straining mass of a horse moving beneath him, launching over the fence. Nor would he forget the feel of Julianne's arms slipping from his waist as she fell to the hard earth.

He could not live with more regrets.

"Have you proposed? Did she accept?" Julianne scooted forward again, looking dangerously close to falling off the sofa.

Staring into his sister's animated face, the invisible band about his chest loosened, knowing this marriage would at least please her. "Not yet."

"But you intend to propose?"

He dragged a hand over his jaw. "Yes."

He would simply have to accept the notion of marrying a woman who affected him in ways that he had vowed his wife never would. So she drove him to distraction with lust. He could resist. He could slake his lust on other women. Women who did not present a threat to the barriers he had erected around his heart.

Chapter 18

By the time Jane returned home, dusk had fallen. She entered through the servants' stairs and hurried to her room. The silence felt loud, oppressive, pressing in as thickly as fog. The servants were scarce, the house still as a tomb. Preternaturally still. The quiet before the storm, she couldn't help thinking as she ducked into her room, relieved for the shelter it offered . . . until her gaze landed on the room's other occupants. Dahlia, Iris, and Bryony.

Bryony sat at Jane's desk, rifling through an open drawer, reading old correspondence. She glanced up as Jane entered the room. "Who's Julianne?" she asked mildly, holding out one of Julianne's many letters.

Jane strode across the room and snatched it from Bryony's fingers. "I'll take that." Stuffing it back into the drawer, she glared at the girls.

"Where have you been all day? You forgot about our lessons." Dahlia propped her hands on her skinny hips, her glare hot with accusation.

"Father is furious," Iris taunted from where she sprawled on the bed, her child's voice deceptively sweet as she swirled her slippered feet in the air.

Jane studied the girls closely, assessing, gauging to see if they knew *why* their father was angry with her.

"Is he?" Jane asked with a mildness she did not feel.

"Indeed. You must have done something awful. Mother has been crying. They've neglected us all day."

"What else is new?" Iris chimed, shoving to her feet in a mess of powder-pink ruffles. "They're in the drawing room." Her eyes glinted with mischief. "I know they'll be pleased to hear you're home."

Jane watched her scamper from the room with a heavy heart, knowing she could not stop her, knowing also she could not pack and flee before Iris alerted them to her arrival.

While every instinct urged her to escape, to hide, she forced herself to trail after Iris, shoulders back and hands clasped before her.

She stepped into the drawing room moments after

Iris, feeling like a prisoner approaching the hangman's noose. A chill evening breeze blew in from the open terrace doors, cooling her flushed face.

Her eyes felt hot and itchy, and she blinked rapidly, horrified to realize that tears burned at the backs of her eyes. *Tears*. And not because she had to face Desmond. No, her burning eyes had more to do with the look on Seth's face today. She had seen that look before, long ago, when half a dozen footmen escorted him from her home, Madeline watching on with a frosty, self-satisfied smile.

Tell him, Maddie. Tell him you're going to marry me!

His hoarse cry was still burned into her soul. Jane had said nothing, merely watched in aching silence. She had never wanted to see him hurt. Not then. Not now. As much as she had wanted him for herself, she had wanted him happy—even if that meant marrying Madeline. His expression the moment her sister's betrayal sank in remained fixed in her mind. It haunted her, and she had seen it again. Today. Only this time she had been the reason.

She couldn't bear knowing that he believed the worst of her, believed that she had schemed to trap him, that she was as manipulative and socially ambitious as her sister.

"See! She's here," Iris cried, motioning to Jane as if she had personally scoured the city to find her.

Desmond's head swung in her direction. "Leave us, Iris."

"But Fath—"

"Now!" he thundered.

Jane jumped where she stood, her hands tightening their hold on each other. Iris turned and fled the room with a noisy sob.

Desmond's lips curled back against his uneven teeth as he spat, "So the little whore returns."

She flinched. Berthe had wasted little time in voicing her suspicions.

"Take a seat." Desmond motioned to the sofa Chloris occupied. "We have much to discuss."

Jane looked warily at the sofa, not keen at placing herself beside Chloris.

"Come, Jane. Don't be skittish. Clearly you possess a more adventurous spirit." His heated gaze raked her. "Had I only known," he murmured.

Heat crept up Jane's face at the unsubtle remark.

Chloris stiffened, the severe lines of her face pulling tight.

"Is it true?" Chloris demanded. "You're with child?"

"I believe so. Yes."

Desmond cursed and swung around, stalking out to the terrace.

"Well," Chloris began, her voice eerily tranquil. "It's of no surprise you've brought scandal on our heads yet again."

"*I've* never brought scandal on this family," Jane denied, not about to let that remark pass. Marcus had been the one to cavort with everything in skirts. A sour taste filled her mouth. To the very end.

Chloris smiled nastily. "Yes, well, if you had been a suitable wife, Marcus would not have had to look elsewhere."

Desmond stormed back inside. "Who?" he demanded, his voice scraping over her like a rusty blade.

Sighing, Chloris smoothed an imaginary wrinkle from her skirt. "Does it matter, Desmond? I think the question at hand is what are we going to do now."

Desmond's black stare engulfed Jane, and she strongly suspected he had not heard a word his wife said.

"Who?" he bit out, back to that again.

"I think we should send Jane to the country." Chloris stared intently at her husband, her brow wrinkling into its many folds. "No one will think anything of it. She is in mourning after all."

"And when the babe comes?" Desmond spoke at last, acknowledging his wife without looking at her. "What then?"

Jane looked back and forth at Desmond and Chloris, stunned that they would discuss her fate and that of her own unborn child as if she were not in the room, as if she had no voice, no opinion.

"We can send the babe to a home for foundlings. No one need ever know."

Cold ice shot down her spine, making her shiver. Jane rose to her feet, clutching the arm of the sofa in a death grip. "No," she pronounced. "I am not giving my child away."

Fury radiated through her, chasing away the cold and filling her with revitalizing heat. There had been little time to ponder her feelings about the child she carried. She had only begun to grapple with the reality of it. Until now. Until the mention of *giving* the baby away. This was her child. Hers and Seth's. No one would take this child from her. Not while there was breath in her body to stop them.

"No?" Chloris echoed, the blunt features of her face tightening with disbelief. She looked to her husband as if seeking confirmation of Jane's refusal.

"Who is he?" Desmond shouted, his face varying shades of red and purple as he stalked to her. "Who?" His hands clamped down on her arms. "I *will* have his name." He shook her as if he could rattle the truth from her.

"Desmond," Chloris hissed in an exasperated voice, and something else. Something Desmond did not pay the least bit of mind to as he continued to manhandle her, a vein bulging in his forehead.

"Let me go," she ground out.

His fingers dug deeper, hurting her. "I'll have his name."

The pain of his grip fed her, poured liquid fire into her parched soul and sent a shot of courage to her system. Noses almost touching, she hissed into his face, "Never."

His pupils dilated, his black, soulless gaze drilling into her until she felt certain he wanted to strike her. Her throat thickened, but she forced her chin higher, finished with submitting.

"Unhand her."

Jane's gaze swung in the direction of the door, gasping at the sight of Seth framed in the threshold. Her heart leapt in her chest and the thickness in her throat intensified, choking her.

Larger than life, he loomed over the room, seeming to suck all energy into himself. Desmond released her, and she staggered back, dropping onto the sofa, her legs as steady as jam. Seth watched her, his square jaw clenched tight, his gaze unreadable, the scar down his cheek all the more vivid against his flushed face. Never had he looked more menacing. Or beautiful.

"If you're so desperate to know," Seth drawled, nonchalant as he tugged free his gloves and shoved them into his coat pocket, "I'll be happy to tell you."

Jane shook her head, her lips parting on a silent breath.

"The Earl of St. Claire," Barclay chimed, suddenly arriving, looking frazzled and annoyed all at once as he tried to wedge past Seth. "Your pardon, Mr. Billings. He insisted on introducing himself."

Desmond's black gaze never left Seth as he addressed the butler. "Leave us."

Barclay departed. The door clicked shut, the noise discordant in the sudden still of the room. No one uttered a sound.

Desmond and Seth stared in silence at one another. A muscle in Seth's jaw jumped madly, just as madly as Jane's heart thumping within her too-tight chest.

Words burned on the tip of her tongue.

What are you doing here?

Why did you come?

Only no sound emerged. She simply stared, watching, waiting, her pulse fluttering madly at her neck. Her hand flew there, pressing the warm flesh as if she could still the frantic tempo.

Chloris was the first to speak. Clearing her throat, she greeted with false cheer, "Lord St. Claire. How lovely of you to call."

Seth's gaze shifted, landing on Jane with a burning intensity that trapped her breath in her chest, pinning her to the spot. "I've come to collect Jane."

Collect Jane. Her hackles rose. She was not a parcel to be fetched. Her chin lifted. He did not miss the gesture. His eyes darkened, the centers glowing fire. The corners of his mouth lifted in a mocking semblance of a smile. "Isn't that so, Jane?"

Chloris saved her from replying. "Indeed?" Gathering a fistful of muslin, she rose, simultaneously gripping Jane's hand. Her cold fingers circled Jane's wrist, pulling her free of Desmond. "We will leave you gentlemen alone. Come along Jane."

Jane twisted free, determined to remain.

"Jane," Seth's voice, deep and potent, stroked some place deep inside her. As if pulled by an invisible thread, she moved to his side, recognizing the significance of doing so. She had finished running. From him. From herself.

Come what may, they were bound. Even before their night in the garden. She saw that now. Now she understood. Seth had never left her. He was in her blood.

She stopped beside him, pressing her palms to her sides in an effort to still their trembling. Seth brought his hand to the small of her back and she jumped at the contact. The feather-soft brush of his fingers singed her through her clothing, reminding her of the fire found in his caress.

"He's the one," Desmond's voice, rough and strangled as if he fought for breath, broke through her thoughts. Judging from his ruddy face, his breath was not the only thing lost to him. Hot words tumbled from his mouth. "He's the one you let crawl beneath your skirts."

Chloris made a sound, a tiny mewl through her fingers as she shook her head.

Seth's lips tightened. A muscle flexed in his cheek, making his scar jump as if it lived, breathed, a serpent writhing upon his face. His eyes changed, gleaming as dark as a fathomless cave.

"Have a care Billings," he warned, his words dropping like stones in the thick air. "This can be easy or hard. Either way, she's leaving with me."

Her blood pumped so loudly in her ears she felt certain the others in the room could hear it.

"Like hell she is," Desmond bit out, pointing a reed-thin finger at his side. As if she were a dog to be ordered about, he commanded, "Jane, come."

Dark fury spiraled through her. All her life she had done what others expected, what others wanted. And what had it gotten her? Parents who cared nothing for her? A faithless husband? Relations that ran roughshod over her? She gave her head a small shake. No more.

She breathed in through her nostrils, drawing the air deep into her lungs. Her single night with Seth had been her one self-indulgence. And for that, she could not summon forth a scrap of regret. Even as her head told her she should feel the deepest shame, her heart could not.

She was done doing as others wanted, finished putting herself last. If she had considered herself first, perhaps she would have told Seth how she felt for him all those years ago. Before Madeline sank her claws into him. Before he set sail. Before she married Marcus and put to death dreams of love and happily ever after.

Shaking her head, she banished *what if* from her head. That road only led to madness.

Compelled to stand on her own, to start living for herself, she stepped away from Seth's side and approached Desmond.

Crossing her arms over her chest in an unlady-like pose, she declared, "I will not."

Desmond drew nearer. Still, she did not shrink away. Not even when he stopped before her, eyes glasslike and unblinking.

"Jane," he said, his voice low with warning, soft with threat. "Don't do something you'll regret. Tell this"—his devil's gaze cut to Seth—"tell St. Claire here you're not going anywhere with him."

"My only regret would be staying another night under this roof."

His eyes flashed with a desperate fury and he snatched hold of her arm. She stifled her wince.

"You heard her," Seth cut in behind her. "Let her go."

Chloris must have recognized how near her husband was to losing control. "For God's sake, Desmond, unhand her," she hissed.

Desmond shook his head in savage denial.

"I advise you to listen to your wife," Seth bit out, the hard edge of his voice scraping her frayed nerves as he stepped alongside her, his body humming with tension.

As if he hadn't heard a word, Desmond's fingers dug deeper into her arm. "Whore," he hissed, "This isn't—"

Seth shot from beside her, his fist connecting with Desmond's face in a blur of movement. Desmond collapsed on the carpet with a thud, his spindly legs stretched before him.

Eyes bulging, he cupped his nose, blood seeping steadily between his fingers as he sprawled on the floor. Chloris shrieked and crouched down beside her husband.

"It's finished," Seth ground out. "Understand?"

Desmond nodded mutely, his dazed expression leaving Jane to wonder if he in fact did.

Grunting, Chloris tugged him to his feet. Glaring at Seth, she spat, "You animal! Take her. Take her and go." Her eyes scoured Jane with loathing as she dragged Desmond alongside of her. "Good riddance."

Unruffled by Chloris's histrionics, Seth lowered himself into a plush wing-backed chair, fingers idly tapping the arm as he watched their clumsy retreat.

Jane buried her shaking hands in the folds of her skirts, more satisfied than she liked to acknowledge over the violent episode.

"Lovely family," Seth murmured.

"They're not my family," she hastily corrected,

then flushed when she realized her true family was little better.

"I suppose I would be in no rush to claim them either."

Pulling back her shoulders, she looked down at him where he lounged, one booted foot at rest upon his knee in a casual pose so at odds with the waves of tension emanating from him.

"Why did you come?"

"Did you not hear me? I believe I made myself quite plain." His eyes warmed as they roamed over her, that amber flame back, lighting the dark centers. "I've come for you."

"Yes, I heard you," she said quickly, the heat in her face intensifying, burning all the way to the tips of her ears. "I—I—"

"You stormed into my house," he broke in, rising to his impressive height and advancing on her with slow, measured steps, "and announced you carried my child." He stopped directly in front of her, the breadth of his chest and shoulders filling her vision. "Did you think you had seen the last of me?"

"I had not thought much beyond confessing my . . . condition."

He rocked back on his heels, eyes narrowing. "You had to know it would come to this."

Jane shook her head, not certain what she had

thought would happen when she told him the truth . . . and not certain it mattered anymore.

"But then," he continued, eyes crawling over her face in a way that made her skin prickle, "I can't claim to know you." Another step closer, and their breaths mingled. "Can I?"

"You did once," she murmured, dropping her gaze from his penetrating stare, a stare that would see all of her if she did not look away—the shadows of her heart, the dark corners of her mind, the deep regret that lived in her soul, eating at her for not confessing her feelings, not taking a chance all those years ago.

She stared at his lips, at the mouth that kept her awake night after night. Her fingers ached to caress the scar marking its upper corner.

The impulse to confess that she hadn't changed that much—at least in regard to her fool's obsession with him—smoldered within her chest.

"Yes," he mused, drawing a finger down the side of her face in a tantalizing stroke. She closed her eyes at the contact, tormented from the touch. At her mouth, he traced her bottom lip, the rough pad of his thumb a slow drag of heat over her sensitized skin. "But you aren't that girl anymore, are you?" That said, he dropped his hand and stepped back with the abruptness of a slap to the face.

"And you're not that boy," she shot back, lips tingling from his caress.

The grim way he looked at her fueled her temper. The boy she had known never toyed with women. Never seduced one and then moved to another without pausing for breath. It did not matter that she had been *both* women. It still marked him a libertine, incapable of deeper emotion for any single woman. A man, she realized, not very different from her late husband. Unable to love . . . or at least unable to love her.

But then perhaps she didn't exist anymore. Not as he had known her. Not as she had once been. Their days of frolic seemed a lifetime ago. All save that day. It haunted her still, teased her with the haziness of a dream. The afternoon had been like all others. Before he fell in love with Madeline.

They had swum beneath a rare sun, splashing and wrestling in the water. Until it happened. A flash of light in a dark sky. The moment had burst upon them, and they had stopped, frozen with a sudden awareness that had not been there before.

She could recall the drops of water clinging to his face, to the lean, exposed flesh. Ripples of muscle and sinew danced beneath his skin. His slicked back hair gleamed darkly beneath the sun's glare, beckoning her fingers. He had looked at her then. Truly looked at her.

Frozen and entangled, every fiber of her had screamed for him to close the distance and end it—or rather begin it. Instead, he had broken away and swam back several strokes to splash her as if nothing untoward had occurred.

That memory had never left her. She thought about it countless times over the years, wondering what he would have done had she only leaned closer. Would he still have given his love to Madeline beneath falling apple blossoms? Or might she have been the one to claim his heart?

"No," he agreed, his tone brusque. "I'm not that boy. Neither of us are who we used to be."

She nodded stiffly before turning and moving to the window. He followed, the heat of his big body radiating at her back. She drew a small invisible circle on the glass, trying to pretend she did not feel him there.

True, the Seth she had grown up with had treated her with affection, entrusted her with his confidences, shared his dreams. The rigid man behind her would never do those things. She would do well to remember that.

"It appears we shall become reacquainted." The low rumble of his voice sent shivers up her spine.

"I'll arrange for a special license. I don't imagine you would want a large wedding again—"

"Why are you doing this?" she demanded in a voice so soft she could scarcely hear herself. "I cannot imagine you actually *want* to wed—"

She felt his sigh at her back. "You carry my child. My heir."

Her stomach tightened. She should feel gratitude that honor guided him, but she felt only a gnawing bleakness. They would marry for the child. A grimace pinched her face. Love had nothing to do with it. Nor would it ever.

Turning, she faced him and her heart clenched at the grim resolve in his stare. At worst, she would live with his quiet condemnation. At best, his indifference.

"We'll marry for the child," she uttered in agreement. Her fingers drifted to her stomach, to the life hidden within. "I can think of no better reason."

"Make no mistake, Jane. Ours will be a practical union. Don't try to make more of it than that. Don't expect love."

Don't expect love. She nodded numbly.

"I ask only one thing."

She forced a smile, praying her face wouldn't crack from the effort. "Of course."

"Look after my sister if anything befalls me."

His eyes drilled into her, stripping away flesh and bone to the core of her. "Give me your word, and I'll believe you." His gaze drifted somewhere beyond her shoulder. "I'll know at least I did not fail her in that."

"Certainly," she agreed. "You needn't even ask."

His gaze shot back to hers. "And you'll have my name." He dipped his head, putting his eyes level with hers. A shock of gold-streaked brown hair fell onto his forehead. She had to stop herself from reaching out and brushing it back. "Don't ask for more."

Jane winced, fighting to hold his stare in the face of words that clawed her heart. "I understand."

He stared at her a long moment before nodding, seemingly satisfied with her response. "I don't suppose it seemly for you to relocate to my residence prior to our vows." His lips twisted in derision. "However, you cannot remain here. Are your parents in Town?"

She could not recall the last time she had seen her parents, although they permanently lived at one of the Duke of Eldermont's many town residences. Too occupied with spending the allowance granted them from Madeline's husband, they would not welcome the intrusion of her into their lives. "I'll go with you."

He eyed the stubborn lift of her chin and appeared ready to argue, then shook his head. "Very well. I'll wait here while you gather your things."

"I won't be long."

She saw no one as she hastened up the stairs. Once in her room, she hurried and packed a valise, realizing that she had very little to pack. Seven years, and there was little to account for. Thoughts awhirl, she swept her gaze over the room one final time, hoping to feel something, anything for the time she had spent beneath this roof. And yet nothing stirred in her heart save a deep sadness for the years wasted to loneliness.

Eager to be gone, she hurried downstairs. To Seth.

Whatever future awaited her had to be better than what she left. Perhaps he evoked feelings too close to those she felt as a girl, those she had no business feeling as a woman entering marriage with a man who vowed to never share himself with her—to never so much as touch her.

But she would overcome that. In time. She must. She wasn't a naive girl anymore. Seth would never love her. She dare not believe he could.

"Ready?" Seth asked, waiting for her at the bottom of the stairs, face impassive as stone, mouth hard and unsmiling—ever the grim warrior.

"Yes," she murmured.

Even as she descended the steps to the waiting carriage, she risked a glance over her shoulder to the dusk-shrouded house, wondering if in leaving its walls she would leave her loneliness behind too.

"Jane."

She turned. Seth held his hand out and she took it, heart leaping traitorously in her chest at the warm hand enfolding her own.

Once inside the carriage, her fingers slid free of his, the loss of warmth immediate, both a relief and a regret. Settling back against the plump squabs, the sound of the carriage door clicking shut echoed in her head like the clang of a great iron gate.

Staring out the window, they began to move, and she could not help wondering whether a future as Seth's wife would prove her torment or salvation.

Chapter 19

A strange tightness gripped Seth's chest as he watched his sister embrace his bride, kissing Jane's cheek with far more exuberance than he had bestowed on her at the pronouncement of them as man and wife.

A chaste kiss was all he could manage. All he trusted himself to give. He had set the rules for this union of theirs. He would not crumble and show himself weak now, on the first day of their marriage. She would not control him. He would not permit her to enslave him with his craving for her.

Jane met his stare over Julianne's shoulder and quickly looked away, making him wonder what she saw when she looked at him. The husband she had duped and snared? Try as he might, he could not muster forth much of his earlier rancor. Not if she had done what she did to escape Billings. He'd been glad to remove her from that bastard.

Theirs had not been a grand church wedding. Merely a drawing room ceremony. No flowers. No candles. No pews full of family and friends.

His eyes flicked over her. The moment she entered the room he had cringed with some distaste that she still wore black, feeling irrationally annoyed to be marrying a woman in mourning for another man. He cursed beneath his breath for not thinking to provide her with something other than black. For not thinking of her at all—only his sense of injustice at being forced to wed a woman he would not have chosen.

Stifling a sigh, he accepted the well wishes of the reverend and his wife, still keeping one eye on Jane as she chatted with his sister. Morning light poured through the open terrace doors, making her brown hair gleam richly in its confining chignon.

His sister looked happy, animated, and his heart loosened in his chest, allowing him to breathe easier. At least he had accomplished what he set out to do. If nothing else, he trusted Jane with Julianne. Even if she was a Spencer. Suddenly reminded of his in-laws, he glanced about the room, almost expecting to see their unpleasant visages materialize.

The Duchesses Shillington and Derring stared

back at him. Lady Derring's dark eyes, a stark contrast to her fair hair, slid over him, as frank and direct as any man's and vaguely threatening.

Lady Shillington was more circumspect, surveying him with sidelong, suspicious glances.

He moved to his wife's side. In a low voice, he asked, "Could your family not attend?"

She inhaled deeply, her chest rising within her bodice, catching his notice in a way that made him scowl. He didn't want to notice her attributes, did not want to remember the fullness of her breasts in his hands—the way they felt, the way they tasted. He would do well to never let himself become caught in her spell again.

Smiling thinly, she said, "I did not invite them."

He studied her a long moment before murmuring, "I trust you did not do so on my account."

Her fragile smile faltered. "It was my wish," she answered in a quiet voice.

He felt something tug at his heart. Relief perhaps. Whatever the reason, she had not forced him to suffer the very people that humiliated him years ago. The realization struck him then that he no longer included Jane in their ranks. For better or worse, she was no longer one of them. No longer a Spencer. She was his. Possessiveness crackled through him like summer lightning. *His*. Who would have thought she could ever elicit such feelings?

Before his icy reserve melted entirely, he turned and addressed the waiting butler. "Are we ready to move to the dining room?"

"Yes, my lord. Breakfast awaits."

"Very good." Extending his arm to his wife, he avoided her gaze, resisting the pull of whatever lurked in those variable depths, reminding himself that she was not of his choosing, no matter how she made his heart beat harder and his blood pump faster.

Her fingers landed soft as a falling leaf on his arm. Together they led their small wedding party into the dining room, to the wedding breakfast Julianne insisted they host. Even though he saw little point in pretending theirs was a happy union brought about through a customary courtship, he relented. A wedding breakfast was a simple enough matter to please his sister.

Julianne and the Duchess of Shillington maintained a sprightly banter, seeing to it that the conversation never lagged entirely—no easy task considering the bride and groom's brooding silence.

The coolly dignified Duchess of Derring concerned herself with her food, feasting with a voracious appetite the likes he had never seen in a lady—the only hint of spontaneity in her icy demeanor. Occasionally she paused to level her dark enigmatic stare on him. He stared back, undaunted.

"To Lord and Lady St. Claire," the lady intoned, dark eyes fastened on him as she lifted her glass high. "May his lordship know the treasure he holds in a wife."

"Astrid," Jane whispered, dropping her utensils and tucking her hands beneath the table.

The Duchess of Shillington heartily seconded the toast.

Seth sat utterly still for a moment before tossing his head back in a release of harsh laughter. Hands gripping the arms of his chair, he surveyed his guests.

The reverend and his wife exchanged uneasy glances, clearly uncertain whether to raise their glasses at the one-sided toast.

Jane's cheeks pinkened.

Her friends held their glasses high, gazes burning into him, ready to carve out his heart if he did not raise his glass. Idly, he traced the edge of his glass in slow circles. Jane followed the movement of his fingers, a shadow falling over her eyes.

Shrugging, he lifted his glass in salute.

Jane's cheeks glowed brighter. Her hands remained tucked beneath the table, far from her own glass as he saluted her.

As they neared the end of the meal, Knightly appeared at his side. "All is in readiness. You best leave now if you wish to arrive by nightfall."

"Thank you, Knightly." Seth rose to his feet. "If you will excuse us. Jane and I must make haste."

Jane looked sharply from Knightly to him. "Where are we going?"

"It's a surprise," Julianne chimed, her face glowing as she tossed down her napkin. "Although I did have a hand in it." She smiled pertly, a dimple denting one peaches-and-cream cheek. "You can thank me upon your return."

Seth shook his head at his sister's naiveté. She seemed to think a honeymoon the natural course of things. As though his marrying Jane were an anticipated event.

Even when he had reminded Julianne that Jane had been married before and would hold no expectations of a young starry-eyed bride, it failed to matter. To avoid disappointing Julianne, he had agreed.

"Come, Jane," he said, holding out his hand. "Let us be off."

He watched, his gut tightening as the tip of her tongue wet her lips. "But my things—"

"Are already packed and in the carriage."

"I see." Squaring her shoulders, she gave a brisk nod, reminding him of men bracing themselves for the cannons of a marauding ship.

Still looking uneasy, Jane accepted his hand, her palm warm and soft against his. Small, he realized. Somewhat at odds with her robust appearance.

Their guests followed them to the foyer, their steps a busy clatter on the parquet floor. He waited patiently as she made her farewells.

"Tell Anna not to fret," Jane said, shooting a quick glance Seth's way as she slipped on her cloak. "Let her know I am well."

"Of course," Lady Shillington assured, fixing her gaze on him, a light of warning in the blue-gray depths that he did not mistake. "Have a marvelous time. Be sure to send word when you've returned. I must hear all about this secret honeymoon."

Nodding, she allowed him to lead her from the house and into the waiting carriage.

Settled against the velvet squabs, she busied herself with arranging her crow-black skirts and repeated her earlier question. "Where are we going?"

He waited until she removed her attention from her skirts, until she met his gaze before answering.

"Julianne wouldn't want me to ruin the surprise. According to her, it wouldn't be romantic if you knew."

"Don't mock," she whispered, those luminous eyes of hers so bloody wounded that he felt like an utter ass. With a shake of her head, she turned to stare out the window. "Let's cease the charade, shall we? Your sister is not here. And you've already schooled me on the precise nature of our marriage. I have no expectations of romance."

He studied her profile, noting the hard set to her mouth.

"Does that disappoint you, Jane?" The moment he asked, he regretted the question. It did not matter if she was disappointed. Their marriage was what it was. It could be no more. He could not allow it.

"Not at all." Her clipped words fell like shards of ice. "I know you don't believe me, but I never intended to trap you." That round little chin of hers lifted stubbornly. "I never intended for you to . . . find out it was me. Never wanted to become a complication in your life."

A complication. The word seemed inadequate to describe Jane. He doubted he could name what he felt for her, but she was vastly more than a mere complication.

"We're wrong for each other," she continued. "Ill-suited at every level. I know you came to Town to find a bride. And you never would have chosen me." She looked out the window again, her fingers thrumming her lips in a thoughtful manner. "For that, I'm sorry. Sorry that I took your choice from you."

Even as she said the words, the image of her eyes, glowing like embers in the night through her domino as he thrust in and out of her flashed through his mind. His body responded instantly and he shifted uncomfortably on the seat. He had chosen her. He just had not known it was her at the time.

And if he were honest with himself, he had chosen Jane, too. He had followed her into Lady Shillington's gallery, suffering no qualms when he slid his hands beneath her skirts, heedless of the risk, uncaring that they could be discovered at any moment. Had they been caught, he would have done the honorable thing and married her.

"I would not say that I was without choice. I am not in the habit of bedding strange masked women. I could have used more discretion. You do not bear total culpability."

Why he felt the need to set her right on that score, he could not say.

She glanced at him, fingers paused over her mouth, hope brimming in her eyes. Hope that he dare not nurture.

"I know my duty," he added brusquely, watching the hope fade from her gaze like a diminishing sun over the Indian Sea. "I will do my best to be a good father and a decent husband. A fair husband. That is enough. For both of us."

His words rang in his head as dismally as the pealing of a funeral bell. *Hell*. Who was he trying to convince? Her? Or himself?

Cursing beneath his breath, he looked away, staring blindly out the window and willing his heart not to thaw one fragment. Not for her. Not a woman who had proven herself less than honest in her dealings with him. He drew a lungful of air, letting it fortify him.

Her hushed voice reached him, quiet as leaves tossing in the wind. "Already you offer me more than I ever had. My last marriage taught me to expect nothing. I would be a fool to start now."

He glanced at her. The coolness of her expression validated her words. She would accept what little he offered.

And he would convince himself that he wanted nothing more from her.

Chapter 20

A salty breeze whipped tendrils of hair across her face as she descended the carriage to face the Tudor-style manor house. Well-trimmed yew hedges, lush as green velvet, surrounded the house, contrasting richly with the light Caen stone. Seagulls sang in the not too far distance. Clouds, fluffy as wool, skidded across a cerulean sky.

"Is this it?" Her gaze flew to Seth's face, hope fluttering in her heart. "The cottage?"

"Yes," he answered, taking her elbow.

Her breath escaped her in an excited rush. Before Julianne's accident, his family spent a fortnight every summer at the cottage. Her eyes skimmed the sizeable house, larger than her own girlhood home. *The cottage*, she mused. An imprecise designation. She had longed to join his family during those summers, to see the ocean, to frolic in the waves with Seth and Julianne instead of languishing at home with her family.

Lifting her face, she inhaled sea air. "Is the ocean far?"

"Not far," he replied, guiding her up the steps just as the front door opened and an elderly couple stepped out. "Mr. and Mrs. Lowery," Seth greeted, "May I present my wife, Lady St. Claire?"

Smiles wreathing their lined faces, the couple sketched a bow and curtsey. "My lady," they greeted.

"Thank you. A pleasure to meet you both."

"Felicitations on your marriage, my lord," Mrs. Lowery offered, studying Jane in her gloomy attire with ill-concealed fascination as they entered the tiled entry.

"Thank you, Mrs. Lowery."

"Would you care to relax in the parlor with some refreshments?"

Seth cut Jane a shrewd glance. "I suspect we would like to visit the beach first off."

Jane nodded mutely, too eager for words. After all these years, she was actually at the cottage. With Seth. Her husband. The latter thought settled heavily in her chest. Certainly she had dreamed of marrying Seth, of spending summers at the cottage with him. With their children. A deep ache pulsed beneath her breastbone. In her dreams, however, there had been the cheering awareness that he loved her, that he *chose* her. He had not been cornered and compelled to marry her.

"Of course. We'll have refreshments waiting for when you return."

Seth led her through a room of richly paneled wood. They skirted a massive mahogany desk and ventured outside through a pair of French doors that opened to a breathtaking garden. Roses, lavender, and iris grew in wild abandon, mingling with colorful shrubbery.

He guided her beneath a long stretch of vine-covered pergola. They strolled beneath dappled sunlight until the arbor ended. Stepping clear, they turned down a path of crushed shells, leaving the well-tended lawn behind. She turned her face to the kiss of a salt-scented breeze. Fat seagulls circled the air as they made their way down a steep path to the beach.

"I can imagine no better place for a honeymoon," she murmured as the pebbled path gave way to golden sand.

He slid her a slow glance before looking straight ahead. "It was Julianne's idea."

A shadow fell over her heart at his gruff reminder. Her stride increased as water, blue as indigo, came into sight. She hurried ahead of him, stopping abruptly at the water's edge to shed her shoes and stockings.

Seth watched her with a curious expression. "What are you doing?"

"I've waited a lifetime to feel sand between my toes."

Tossing her last stocking aside, she straightened and stared ahead, hands braced on her hips, determined that the stern, unsmiling man at her side not ruin the long-awaited moment. The water was calm, the wind rippling its surface only slightly.

"A lifetime?" he echoed. "Your husband never took you abroad? No extravagant honeymoon to the Continent?"

She had enjoyed no honeymoon with Marcus. They married in the spring and he had not wanted to miss the festivities of the Season. Studying the endless blue horizon, she wondered if it was worth explaining that Marcus had preferred to plow the thighs of ladies fresh to Town rather than honeymoon with his new bride.

Lifting her skirts, she hurried to meet the sea lapping at the golden sand—almost as though she fled the unpleasant memories.

Gasping, she laughed as water washed over her toes. "Ah, that's cold!"

"You look like a girl again," he murmured, and something in his voice prompted her to look over her shoulder.

The intense look in his eyes as he surveyed her snatched the breath from her throat. Flustered, she faced the sea again and tried to still her racing heart.

Seeking to fill the charged air, she asked, "Did you miss it? This? Home?"

Silence met her question. Only the sighs of the sea and squawking gulls filled the air. For a moment, she thought he would not reply and warned herself not to expect friendly banter from him. He only brought her here because of Julianne. Not because he wanted to spend time with her. Not because he wanted to give her a real honeymoon. Her hands grew damp where they clutched her skirts.

"I missed my family. My sister. My brother," he answered at last, his voice gravelly and thick with an undercurrent of emotion. "I did not know Albert had died until I returned and found my cousin ensconced at the Priory."

"It was rumored that you were dead."

"Rumors put forth by my cousin," he growled.

"In any case, I was glad to hear the rumors were untrue."

243

"Indeed," he replied, a curious edge to his voice. "And did you think much of me over the years?"

More than a married lady should. More than you will ever know.

Deliberately avoiding the question, she said, "It must have been a shock to return and find Albert dead."

He snorted. "That I should return home unscathed from years of war to find my brother died in his bed from fever?" He laughed, the sound bitter and caustic, twisting inside her belly. "Yes, you could call it a shock."

She nodded, staring hard ahead, afraid to look over her shoulder at him again, afraid that he might suddenly stop when he realized he was *talking* to *her*. As he used to. As friends. Despite the painful subject matter, she did not want him to stop, to seal himself off when he recalled the nature of their marriage.

"I had received word of my father's death," he continued, "but he was lost to me before I ever left."

Her stomach knotted, well remembering the day he had earned his father's undying reproach.

Their mounts had jumped that fence countless times. There was no reason to expect any of them would not clear it. No reason for Seth to blame himself for Julianne's fall. But he did. That much Jane had known as she stood with him outside Julianne's bedchamber, her hand squeezing his as they waited for the physician to finish his examination. When the earl emerged from the room and struck Seth, her own heart had broken.

"Your father loved you," she murmured, not entirely convinced she spoke the truth.

"Once," his voice cracked the air. "He loved me once. Before I ruined Julianne."

Swallowing, she crossed her arms and faced him, "He needed someone to blame."

"He blamed me because it was my fault," he snapped, then, shaking his head, dragged a hand over his face. "Never mind. I did not bring you here to discuss such things. My father is dead. Whether he loved me is not a question I ask myself."

Dropping his hand from his face, the familiar steel returned to his gaze. "I'm sure you would like to rest in your room before dinner."

"Of course," she replied, not the least bit weary.

Crouching, he gathered her shoes and stockings. Before she quite realized what he was about, he was brushing the sand from her foot, each swipe of his fingers a caress that sent a spark of heat up her leg to the core of her. Her stomach quivered and contracted.

A lump formed in her throat as he delved higher beneath the hem of her skirts, his fingers closing around one ankle. Her breath caught at his warm touch on her damp skin.

She looked down at his bowed head. Sunlight gilded the brown strands. Whiskey trapped in cut glass. Her fingers itched to caress the tendrils, to feel the softness against her open palm.

He slid her stocking up her calf, his touch burning a trail toward her garters, fingertips light as a feather stroke on the sensitive flesh of her thighs. Her throat tightened, the lump growing into a painful knot as he turned his attention to her other leg.

By the time he slipped on her shoes, she was a quivering wreck, biting her lip to keep from crying out. Rising to his feet, his gaze snared hers, the centers of his eyes glowing with the knowledge of her arousal.

Without a word, he took her arm and led her back to the house.

Her mind drifted, moving to the night ahead. Would he come to her?

The pulse at her neck shuddered wildly at the prospect. She prayed he would. Her flesh longed to join with his again, to feel with her body what her heart could not.

* * *

Gregory rose from bed at the soft knock on his door. Hastily donning a robe, he opened the door, sensing, as he did so, who would be standing on the other side. Yet even knowing, he did not hesitate. Could not stop if his life depended on it. With his heart in his throat, he pulled open the door.

"Julianne," he greeted, his voice a croak as he drank in the sight of her. The upturned angle of her face, so expectant, so hopeful, so pure, captivated him and made him ache in a way he never had. He clenched his hands at his sides to stop from reaching out and touching her.

With Seth on his impromptu honeymoon and Rebecca visiting relations, he had been thrust into the role of companion, something that had been both a pleasure and a torment. He almost wished he hadn't suggested that Seth leave him behind. A consummate romantic, Julianne had jumped at the suggestion, insisting that Seth eschew his use for a valet during his honeymoon.

As a gentleman lacking wealth and property, he could never hope for a life with Julianne, yet that was what he had found himself doing. Daring to hope, to want. Imagining them together as only a man and woman could be. He longed to chase the shadow of loneliness from her face.

He should have put a halt to their growing relationship, knowing her brother would disapprove, knowing Seth would in fact see it as a betrayal, but he hadn't possessed the strength.

"May I come inside, Gregory?"

The question was simple—as his answer should be. Yet the word stuck in his throat alongside his heart. He swallowed. Despite what the blood pumping through his veins urged him to do, he found the strength to utter, "No."

Her face fell. "No?" she echoed, tightening her night rail about her and stepping back. "I understand." She shook her head, her unbound mane of auburn hair tossing over her shoulders. "I thought you liked me, Gregory. I thought—"

He caught her wrist. "No. You don't understand. What I feel for you cannot be diminished to mere liking. It's because of the way I feel for you that I'm telling you—" He broke off with a growl of frustration, his fine thread of control snapping as he hauled her hard against him for a hungry kiss.

Her hands crept up and wrapped around his neck, the touch of her fingers silk against his nape. She moaned deep in her throat and the sound vibrated through him. Dangerously close to forgetting every reason he could not have this woman, he wrenched free of her, stepping back several paces.

"Go," he rasped. "Leave and never come to my room again."

Tears sheened her eyes. "Why must you send me away?" She stepped toward him again and he set her back gently.

"Don't be foolish, Julianne. Nothing can come of this. An earl's daughter does not carry on with a valet."

"I don't care—"

"Well, you should. A woman of your station, your rank—" He broke off shaking his head. "In any case, I care enough for the both of us and I'm ending this now." He gentled his voice. Unable to resist one more touch, he ran his thumb over her kiss-bruised lips. "It can never be, Julianne."

Her expression changed, the soft lines of her face hardening. "We'll see about that," she uttered before swinging around and striding down the corridor, one hand lightly skimming the wall as she marched off with martial stiffness.

We'll see about that.

Part of him worried over her words, fearing she would pursue her infatuation with him—pursue him. But there was another part of him, buried deep in his heart where impossible dreams clung, that fervently hoped she would persist and break down his resistance, that what she felt for him amounted to more than one overly sheltered woman's first foray into love, that it was genuine and lasting and could conquer good sense and the strictures of Society.

Then perhaps he could consider breaking every principle that governed him and spend his life with a woman with whom he was fast falling in love.

Chapter 21

Three nights and Seth had not come.

Jane spent her days alone, discounting the occasional company of Mrs. Lowery. Seth occupied himself with estate business. Presumably the cottage required a great deal of attention. She had gleaned from conversations with Mrs. Lowery that Albert had not given the seaside manor much care over the years, more concerned with the Priory and the profits yielded from the labors of its many tenants. Sound justification for Seth's absence she supposed.

And yet she spent her nights staring into the dark, waiting, listening, her body hungering for his touch, aching to hear his footsteps in the adjoining room, praying they would cross the threshold into her room.

Jane read the pity in the housekeeper's eyes

and did her best to appear unbothered by Seth's neglect. She had been duly warned. A practical arrangement, he had said. She should not harbor expectations for anything else. Yet she could not help herself. Longing had wormed its way into her heart.

Her days fell into a pattern. Nausea plagued her in the mornings, leaving her weak and shaken as a newborn foal. On those mornings, she told herself it was best that Seth left her alone. It would only embarrass her for him to see her in such a condition.

She felt improved enough in the afternoons to take lunch. Alone in the dining room, a silent footman hovering in the corner, she picked at her meal, staving off the aching loneliness and disappointment she had no business feeling. Especially understanding full well the sort of marriage she had entered. She was no stranger to loneliness, no stranger to an empty marriage bed.

Walks on the beach were her one solace. She strolled up and down the stretch of pale sand, her pace brisk, as if she could leave herself and the hollowness inside her chest behind with each step. Eventually, she had to stop and return to the house to prepare herself for dinner. Tiresome affairs where Seth sat cold and distant across from her.

Something had happened since the day they arrived. A change had come over him, as tangible as the salt in the sea air that tickled her tongue. He spoke little . . . looked at her even less. The man she married had become as cold and unrelenting as stone.

Sitting at her dressing table after another grim dinner, Jane brushed her hair until it crackled and shone in the lamplight. Her gaze drifted to the adjoining door. She knew it would not be locked. She knew because she had tested it earlier in the day, when there had been no risk of running into Seth. Curious, she had investigated his chamber, trailing her hand over the brocade counterpane, bringing his dressing robe to her nose for a lingering smell.

Rising from the bench, she rose and approached the adjoining door. Her heart fluttered like a wild bird in her chest as she eyed the thin line of light glowing beneath.

He had wanted her once. Perhaps he could again.

Ignoring the nagging little voice that whispered through her mind, *He did not know it was you*, she dragged a breath into her lungs and rapped twice.

At his muffled command, she squared her shoulders and swept inside the room.

"Forgive the interruption," she began, watching

as his lean form rose from the bed in one motion. Muscles danced beneath the fine lawn of his half-opened shirt like wind on water. He moved like a jungle cat. Swift and purposeful.

Her mouth dried, suddenly uncertain now that she stood before him.

"Jane," he acknowledged, his deep voice a drag of silk against her highly sensitive nerves. At her silence, he pressed, "Is there something you wanted?"

Was it not evident? She stood in the midst of his bedchamber in her nightgown, shaking like the sea wind against the shutter. Heat swept up her face. "I thought you may have use for me tonight."

Use of her? She cringed. *Blast it.* She made herself sound like a handkerchief to be used and discarded.

"I—I mean to say, I thought you might desire my company."

The word desire hung in the air like smoke between them.

Crossing his arms, he studied her in brooding silence, his eyes skimming her, from the top of her head to her bare toes peeping beneath the hem of her nightgown. His jaw hardened, the uneven line of his scar stark as ever against his face, leaving no doubt that he understood her meaning perfectly.

"You are familiar with my reasons for wanting a wife."

Like sand settling to a riverbed, dread sank in the pit of her belly. She braced herself, knowing he would say more and knowing she would not like it, knowing she had been a fool to come to him, to expect more when he had warned her against such longings.

"Indeed." Her legs trembled beneath her. "You wished for a wife that could care for your sister. Oh, and provide the requisite heir."

His brown eyes glimmered darkly in the dim room and he gave a quick nod. "Anything more is superfluous."

Superfluous.

The word blew a chill through her heart.

Instead of fleeing as common sense—pride— urged, she fiddled with the ribbon that tied her wrapper at the front.

His gaze dropped to that gossamer-thin ribbon keeping her wrapper closed. A sudden charge of energy filled the air, raising the tiny hairs at the back of her neck.

His hand lifted with a dreamlike slowness and her breath lodged in her throat. He stepped closer. Eyes wide and unblinking, she watched as his fingers unraveled the ribbon and pushed her wrapper from her shoulders in one smooth motion. It fell to the carpet with a whisper, puddling around her bare feet.

His fingers skimmed the thin cotton of her night-gown, down between the valley of her breasts. Eyes darkening, his touch grew bolder, moving to the outside swell of one breast, tracing the rounded outline with agonizing gentleness.

Her breathing grew ragged, filling the silence. His hand, large and burning through the thin cotton of her gown, uncurled over her rib cage, sliding upward until he lifted her breast higher between his forefinger and thumb.

The harsh rasp of his breath mingled with her own. His thumb shifted, sliding over her nipple, grazing the peak. She bit her lip to stop from crying out.

His thumb moved faster, rotating in small circles over the turgid crest, his touch growing firmer, harder until he finally squeezed, rolling her nipple between two fingers, the sweet pain of it ripping a loud sob from her throat.

As if her cry woke him from a spell, he blinked and dropped his hand. Clearing his throat, he dragged a shaking hand through his hair.

Lifting his glittering gaze, he commanded hoarsely, "Dammit, Jane, go."

Bewildered, she shook her head. "I don't understand—"

"Go!" he shouted.

Sucking in a ragged breath, she snatched her wrapper off the floor. With as much dignity as she could manage, she shrugged into it.

In a blink, she was nineteen again, stumbling upon Marcus with Berthe. On that day, she had realized he had no need for her either.

And now, mere days into her second marriage, another husband had turned her from his bed. The humiliation burned at the backs of her eyes.

"I see." And she did. Perfectly. Resisting the overwhelming urge to lash out at him, to wound as she felt wounded, she spun around to leave.

"Jane, wait." His hand fell on her arm, hard as granite as he forced her around.

Before he could say anything, words tumbled from her mouth in a furious torrent, "I don't suppose *you* shall live as a monk."

Her frowned, saying nothing.

She snorted, attempting to twist free from his hold. "I know all about the faithfulness of husbands. *You* shall not be lonely, I am certain."

Something in the brown of his eyes softened. "Was that the way of it, then?"

"No," she snapped, despising him in that moment. She would not have his pity. The need to hurt, to lash out, burned a fire in her chest, fueling her. Before she could consider the wisdom of her words, she spit out, "We may not share a bed, but don't expect me to live as a nun. I've walked that path before and I won't again."

"Tread carefully, dear *wife*," he growled, the endearment a foul epithet on his lips as he pulled her closer. "No man will have what is mine." Despite the softness of his voice, his words fell roughly on her ears.

"*Yours?*" She struggled against his hold, laughing wildly. "It takes more than the words of a reverend to accomplish that."

He shoved his face closer, brown eyes so close she could see the countless flecks of amber burning feverishly in the centers. "Don't push me, Jane."

"Or what?"

Their rasping breaths mingled. His eyes dropped to her mouth and for a moment she thought he would kiss her—*prayed* he would. Instead he flung her from him with a stinging curse.

"Look at us." He laughed mirthlessly. "Days married and already at each other's throats."

Yes. And why? Because of her. Because she wanted more. Wanted him. Would she have a child's tantrum because her husband did not want her in his bed?

Suddenly shamed, she peeled his fingers from her arms. "We won't fight anymore."

"We won't?" he asked, a dark brow arching in skepticism.

"I understand now. I thought I did before. But I didn't." Despite her claims, she had harbored hopes that their marriage of convenience might lead to something more. A marriage in the truest sense.

He stared, his jaw flexing.

Moistening her lips, she announced, "You ended up with the wrong sister—"

"Don't drag her into this," he cut in.

Her heart twisted. "Do you love her still?" she asked, knowing she sounded jealous and foolish, but she couldn't stop herself. She had to know if he still loved Madeline. If Madeline would always be there, a wall between them, she best find out now.

"She has nothing to do with us."

Not precisely the answer she sought.

"She has everything to do with us. You're punishing me because of her—"

"That's not true."

"No?" She angled her head. "If Aurora had turned out to be another woman, any woman besides me, would you be sleeping alone tonight?"

She waited, her breath lodged deep in her chest.

He stared at her in silence, his eyes dark and unfathomable. A muscle ticked in his jaw, the only sign that she perhaps struck a nerve.

The silence grew, a terrible thing between them, confirming that it was Jane he found objectionable. Finished standing before him, an offering that he would refuse as if foul, she swallowed down the thickness in her throat. Gathering the scraps of dignity left to her, she thrust her chin forward. "Forgive me for disturbing you." *I won't do so again.*

"Jane," he called, but she had already passed through the door. Even knowing he would never cross its threshold, she locked it behind her, collapsing against its solid length, her chest heaving as if she just raced a great distance.

He knocked, the wood reverberating at her back. "Jane, let's talk about—"

"We've talked enough. Good night, Seth."

She held her breath, waiting to see if he would say more, unsure whether she wanted him to or not . . . knowing she only wanted to hear what he could never say.

She pressed the base of her palms to her burning eyes and willed the pain away, choking back a sob as she commanded herself to forget she had ever loved Seth. *That she still did.*

The sob swelled higher in her throat, threatening to burst free as that realization washed over her.

She had never stopped loving him. Even after all these years.

The journey back to Town was a miserable affair, even without the waves of tension, palpable as fog, swirling around them. She stared out the window, watching the rolling countryside, convinced she could never look Seth in the face again. Not without reliving the shame of his rejection, at any rate.

The swaying and rolling motion of the carriage heightened the sickness she had thought mild and endurable at the cottage. A queasy belly that cramped and twisted insistently soon pushed thoughts of Seth from her mind. After the first hour, she fell limp against the carriage wall, slipping in and out of misery-induced sleep.

"Are you well?" Seth asked at one point, his hand falling on her shoulder.

She whimpered at his touch, as if it somehow compounded her misery.

"Fine," she mumbled without opening her eyes, concentrating on not retching all over the carriage floor. "Just tired."

At some point, her dozing must have turned into a full-fledged slumber because the next thing she knew she was being lifted from the carriage and carried up the steps of the St. Claire townhouse.

Her cheek rested weakly against Seth's hard chest, the thudding of his heart filling her ear as her head lolled with the pound of his footsteps. She lifted her head, determined to escape his comforting nearness, to neither need nor want it, but that still left the hard bands of muscle holding her securely, and the unyielding breadth of a very male chest against her. She gave up the fight, telling herself she took no pleasure in his holding her.

He deposited her upon a large tester in the room that she had occupied prior to taking their vows. Relieved to be free of the rollicking carriage, she curled on her side, closing her eyes as she sank into the down-filled mattress, so grateful she did not even protest when he removed her slippers and stockings.

Slipping her hand beneath her cheek, she released a shuddery sigh as warm fingers squeezed the blood back into her feet. "Mmm," she moaned, rolling onto her back, afraid to open her eyes and find him gone and the pleasant sensation a dream.

He rubbed deep, languorous circles over the arch of her feet. His fingers slid up, those marvelous thumbs moving over her calves in long, penetrating strokes until she felt boneless, a weakened mass of her former self.

Instinctively her knees parted and she groaned as he moved up even more, his fingers digging deep, sweeping strokes along her quivering thighs. Her hands stretched out to her sides, fisting the brocade counterpane as small noises of pleasure escaped her.

She opened her eyes, letting herself look at him at last.

Seth stood poised over her, hands digging into her thighs, a feverish look in his eyes that brought a rush of moisture between her thighs. Her body reacted, an aching throb tugging low in her belly, demanding and insistent. She bit her lip, wanting badly to assuage that ache—wanting him to pound it into submission as only he could.

"Jane!" a voice intruded.

Seth's hands dropped from her thighs as though burned and he took a hasty step back.

Anna charged into the room, her broad faced creased and lined with worry. "I heard you were carried inside the house. Are you unwell?" The older woman looked Seth over accusingly.

Jane rearranged her skirts, sitting up. "I'm fine. Only a little travel-weary."

"Hmm," Anna murmured, casting Seth a side-long glance.

Blinking with the realization that Anna stood

before her, Jane exclaimed, "Anna! What are you doing here?"

Anna nodded at Seth, folding her hands before her substantial figure.

Jane's gaze jerked to Seth.

He gave only a curt nod.

Anna explained, "Before you left for your honeymoon, his lordship hired me."

Jane stared hard at Seth. "You did that?"

He shrugged one shoulder. "It was a small matter."

Why would he do something so thoughtful, so generous . . . for her? And before they ever left Town. Before that wretched night when she had thrown herself at him and shamed herself.

"You do look peaked," Anna observed, her sturdy, callused palm brushing Jane's cheek. "Are you feeling poorly?"

"I'll leave you now," Seth announced. Looking to Anna, he advised, "Do see that she rests and eats."

"Yes, my lord." Anna sketched an awkward curtsey, watching as he strode from the room. As soon as the door clicked shut, Anna whirled about. "Out with it now. What has he done to you?"

"Nothing. I'm merely a bit under the weather," Jane confessed. "I'm sure it's no more than exhaustion from the journey."

"It's the babe," Anna pronounced, shaking her head with a dogged resolve. "Your mother was violently ill with both you and your sister—especially you."

Jane's hand flew to her belly. "Violently ill?" she echoed, praying it would not be so with her. She did not want Seth to think her weak and sickly. He already thought low of her. She would have that he not view the mother of his child as frail and unfit for the rigors of motherhood.

"Come, lie down. I shall send for a tray."

"No," Jane said, her voice falling hard. "I won't have him think I need special care."

Anna observed her keenly, lowering herself to the bed beside Jane. The bed dipped from her added weight and Jane had to stop herself from rolling to the edge. "You seem to care a great deal about what he thinks of you."

Heat warmed her cheeks. Jane splayed a hand over her belly and rubbed idly. "Clearly I am not immune to him. He is an attractive man."

"And that's the sum of it, then." Anna smirked, cocking a bushy gray brow. "He's merely . . . attractive."

"Of course," Jane said, fighting the wave of emotion that told her she lied.

Leaning down, Anna removed the pins from

Jane's hair, shaking the heavy mass free. "Rest. All this excitement . . ." She clucked and shook her salt-and-peppered head in disapproval. "First that rushed business of a wedding—"

"I had a church wedding once," Jane interrupted. "It's not everything."

"Then that ill-conceived honeymoon. You've no business traveling in your condition," Anna continued as if she had not spoken. "You need peace and quiet. Let your mind and body settle." With a decisive nod, Anna shoved to her feet. Jane grabbed her hand, stopping her.

"Anna . . ." she hesitated, scanning the woman's heavily lined face, needing approval from the woman who had been more of a mother to her than her own. "Have I disappointed you?" Her hand curled over her stomach protectively, almost as if she wanted to shelter the child within.

Shock crossed Anna's face. "You? Never." Moving close, she smoothed a chapped palm over Jane's brow. "You're a good girl. Misused by the very people God intended to love you, is the sorry truth. You'll have a child to love now. Who will love you back." Her lips twitched and her eyes twinkled with humor. "And you're with the boy you always loved. You deserve no less."

Jane shook her head fiercely, seeing no humor in her present predicament.

Anna continued, "You may fool yourself, but I know you. You never stopped loving that boy."

Jane fought the sudden, infuriating burn of tears in her eyes, wishing she could deny the claim.

Swiping the back of her hand against her eyes, resolve steeled her nerves. She may love him, but she would not torment herself with the hopes that he could love her back.

Seth sought refuge in his bedchamber. He needed to greet his sister, but not before he collected himself. Not before he gained control of his raging lust.

Pacing the room's length, he dragged both hands through his hair, cursing when he realized how they shook.

Damn her. And damn him. He couldn't even touch her in the most innocent way without fondling her. How was he to keep his hands to himself?

He had defined the parameters of their marriage. He could not change the rules now. Not without looking a bloody ass. Not without revealing himself weak and without control—precisely the type of man he vowed never to become. He'd lost control before. He would not permit a woman to hold such power over him again.

Not that he needed to worry. Even if he failed and succumbed, she would never give him another chance. Not after he rebuffed her. He'd seen the look in her eyes that night. The utter devastation. The deep hurt. He had felt its echo in his own heart, so much that he almost surrendered. Almost caved and took her in his arms, claimed her body as he yearned.

She hardly looked at him now. And when she did, her gaze flitted over him as if he were nothing—something to be scraped off the bottom of her shoe.

He sighed. At least it kept her from coming to his room in the dead of night garbed in a nightgown that did more to accentuate her curves than disguise.

He could never survive that. Not again. It had killed him to watch her walk away when every inch of him wanted to strip her bare and sink himself to the hilt in her softness, to join with the body that haunted his nights.

If only the woman who drove him mad with desire weren't Jane—weren't his wife.

If only he didn't feel his control slip each time he looked at her.

Chapter 22

Jane smoothed her hands over her wide pleated skirts. The blue and yellow striped dimity was heaven to behold. No more ghastly black. She could have wept with elation.

It had taken less than a week to outfit her with a new wardrobe. The little Frenchwoman Seth had sent wasted no time, barking orders with military precision. Even Anna jumped to her commands. In a flash, the seamstress had stripped her wardrobe with the clipped command, "burn them" and began measuring Jane for ball gowns, day dresses, riding habits, nightgowns, filmy undergarments that made her blush. Nothing was overlooked, including future clothing for her confinement.

Pulling on the tidy white cuffs of her dress, she knocked on the door to Seth's office, anxious to see his reaction to her new attire, to show him that she could look the part of a countess—even if a name only wife.

They had not seen each other since he deposited her in her bedchamber, leaving her to Anna's care. His summons today mystified her.

His voice carried through the door, bidding her enter.

Squaring her shoulders, she fixed a neutral expression on her face and did her best to ignore the way her blood rushed at seeing him. He sat behind his desk, papers and ledgers littering the surface. Strands of golden brown hair fell over his forehead. As always her fingers itched to touch his hair, to delve through the sun-kissed mess and push it back from his brow.

"Jane," he greeted, his gaze sweeping over her as he rose to his feet, tossing his hair back with a shake of his head.

Her fingers flew to her clammy cheek, realizing she mustn't look her best despite her lovely new gown. With each day, she felt as if she were being turned inside out. Her stomach a rolling, twisting beast that dictated her actions. Every smell, good or bad, had her covering her nose, fearful to draw too deep a breath lest she become sick.

He motioned across from him.

She followed the gesture and noticed the room's

other inhabitant, immediately recognizing Mr. Younger, the Guthrie family solicitor. A sour taste filled her mouth, and she gave him a grim nod. He had always treated her as though she possessed half a brain. Fortunately, she had not seen him since Marcus's funeral.

Rising to his feet, the reed-thin gentleman bowed. "Lady Guth—" he stopped and corrected himself, "Lady St. Claire."

"Mr. Younger." She smiled tightly and took the chair beside his. "A pleasure to see you again," she lied.

"Jane, Mr. Younger has some startling news."

"Indeed?" She looked to Mr. Younger.

"Yes, it seems I owe you an apology, my lady."

She cocked her head to the side. "Whatever for?"

The solicitor's Adam's apple bobbed wildly. "It appears I should have monitored your brother-in-law's supervision of your jointure—"

"My jointure?" she interrupted. Her gaze flicked to Seth. "Marcus left me no jointure."

Mr. Younger pulled at his starched collar as if it choked him. "In fact, the late Lord Guthrie did."

Marcus left her a jointure? She considered this news, accepting it as a possibility. It was what most gentlemen did, and Marcus had been the consummate gentleman, infidelities withstanding.

"Mr. Billings convinced us that you were too grief-stricken over Lord Guthrie's sudden death to attend to your affairs." Releasing his collar, he gave a small shrug of his slight shoulders, his gaunt cheeks flushing. "Given the circumstances of your late husband's passing, I deemed that very likely."

"Could you not have asked me?" she bit out, her hands clenching the arms of her chair.

He reddened further at her simple question. "I found it quite credible that you lacked the proper frame of mind to oversee proceedings usually left to the domain of men. Mr. Billings and I decided he was best suited to manage your affairs." He looked to Seth as though expecting agreement.

Suddenly it all made sense. Desmond had worked so hard to keep her beneath his thumb in order to maintain control of her jointure. Her cheeks burned, indignation firing her as she focused her wrath on the hapless solicitor. "Well, which is it, Mr. Younger? Was I too grief-stricken or too feeble-minded to be versed in my affairs?" She fisted her skirts to stop from swinging at the arrogant popinjay.

Her own jointure would have altered everything. Granted her the means to be independent. Perhaps she would not have risked attending Madame Fleur's masquerade, so desperate for a night of freedom. Perhaps she would not have seduced Seth at Vauxhall. Would not now find herself married— once again—to a man who cared nothing for her.

Nor would she carry his child. Her hand drifted to her stomach and her anger dissipated like a ring of smoke in the air. As simple as that her wrath vanished.

Mr. Younger inclined his head in a show of remorse. "My deepest apologies, my lady. It was not well done of me."

Seth's voice broke in, "I would like my wife's funds transferred at once."

"That, my lord, is the issue that brings me here today," the solicitor murmured in a near whisper, his eyes downcast. "Upon learning of Lady Guthrie's marriage, I set myself to that precise task. And yet . . ." He pulled on his collar again.

"Spit it out, Younger," Seth demanded.

"There is nothing left," he choked. "Mr. Billings has gone through all of it."

"Gone through all of it?" Seth echoed, dark brows dipping in a frown.

Jane shook her head. A bitter laugh bubbling up from deep in her chest. "Of course."

The irony galled her. Desmond had convinced the solicitors she was incompetent to oversee her affairs, and then *he* proceeded to squander her money.

"We greatly misjudged Mr. Billings, my lord. He is quite the swindler," Mr. Younger rushed to say. "I've visited him and he claimed that your wife's portion was spent on her upkeep."

"Indeed," she inserted hotly, thinking of all she had gone without since Marcus's death. She had not shopped, traveled, or done the usual things that a lady of the *ton* might do.

Younger continued, his nasal voice grating her nerves, "Seeing as there is no way to prove or disprove this claim—"

"Nothing can be done," Seth finished, the edge to his voice sharp as cut glass. Jane watched as he unfolded his great length from behind the desk.

Mr. Younger shrank back in his chair, the leather creaking beneath him.

"You may take your leave, Younger. And thank you. It's of use to know one solicitor whom I shall never entrust with my affairs. I shall be sure that all of Town knows as well."

Mr. Younger's mouth fell slack and his eyes bulged. Leaning forward, he raised a hand in supplication. "L-Lord St. Claire, you cannot mean to spread tales—"

"Of your incompetence? Indeed, I do. Good day, sir. I'm certain you remember the way out."

His face pale as chalk, Mr. Younger gave a reluctant nod before rising and departing the room.

Jane stared after the solicitor for a moment before murmuring with a shake of her head, "I'm sorry, Seth. It seems I should not have come empty-handed into this marriage."

"I never expected money when I married you."

"Just the same, anything Marcus left me should have gone to the man I married—"

"Don't apologize. Your jointure would have been yours to do with as you wished. I wouldn't have touched a penny of it."

Jane stared at his resolute expression. "You would have let me keep what I brought to the marriage?"

"Your late husband left it to you. Not me." He leaned against his desk, crossing his arms. The motion pulled his jacket taut against his shoulders and biceps and she forced her gaze to his face. "Money has nothing to do with why we married." His stare held hers, the molten brown steadily trained on her. "You know why we married."

For the life of her she could not look away. Nor could she breathe as she gazed into those warm brown pools, eyes that ensnared her, that seized her by the heart and refused to let go.

You know why we married. Indeed she did. Her

hand brushed her stomach, to the child within who made his presence known daily. She knew why Seth married her. Duty drove him. Duty to his sister. To his unborn child.

Her reasons, however, had nothing to do with duty and more to do with hope. With dreams of love that her foolish heart refused to release.

He blinked. And just like that a shadow fell over his eyes. Abruptly, he turned, circling back around his desk. "I've work to do."

She rose as if a poker prodded her backside.

"Of course," she murmured, moving to the door, calling herself the world's greatest fool to ever hold out hope that his feelings for her would change, that he could love a woman he had never wanted to wed in the first place.

Jane clutched the edge of the basin, her empty stomach clenching until her fingers turned numb and bloodless. After several more heaves, her stomach stilled, and she prayed that the worst had finally passed. Heavens knew there was nothing left in her belly.

The air sounded fuzzy, a humming quiet after the harsh sound of her retching. Blinking through watering eyes, she pulled back on unsteady limbs. Cold tears streamed silently down her face and she dashed a shaking hand over each cheek. The gray light of dusk washed over the chamber and she marveled at the day lost to illness.

She didn't attempt to stand, simply crawled toward the bed, grasping the hem of her nightgown so that it did not become caught beneath her. Halfway there she gave up and collapsed, curling up on her side with a shuddery sigh. For the best, she supposed, eyeing the basin. She shouldn't stray far.

She hugged herself, trembling like a leaf on the wind—a dreadful full-body shake that made her feel weak and helpless at the same time. For the moment, her belly was still, the nausea at bay, but even as she tried to hope that her stomach had settled, that she couldn't possibly feel any sicker, she knew she could. She knew she would. Today had been an endless misery.

Not for the first time, she agonized that something was wrong with her—with the babe. Even though Anna had assured her that such things were normal, even common, she could only feel a deep, gnawing anxiety.

Her hand drifted to her belly, love swelling in her for this life that was a product of her and Seth. Something good. Sweet and innocent. Love would result of their union. One way or another.

Fierce determination gripped her. No harm

could come to him, this person that she already loved. Who would love her in turn—as her own family never would. As Seth did not.

She curled herself into an even tighter ball. *Please, please make him well and strong.* The litany rolled through her mind with the ferocity of a rushing river.

The door opened. Relief coursed through her. No doubt Anna had returned with the mint tea. She had vowed the brew would help settle her stomach.

"Anna," she whispered through parched lips and a throat that felt ravaged as plowed earth.

A moment later, warm, firm hands were pulling her up.

"Seth," she murmured, confused, instantly knowing his touch, his smell, his enlivening heat. *Blast.* Would she never be immune? Indifferent?

He swung her up into his arms and gently laid her on the bed.

"No," she protested, one arm motioning weakly for the floor. "The basin," she managed to get out.

"I'll fetch it."

Mortification stung her cheeks. Seth playing nursemaid was the height of humiliation. She could not bear for him to see her like this. At her worst.

"Go away," she choked, jamming her eyes shut.

"Hush," he murmured, pressing the cool cloth that Anna had used against her forehead.

With a sigh, she turned her face toward that soothing coolness. Her heart should not leap at the gesture. It didn't mean he cared for her. It didn't mean she meant anything at all to him. He was an honorable man. An honorable man would stop to help an injured animal. Certainly his wife would not be excluded from that basic impulse to offer aid.

Even a wife he did not want.

Worry hammered Seth's chest as he bathed Jane's brow. She looked the image of death. An image he knew well. Lips as gray as gunmetal. Eyes glassy with agony. He'd seen the face of death before. On brave men cut down in their prime, vital one moment, refuse on the deck of a ship the next— the loud whistle of the bosun's mate a sorrowful salute on the wind as their wrapped bodies slid to a watery grave.

"How long have you been like this?" he demanded, chasing thoughts of death from his mind and focusing on the present, on Jane.

Why had no one fetched him? He assumed she had been avoiding him, retreating rather than face him. As he had been doing. Never had it occurred to him that she was ill. Passing her door, he had heard her terrible retching. For no other reason would he have entered her room, too determined to avoid the temptation she presented.

"For a while," she whispered, her voice a dry croak. "Anna says it will pass."

"This is . . . normal?" Seth asked, feeling frighteningly ill-equipped. He could stitch up a wound and dig out a bullet if necessary, but this . . .

The last time he had felt this helpless was staring at Julianne lying twisted and still as stone amid the bluebells. He'd thought her dead. Thought he had killed her.

"According to Anna, the sicker I feel, the healthier the babe." A tremulous smile curved her lips, as if she did not entirely believe such counsel.

His gaze flew to her stomach, as if he could see the child within her. His child. *Theirs.* Until this moment, none of it had been quite real. Suddenly he could imagine their child. A little girl with Jane's glossy brown hair and hazel eyes. His heart constricted.

"Perhaps we should send for the physician, just to be safe," he suggested, the protectiveness gripping him fierce, an emotion, welcome or not, he was coming to anticipate around her.

"My lord? What are you doing here?" The sound of Anna's voice brought him to his feet.

"Seeing to my wife," he answered.

Anna studied him warily as she carried a tray holding a steaming cup and set it on the table beside the bed.

"Your wife," she harrumphed, folding her arms over her great bosom. "Wouldn't know it for all the notice you've given her."

"Anna," Jane scolded, color washing the green tinge from her face.

He scowled. "I'm sending for the physician."

Anna snorted. "What does a man know of female matters?"

"It's unnecessary," Jane interjected, her weak voice firm with decision. "I'm in good hands with Anna."

"Perhaps," he conceded. "But I'm staying. And if I think you're worsening, I'm sending for a physician."

Anna began to protest.

He arched a brow in warning.

Snapping her mouth shut, the maid nodded and motioned to the tea on the bedside table. "See that she drinks."

Seth settled down beside Jane, stretching his legs alongside hers. Nestling her head against his shoulder, he brought the tea to her lips.

"I'm not an invalid," she complained, looking up at him with weary, bemused eyes.

"Hush," he murmured. "Drink."

She sipped from the cup, watching him drowsily. "Thank you," she murmured, eyes drifting shut.

"You may leave us, Anna." He didn't look up as the maid departed, too occupied with studying Jane's face as she fell asleep in his arms, her soft curves nestled against his a tormenting reminder of all he was denying himself each night he slept alone in his bed.

He squeezed his eyes tightly, struggling to forget what it felt like to have her, to sink himself into her heat.

Despite his struggles, it was a memory that plagued him long into the hours of the night.

Chapter 23

"**G**ood morning," Jane greeted upon entering the dining room and moving to the sideboard.

"Jane!" Julianne's face brightened as she stared in Jane's general direction. "How lovely to have you up and about again. Seth was beside himself with worry."

Jane glanced Seth's way. Heat flooded her face at the memory of yesterday, of falling asleep in his arms, of waking up in his arms.

Lowering his paper, he watched her with unreadable eyes as she placed one slice of toast upon her plate, not yet ready to try her stomach with her usual fare of eggs and kippers.

"Good morning, Jane." He inclined his head, the sound of her name on his lips low and deep, making her shiver.

Sinking into the seat across from Julianne, she snapped her napkin free and murmured, "I feel much better. I actually woke hungry this morning." Her gaze darted to Seth again, wondering if he had yet explained to his sister the reason for her illness, or, for that matter, the reason for their marriage.

"Are you up for a drive in the park then, Jane?" Julianne asked, carefully reaching for her teacup. Closing both hands about it, she brought it to her lips for a small sip. "I confess I've been eager for your company. Rebecca's sister lives in Eppingham. Since we're so close I insisted she spend a few days with her."

Seth grunted at this before taking a crunchy bite of his toast.

"Seth is not pleased with me doing so," Julianne added in a not so conspiratorial whisper.

"I'm sure even the most loyal companion deserves the occasional time off," Jane volunteered.

One of Seth's brows cocked. "Quite. Only perhaps not when Julianne is in a house virtually unknown to her and requires more help than usual."

"Oh," Jane murmured, looking with concern to Julianne.

She flicked a hand in dismissal. "Nonsense."

"Then why have you pilfered Knightly, claiming

to need his assistance?" Seth reopened his paper, missing the telltale blush stealing over Julianne's face. But Jane did not. She noted the flood of color and wondered at it. Why should Jane blush at the mention of Mr. Knightly?

"I think a drive too soon for Jane," Seth announced.

She snapped her gaze back to him, nostrils quivering. As much as she resented his answering on her behalf, she could not disagree. The thought of ambling along curving paths made her stomach tighten.

"I suppose you can prevail upon Knightly again, Julianne. I've a meeting with my solicitor this morning."

"Certainly I wouldn't want Jane to relapse." Julianne cleared her throat, tracing the rim of her teacup with an elegant fingertip. "If you're sure Greg— Mr. Knightly isn't otherwise occupied."

Seth looked up at her slight slip, observing her intently. For a moment, something flickered in his gaze. Doubt. Uncertainty. Something. Then he shook his head and it was gone. He returned his attention to his paper.

Jane studied Julianne as she slowly chewed her toast.

"Excuse me, ladies." Seth rose to his feet. "I

have an appointment to keep. Julianne, I'll send Knightly along."

Julianne dabbed a napkin over her broad smile. "Thank you."

Seth faced Jane. For a moment, his eyes darkened with something indecipherable. "Jane." He gave a single tight nod.

Heart in her throat, she watched him depart, stirring her tea absently as his broad back disappeared from sight.

"Jane." At the sound of her name, she returned her attention to her sister-in-law. "You've met Mr. Knightly . . ." Julianne paused, her slender throat working for words.

"Yes?" she prompted.

"What do you think of him?"

Jane answered slowly, "He seems a fine gentleman." Unsure she knew enough about him to assess his character, she added, "Although I've not had the chance to make his acquaintance to any great degree."

"I have," Julianne confessed, leaning forward in her chair, her expression rapt, reminding Jane of the girl she had once been, full of anticipation and wide-eyed naiveté. "He's brilliant! So witty and charming. Oh, Jane!"—she clasped her hands together before her—"he *listens* to me. No gentleman has ever listened to me as he does. And he treats me as though I'm whole and not some invalid. My own family has never even treated me like that."

"It appears you've grown quite attached," Jane murmured, concerned over the *tendre* Julianne was clearly forming for Seth's valet.

"Jane . . ." Color flooded Julianne's face.

"Yes. What is it?" Jane prodded.

"Mr. Knightly. Is he . . . handsome?"

Jane stared in surprise.

At her silence, Julianne rushed forth, babbling, "Not that it matters a great deal. It wouldn't change my feelings for him. I'm simply curious and would like to hear a woman's opinion."

"Yes. He is attractive. Any lady would think so, but Julianne—" She shook her head as if to clear it. "What sort of feelings do you speak of?"

"I'm in love with Gregory." Julianne leaned forward, hands flattening on the linen-covered table before her. "You mustn't tell Seth, Jane. He wouldn't understand. Swear it, Jane. Swear to me."

Jane's mouth worked for a moment, wondering how she could keep such a thing from Seth. He cared deeply for his sister. He had *married* for Julianne's sake! How could she keep such a thing from him? What would he do if he discovered she harbored such a secret?

"Jane," Julianne's voice broke into her musings, insistent and desperate. "Promise me you will not tell."

Feeling as though a deep and lasting noose settled about her neck, she relented with a sigh. "I promise."

A sour taste flooded Seth's mouth at the sight of the woman lounging on the chaise, the morning sunlight streaming through the window gilding her fair hair.

Madeline. The mere sight of her had once sent his heart pounding. Crossing his arms over his chest, he surveyed the woman that had once filled his every dream, an odd sort of detachment coming over him as he eyed the impeccably coiffed lady idly caressing a figurine of cut glass in her hands.

She had changed over the years. Her face had narrowed, the rounded curves of her cheeks lost to delicate angles and hollows. Her girlish figure had filled out. The waist was no longer so small. The breasts she had permitted him to caress beneath the summer sun had grown fuller.

Changes aside, she was still one of the most beautiful creatures he had ever seen. And yet he felt nothing. Nothing save a rueful regret for losing his head over such pretty packaging. And a renewed determination to never lose his head over any woman again.

"Your Grace," he greeted, executing a sharp bow.

Her head swung in his direction. "Seth, dearest." She set the figurine back down on the table with alacrity and rose in one graceful move. Her glossy lips curved in a hungry smile. "Surely we are beyond such formality. We're family now, after all." She walked toward him, her hips swaying seductively.

Family. A cold wind swept through him at the very idea.

She stopped before him, one hand propped on her cocked hip. "Although I was not invited to the wedding"—the fine porcelain skin of her nose wrinkled—"a rather slap-dash affair, I imagine." Her hand toyed with the ivory lace fringing her low-cut bodice, beckoning his gaze. "But then Jane was never one to expect much from her husbands."

His hands clenched at his sides, unsure if the gibe was an insult to him or Jane. And the reminder of Jane having been married to someone else—though not news—caused an unfamiliar tightness in his chest. "The goal was expediency, Maddie."

Her gaze softened. "You were the only one to

ever call me that." Her fingers brushed his cheek, where the scar split his flesh. A feral glow filled her eyes. "How fierce you look now. Dangerous. Quite appealing, really." Her voice dropped to a rhythmic croon. "I'm so sorry, Seth. It should have been you and me—"

"Don't," he bit out. "What we had is dead."

And in that moment, he realized he spoke the truth.

Staring at her ice-like beauty, so perfect she could have been chiseled from stone, he realized with a jolt that the love he once held for her had been grounded in infatuation—in a determination to possess the one person everyone told him he could never have. Looking at her, he could not recall what he had loved beyond her face.

Acute relief flooded him that he had not in fact married her. That he had grown into a man that could see beyond her beauty to the shallow core of her.

And with this realization came another. There had been more to his relationship with Jane. They had romped, talked, laughed, and shared. Loved, he supposed. Only he had allowed his infatuation for Madeline to put an end to that. No wonder his thoughts had turned to Jane so often over the years. Their relationship had possessed more substance.

Madeline's smile faltered. "I think military life has quite robbed you of your manners." Her eyes glittered with irritation.

"What do you want?" he asked baldly, removing her hand from his face.

"Is that any way to address me?" She straightened and whirled around in a cloud of perfume. "I hoped that we might be friends again."

"We were never friends, Maddie." She had been his obsession. Never his friend. Not like Jane.

"No?" she challenged, smirking. "I seem to recall you begging my father for my hand in marriage?"

Bitter bile rose in his throat. "A whim of youth."

Her lips compressed into a tight, angry line. "I don't believe you," she announced with a toss of blond curls. "You've never stopped loving me."

Seth shrugged. "I don't care what you believe."

Bright splotches marred the fragile perfection of her face. "You still want me," she insisted, flinging her shoulders back and thrusting her breasts forward until they strained against the low-cut bodice.

She advanced on him, a cat on the hunt. "Do you think of me when you plow my sister? Pale comparison, I would think." She brought her hands to his chest, rubbing her palms over him and flexing her fingers like talons. "I've learned many things over the years. Including how to please a man." She wet her lips slowly with the tip of her tongue. "Are you too proud to take what was once denied?"

"Madeline," Jane's voice scraped the air like a rusty blade, sudden and startling.

Seth swung around.

His wife stood framed in the threshold, the color high on her cheeks as she surveyed them. Even across the distance her eyes sparkled like sunlit moss, the exact shade of the green muslin gown she wore.

"Jane," Madeline tittered, slapping Seth's arm playfully. "You startled us. You should have knocked. Seth and I were becoming reacquainted." Her eyes flicked over Seth mischievously. "So many years. So much to catch up on."

Jane's face reddened further.

An angry heat spiraled through him. Seth's blood burned knowing what Madeline would have Jane think. The little witch.

His gaze clashed with Jane's, willing her to see the situation was not as it appeared. That he wanted nothing to do with Madeline. That he would much rather have her in his arms, in his bed.

A fact, he suddenly realized, he was damned well tired of fighting.

* * *

Moistening her lips, Jane advanced into the room and pressed a cool kiss to her sister's cheek. No simple feat when she would rather have clawed her eyes out.

The sight of her sister rubbing against Seth like a hungry cat stirred a host of hot, uncomfortable feelings. Made her feel like a girl again, watching them in the orchard, oblivious to her, to the world. Aware of only each other amid a swirl of apple blossoms.

"You should have sent word," she said tightly. "I did not expect you."

"Desmond came to see me." Madeline's mouth puckered with censure. "He is beside himself with worry over you. Poor man."

Seth snorted.

Madeline tossed him a less than friendly glance. "He fears you've rushed into this marriage and have made a grievous mistake."

"The only mistake I made was in living beneath Desmond's roof for as long as I did," Jane rejoined.

"Come now, dear." Madeline sidled near, fingers closing around Jane's arm like a clinging vine. Jane resisted shaking off the unwelcome touch. "You did not have to marry him." Her shrewd gaze cut to Seth. "You could have lived with me. You still can, in fact."

Jane blinked. "I'm carrying his child," Jane pointed out.

Seth growled low in his throat. "Nice of you to offer now. Where were you when Jane was widowed and forced into servitude?"

"You exaggerate—"

"Not by much," Jane interjected, her pulse suddenly skittery at her throat. "You knew how things were for me and you never once made such an offer."

"Jane." Madeline pouted prettily. "If I thought you truly suffered I would have insisted you live with me." Madeline squeezed her arm, her sharp nails digging painfully. "As I'm insisting now. You cannot mean to endure this farce of a marriage. Do you really think Seth loves you?" Her eyes gleamed in pity, seeming to say: He cannot. He loves me.

"I'll stay with my husband," Jane answered, twisting her arm free and telling herself not to take too much satisfaction in the declaration. They were only husband and wife in name. Not in the proper sense. But at least Madeline need never know that.

"Indeed." Madeline's lip curled as if tasting something foul.

"Indeed," Seth echoed, tucking Jane to his side. Her breath caught at the feel of his big hand sliding around her waist, his fingers splaying over her rib cage. "I couldn't abide not having her."

Madeline's lips worked. "You cannot expect me to believe—"

"I already told you I care not what you believe."

As if to make his point, he folded Jane into his arms and smothered her lips with the hot seal of his mouth.

Jane froze for the barest moment before melting against him. Her mouth opened, allowing his tongue access. And just like that she was back in the garden again.

His hands slid into her hair, loosening the mass as he plundered her lips. Leaning into him, she clutched his biceps, fingers curling into the sleeves of his jacket as blistering flame shot through her veins. Desire simmered in her belly like liquid heat and she moaned into his mouth.

One hand slid down her back, cupping her derrière through the voluminous folds of her gown.

Loud throat clearing broke the spell, and she jerked her mouth free. Still standing in the circle of his arms, she stared up at him, dazed, mouth throbbing from the assault of his.

His chest lifted with labored breaths, as though he had run a great distance.

"See now, Madeline. I can't even control myself in broad daylight when guests are present. I simply cannot manage a moment without Jane."

Jane gave her head a swift shake and glanced at her sister's livid face. Nostrils quivering in a most unbecoming manner, Madeline stormed from the room, wide skirts nearly knocking a vase from a side table.

After a moment, Jane realized Seth's arms still hung about her. "You can let me go now."

His arms fell away.

Jane stood there a moment longer, looking down at her satin slippers peeping from beneath her emerald green gown. She could feel his eyes on her, blistering into the top of her head.

"Why was it so important for Madeline to see that?" Silence answered her and she lifted her face to stare directly into his eyes. "Was it to make her jealous?"

"God, no," he bit out.

She frowned, unconvinced. She could still recall that day in the orchard when he had been playing Madeline's knight in shining armor. The love in his eyes had been profound and deep.

"Then why?" she demanded, brushing fingers

over lips still pulsing from his kiss. "I wouldn't have left you. I've more honor than that. I carry your child." Sucking in a deep breath, she pressed. "You haven't kissed me since we married. Why now?"

He dragged a hand through his hair. "Perhaps I worried she would convince you to leave with her."

"I would not have gone with her. Even if she knew the truth."

"And what's the truth, Jane?" he asked in a quiet voice, stepping closer, his big body crowding her, warming her in the most disturbing way.

The truth? Not that kiss. Not the way he looked at her, with dark fire in his eyes. His kiss was nothing more than a ploy to get back at Madeline.

"Our marriage is one of convenience. You've made that abundantly clear."

Her heart pinched. Before he could read any telling emotion on her face, she turned for the door.

"We need not feel compelled to convince Madeline that our marriage is a grand love affair," she tossed out, glancing over her shoulder. "It was lovely of you to put forth the effort. Very affecting really."

He made a sound, perhaps speech, but she could hear nothing else. Not with blood rushing through her head in a dull roar.

"You needn't play at such pretense again," she added, ignoring the way a muscle ticked madly in his cheek, indicating she had hit a nerve.

Resolve sealing her heart, she strode from the room.

Chapter 24

Seth walked an uneven line into his room, stopping before the adjoining door to Jane's chamber and squaring off as though he faced an armed adversary.

The light beneath her door glowed, taunting him, beckoning. *You needn't play at such pretense again.* Her words echoed in his head, mocking him. *Pretense? There had been no pretense in that kiss.* His body throbbed at the memory of sucking her tongue deep into his mouth, of fondling that delicious flesh beneath the green satin dress.

With a fierce curse, he swung about and shed his garments with hard, angry movements, never taking his eyes off her door. His sudden movements made his head swim, and he stopped, pressing a palm to his temple. Perhaps he should not have drunk quite so much at dinner. And after.

Only dinner with his wife at his side, her sweet scent drifting toward him, tormenting him, he found the overpowering need to drink—to wash her from his mind, his blood, his soul. Fool that he was, he had thought a snifter of brandy would do the trick. Now, staring at the door that barred her, his wife, the very woman whose charms he ought to feel free to enjoy, he felt only bleak frustration. Nothing would rid her from him. Not as long as she remained near, yet beyond his reach.

He gave his head a hard shake, which only made him stagger sideways. Gripping one of the thick mahogany bedposts, he steadied himself.

He clutched the bedpost in both hands, as though he could claw the barrier down he had erected between them. The barrier *he* had erected.

He had set forth the requirements of their marriage, had thought he was being wise. Only with the taste of her still burning on his lips, he knew he was the greatest idiot alive. Why had he turned her away when she came to him on their honeymoon? Why hadn't he embraced what she so sweetly offered?

Shoving from the bedpost, he moved to the door, heart in his throat.

The time to change the rules had arrived.

* * *

Jane paced the length of her room, listening, as always, for Seth in the next room. Dinner had been a strain. Since her promise to Julianne, Jane could hardly sit at the same table with Seth.

Julianne glowed, her love for Knightly hovering on the air, unspoken but tangible as heavy fog. Seth had to feel it. The truth would eventually surface. And he would never forgive her for keeping the information from him. It would be another mark against her. One of several.

She started at the sudden rap on the door adjoining their rooms.

"Come in," she called, the pulse at her neck beating a furious staccato as she watched Seth enter the room garbed only in his dressing robe.

"Seth," she breathed, wondering if her thoughts had somehow conjured him, wondering if Providence had not sent him to her, presenting her with a chance to confess everything she knew about Julianne and Mr. Knightly.

His expression was stark, almost angry. His eyes gleamed liquid heat, dispelling the notion of confessing all in a cowardly flash. She shifted nervously on her feet.

"I need to speak to you," he declared, stopping before her.

His gaze slid over her in a slow, body-heating

appraisal. The faint scent of liquor wafted about him, mingling with the musky smell of him. Not unpleasant. Still, the smell of alcohol reminded her of her father and the subsequent foul mood it always foretold. The old instinct to run for cover reared its head.

"You're drunk," she announced, nostrils quivering as she edged back a few steps.

"Bloody right I am," he rasped, stalking forward another step. "You, my dear, would drive any man to drink."

She stiffened. "I've done nothing—"

"You exist," he declared, the heat in his eyes making her heart jump against her chest.

"I—I don't understand," she stammered.

Something wild and dangerous glittered in his eyes.

She stumbled back until she bumped the bed and could go no farther. Lifting her chin, she propped her hands on her hips and inhaled, trying to appear taller, more confident than she felt in the face of his strange mood.

"You merely walk into the room and I'm undone." His words stroked some place deep inside her, made her hot and cold and quivery all at once.

"My apologies," she snapped, her indignation

rising to the fore. "I had no idea my presence caused you such . . . *discomfort*."

His lips twisted in a semblance of a smile. "You have no idea the *discomfort* you give me," he rejoined, his voice hard, brutal. A predatory light entered his gaze. "Or perhaps you do," he challenged, snatching one of her fists from her hip and folding it into his large hand.

Caught off balance, she staggered. Her other hand landed on his chest to steady herself. Immediately, she felt his heart, strong and fast beneath her palm. She shook her head, resisting the urge to flex her fingers, to slide them over him and better explore the hard contours of muscle and flesh beneath his robe. She tugged her fist, but he held fast.

"You're drunk," she hissed.

"Quite," he agreed with a brisk nod, forcing her hand lower, down his chest, down the firm ridges of his belly. "And in great *discomfort*," he murmured, flinging her word back at her.

Prying her fingers open, he placed her palm over the erection tenting his robe. Air escaped between her teeth in a loud hiss. Warm fingers circled her wrist, guided her hand to move. Up and down. Up and down. His gaze scorched her, blistering her very soul as he worked her.

He swelled beneath her touch, growing in size. Desire pooled low in her belly. She squeezed her thighs tightly beneath her nightgown, attempting to relieve the growing ache between her legs.

"See what you do to me?" he asked, dragging her palm over him, faster, harder, the stiff feel of him making her breath come harsh and swift.

She longed to feel him without the silk dressing robe. His texture, his heat pulsing in the palm of her hand. No barriers. Slipping her hand inside his robe, she closed her fingers over the naked length of him. Silk on steel in her hand. She ran her thumb over the satin-smooth tip of him. His groan tore through her, thrilling her, emboldening her.

"Seth," she whispered, scanning his face, the square jaw, the hard lines and shadowed hollows. The throat that worked in speechless wonder at her ministrations.

His eyes blazed down at her, the fire there unmistakable.

An answering flare burned through her blood, her soul, filling the emptiness, the lonely ache that had been there for too long now.

He pulled her to him, lifting her onto her tiptoes and swallowing her cry with his mouth. He drank long and deep from her lips, obliterating her senses. His kiss, his rough hands moving over her arms, flamed her passion.

"Jane," he rasped, the softness of his lips against hers a direct contrast to the rough sound of his voice. "I tried. God, I tried . . ."

She shook her head, not understanding the agony in his voice, not able to make sense of his words. The taste of him made her head swirl, brandy and desire, warmth and spice in her mouth. Her shaking hands slid farther inside his loosened robe.

He could have been speaking Greek for all she understood him. Words were beyond her. There was only him. And the delicious things he made her feel. She didn't want to wonder what brought him to her. Wanted only to savor.

Her palms skimmed his firm chest, curving over warm flesh, velvet skin stretched tight over muscle and sinew. As a girl, she had often watched his body, young and lean, on the cusp of manhood. The sight of him had excited her even then—when she hadn't a clue what caused the burn in her blood.

Incredibly, it seemed he was hers now. His body, at any rate.

He took her bottom lip between his teeth, biting gently and murmuring against her mouth, "I don't care what I said." His hoarse voice stoked the warmth in her belly into a nest of writhing flames. Pulling back, his hands skated up her arms, burning through the thin cotton of her gown. "I want you."

Delighted relief rippled through her at his words. Words she thought she would never hear from his lips.

His brown eyes burned golden in the lamp's glow, searing a path directly to her heart. "Tell me you want me to stay. Tell me—"

"I want you to stay," Jane cut in, closing the distance separating them in one step. "I want *you*." A sob welled up from deep in her chest. "I've always wanted you—" Her voice cracked and she turned, determined to hide her face before she completely crumpled before him.

"Jane," he groaned, hauling her into his arms, showering fierce kisses over every inch of her face before his mouth fell on hers in a savage kiss.

He lifted her in one sweep and dropped her on the bed. Still standing, he shrugged free of his robe and stood before her as she had never seen any man. At Vauxhall it had been too dark, and they had been clothed—for the most part. She had barely made out his face in the shadows. He came over her then, his body a thrilling weight, hard and large upon her. Tonight there would be no darkness.

Her hands roamed his broad back, nails digging into supple skin as he lowered his head to suckle one breast through the thin cotton of her gown. Pleasure-pain lanced through her. His teeth abraded her nipple into a hard point, and she arched against him, crying his name. One of her hands flew to fist in his hair, urging him closer.

Turning his attention to her other breast, he laved her nipple with his hot tongue, inching her nightgown up as he worked.

Cool air licked her calves, her thighs, her hips. With startling deftness, he pulled her nightgown over her head leaving her bare, exposed before him, shaking with both desire and trepidation.

"Jane." His hand hovered above her abdomen, long fingers splayed wide, shaking ever so slightly. His hair fell over his brow, hiding his eyes as he gazed down at her. She didn't need to see them to feel their heat, intent and searing on her. Slowly, his hand lowered to cup the slight swell of her belly. "You're so small," he murmured.

"Not for long."

His gaze shot to hers, amusement flickering there. A smile hugged his well-shaped mouth.

She stopped breathing altogether when his head dipped and he pressed a series of open-mouthed kisses over her belly, working his way down her navel.

Warm fingers slid between her legs to tease at her entrance, stroking, spreading her moisture over herself in erotic circles that dragged animal-like mewls from deep in her throat. His finger plunged inside her warmth and she lurched off the bed with a ragged sob.

"Easy," he crooned, his touch magical, working her to a fever pitch. His eyes glowed darkly as he watched her twist and writhe beneath him.

"Now," she pleaded. Her head came off the bed. Legs opening wide, she welcomed him to her as the sky welcomed the sun at dawn. Her fingers trailed the line of his spine, cupping his tight buttocks in her hands and urging him to her—in her.

"Seth," she pleaded, her voice low and desperate, unrecognizable.

"Jane," he groaned, sliding into her in one smooth thrust, filling her with stunning force.

For a moment, he remained still, lodged inside her, pulsing in rhythm to the squeezing burn at her center. Every nerve in her body stretched and sang, humming in sweet, agonizing tension as he held himself over her.

An elusive smile played about his mouth as he restrained himself, hands braced on either side of her head. Gradually, he moved his hips, pumping slowly, torturing her with deep, unhurried strokes.

Her gaze devoured the man stretched above her, his beautiful bronze muscles straining over her in a way that made it clear he held himself carefully in check.

The hair fell over his forehead in a straight veil, the lamplight gilding the brown to golden flame. Her trembling fingers brushed it away, watching as it fell back with a will of its own.

Her body arched like a bow beneath his thrusts. She flexed her inner muscles around him. His groan filled the air and his thrusts grew harder, slamming into her, stoking the fire he had started within her into a savage blaze. Higher and hotter the flames rose until her skin, her very bones, felt as though they would combust, leaving nothing but ashes behind.

"Seth!" she cried, digging her nails into the smooth muscles of his back.

His head dropped to her neck. "That's it, sweetheart," he muttered beneath her ear.

One of his hands slid the length of her bare thigh, lifting her leg to better meet his thrusts. He pumped harder, deeper, the friction unbearable, an exquisite pleasure-pain that drove her mad, left her gasping, sobbing, pleading, blubbering incoherently.

But he understood, knew just what to do. Answering her need, he hooked his thumbs beneath her knees and pulled back her legs for a deeper invasion.

At last, she burst, exploded into fire and ice, wind and rain. Shattered until she was a quivering pile of flesh and bones beneath him. Replete, sated, she sank back on the soft bed like a petal landing, content to still feel him over her, thrusting a final time with a loud shout of release.

A lazy smile lifted her lips. Rolling off her, he kept an arm loosely about her waist. She waited, expecting him to leave. Marcus had never remained.

Staring at the canopy above her, she stroked his hard bicep, taking pleasure in the sound of his ragged breath near her ear. She had done that to him—robbed him of breath, control. Pleasure suffused her and she snuggled deeper into his arms, her heart clenching when he tightened his hold on her. After awhile his breathing slowed and his hold relaxed. Convinced he slept, she whispered, "You should have been my first." A small ache pinched her heart.

His chest vibrated beneath her hand, sending a thrilling shiver up her spine as his deep voice rumbled through the air, "I'll be your last."

Smiling, she closed her eyes and drifted to sleep.

Chapter 25

Seth opened his eyes and squinted against the dimness. The drapes had not been drawn and the early morning air, chalky with the city's usual fog, pressed against the windowpanes.

He reclined on his side, Jane's body curled into his. His arm clung to her as though he feared she might somehow vanish with the fading night. Inhaling the subtle apple scent of her, he skimmed his hand over the smooth curve of her hip, hardening at the feel of her, warm as velvet, soft as silk. Knowing he was on the verge of taking her again, he sucked a steadying breath into his lungs and unwrapped himself from her tempting curves.

Standing, he donned his robe, studying her in the gray light of dawn as he tied off the belt. His gaze slid over the sleek lines of her legs and a familiar burn ignited his blood as he recalled their silky texture wrapped around him.

He wanted nothing more than to crawl back into bed with her—crawl back *inside* her. To never part from her.

She made him feel . . .

He dragged a hand over his bristly jaw. Hell, she made him *feel*.

The realization unsettled him, rocked his heart from the cave where it lodged.

He took a sudden step back as if a snake coiled before him. The last time he had felt this strongly about a woman, his soul had been razed, his heart bled dry.

Love carried a price. He knew that. And he would never pay it again.

His gaze swept over Jane, devouring the sight of mahogany hair tangled about shoulders that gleamed like polished marble in the dawning light. Not that he would ever deny himself of her again. He was not fool enough to try, to think he could.

But that did not mean he had softened and turned into the fool of his youth, hungering for love.

He would have her whenever the urge took him. That did not mean he loved her. Did not mean he had yet again lost control of himself.

Determined, he turned and strode into his room, heart sealed tightly.

Jane woke smiling, her body warm and sated, a lethargy she had never known weighing her down, liquefying her bones, making her feel heavy as lead.

Memories of the night before assailed her. Of Seth. Of her. Of thorough, exhaustive lovemaking she hoped to repeat at the first opportunity.

Twice now, she had fallen asleep in his arms. Her smile deepened. She stretched out an arm, eager to touch him again, to feel his warm skin. Her hands met cool linen. Smile slipping, she sat up and looked around her, staring at the rumpled, sun-dappled bed.

Her brow creased. Seth was gone. Without a word, without a touch.

She drew the counterpane over her nudity and curled into a small ball, trying to imagine it was Seth's arms around her and not merely her own.

Jane hovered in the threshold, observing Julianne sitting alone at the dining table, a forlorn expression on her face as she fiddled with the food on her plate.

"How long are you going to stand there?" Julianne asked, lifting a spoonful of porridge to her mouth.

With a rueful smile, Jane stepped into the room. "How did you know I was here?"

"Apples. You always smell of apples."

"It's my favorite jam." Jane moved to the sideboard and selected two slices of toast. Taking a seat across from Julianne, she began applying a generous amount of said jam to her toast, staring thoughtfully at Julianne as she did so. The secret of Julianne's relationship with Seth's valet rested heavily on her shoulders. Especially after last night. He had come to her. Sensible or not, hope filled her heart. She did not want secrets between them.

"I wonder," she began. "Why not try and explain to your brother how you feel about Mr. Knightly?" Jane bit into her toast, briefly closing her eyes in appreciation of the sweet tang of apples on her tongue.

"You think he would listen?"

Jane swallowed her bite. "Perhaps. Perhaps not. But what can come of keeping it secret?"

Julianne lifted her teacup carefully to her lips. "I suppose it unfair of me to ask you to keep secrets from Seth. He is your husband."

Jane inhaled deeply. "I confess it makes me uncomfortable, but I won't tell him. You should. If what you and Mr. Knightly feel is true, I can't imagine Seth not encouraging the relationship. He loves you."

"And that would certainly make things better for you and Seth."

Jane cocked her head to the side, failing to understand. "What do you mean?"

Julianne lowered her cup to her chin, saying, "To permit me to marry, Seth would have to see me as . . . whole. Not an invalid he must devote his life to tending. And that wouldn't be so bad for you, would it? A husband free of guilt, free to love."

Jane's chest contracted, her skin suddenly tight and itchy as she shifted in her chair. "I don't know what you mean."

Julianne set her teacup down with a noisy clack. "I can still see your face in my mind, you know. Do you still wear your heart on your face? I know you loved him, Jane. Everyone knew." Julianne's mouth slanted in a grin. "Well, everyone but him."

"It was a long time ago." Jane fiddled with a spoon beside her plate, seeing no sense denying what was past. "I was just a girl. What did I know of love?"

"Apparently more than you know now if you don't recognize that you're still in love with him."

Still in love with him.

Yes. She accepted that.

Shoulders slumping, she leaned back in her chair. But Seth wanted no love from her. And would give none. The most she could expect were nights like last night.

It seemed like an aberration. Something invented by her overactive imagination and wishful heart. If it meant anything to him, would he have not been there when she awoke instead of sneaking off like a thief in the night—like Marcus?

Clearly he regretted it. In the light of day, mind free and clear of the influences of brandy, he doubtlessly regretted breaking the terms he had set forth regarding their marriage.

"Don't take it for granted, Jane." Julianne leaned forward, her expression earnest. "You've been given a second chance. Both of you have. Don't be idiots. It's no common event to find yourself married to someone you love—" Julianne stopped abruptly, lips quivering.

"I know, Julianne," Jane murmured, heart squeezing at the longing Julianne felt for a man beyond her reach. A longing she understood.

Eyes suspiciously moist, Julianne surged to her feet, bumping the table and rattling dishes. "If you'll excuse me."

"Do you need any—"

"I can manage," Julianne cut in, clearly anticipating Jane's offer for assistance.

"Of course," she mumbled, watching with some

bewilderment as Julianne made her way from the room.

Jane finished her breakfast alone, her toast suddenly dust in her mouth despite her favorite apple jam. She forced herself to chew as she mulled over Julianne's words, wondering if she perhaps needed to make Seth see that their marriage could be more, could be everything he had once dreamed of finding with Madeline. If he let himself love her. And she him.

Shaking her head, she pushed from the table, no closer to understanding what was possible and what was not. She only knew she couldn't force love on someone who didn't want it. She had known that at seventeen. A painful lesson, but one she never forgot.

Deciding to escape the house and perhaps clear her head, she hastened up the stairs. Turning the corridor to her room, she collided with Seth. His hands came up to grip her arms and steady her. Immediately, heat spread through her. Her body leaned toward his. The reality of time and place fled. She no longer stood in a corridor. It was last night again and her body reacted. Needed his skin against hers, his hands on her.

"Seth," she breathed.

As if burned, he released her. His eyes slid over

her, a bright flame glowing in the brown depths. "Jane."

She opened her mouth to speak, but nothing emerged. She searched his face, looking for answers carved in the hard lines and unsmiling mouth. Answers to questions she could not bring herself to voice. Did last night mean anything to you? Do you regret it? Had it been nothing more than the brandy?

"I was going to my room. To change. I thought I might take a walk." Thinking on her conversation with Julianne, she drew a fortifying breath. She would never know if their marriage could be more, would never find out if she did not at least try. "Perhaps you would care to join me?"

"I have an appointment."

"Oh." She dropped her gaze, studying her hands and feeling foolish.

"Jane." He placed a finger beneath her chin and forced her to look at him. His eyes drilled into her as he shook his head side to side, slowly, almost regretfully. "Last night was—"

"Last night was last night," she blurted, suddenly not wanting to hear anything from his lips that faintly resembled regret.

Stepping around him, she stared straight ahead, careful not to meet his gaze, content to let the vagueness of her words be all that was said.

"Excuse me. I need to change for that walk now."

Jane woke abruptly that night, blinking in the oil-fed light, the book she'd been reading lay haphazardly on the bed to her right. Blast, she'd fallen asleep and forgotten to put out the lamp. She picked up the book and snapped it shut. Sitting up, she rubbed her sleep-clouded eyes and swung her legs over the side, intending to put out the light.

A large shadow fell over her and she fell back on the bed with a yelp, clutching the book to her chest like a shield.

"Seth," she whispered, eyeing the hard naked length of him looming over her.

Her body sprang to instant, singing life. Shadows flickered over his bronzed flesh and her palms tingled to feel him again.

All Seth had done to her, all she had let him do, all she wanted him to do still, rushed over her with an urgency that stole her breath and left her a mass of tingling nerves. She clenched her thighs, the ache low in her belly deepening, clawing, demanding for him.

"Last night," he growled, plucking the book from her clenched fingers, "will be repeated." His eyes glittered beneath the dark slash of his brows. "Tonight, tomorrow, and the next night . . ."

Her heart contracted with each delicious word.

His voice continued in its low rumble, "Again and again and again . . ."

His hand shot to the hem of her nightgown, leaving no doubt the purpose of his visit as he pulled it up and over her head in one smooth motion. Cool air swept over, followed by the burning trail of his eyes. "In the future, you'll sleep in my bed."

He dropped his body over hers, arms caging her in. She turned her head, the sight of the bulging biceps on either side thrilling her, igniting a burning ache at her core that had her instinctively thrusting her pelvis forward, nudging at his hardness, begging for him to fill her, to ease the infernal burn that demanded quenching.

Without a word, he moved her to her side and spooned her, his big body pressed tightly against hers. His manhood prodded her backside and she rubbed against it. His deep, primal groan, vibrated from his chest into her back. Her breasts grew heavy, the nipples tightening.

His large hand splayed her belly, his wide palm sizzling hot on her flesh. Looking down, she studied his darker hand on her pale skin. His hand shifted, moving downward, the blunt tips of his fingers brushing the soft hair between her legs, sifting through the short curls to her wetness. She unclenched her thighs and allowed him entrance, thrilled and scandalized as he stroked her, his touch teasing at first, then harder, tearing short, quick gasps from her throat.

She surged into his hand and ground her backside against his erection. His chest muscles flexed behind her, the crisp feel of his hair exciting and tantalizing, chafing the tender skin of her back.

His fingers worked faster, the rasp of his breath loud in her ear as he furiously rolled his fingers over her tiny nub, tearing a cry from where it hid deep in her throat.

She shuddered, release washing over her in sizzling waves. Boneless and sated, she rolled onto her back, her eyes seeking his. Nothing prepared her for the smoldering intensity of his gaze, for molten brown eyes that seared her with a hunger that matched her own.

He came over her swiftly, settling between her legs. Her fingers dug into his shoulders and her hips rose up off the bed to meet his first thrust.

He tossed back his head, tendons stretched taut in his neck as he impaled her. Neither spoke. Neither made a sound. Lodged deeply inside her, she could not tell where either one of them began, could never imagine not having this—not having *him*.

His gaze recaptured hers. Leaning his face close to hers, noses almost touching, he held her gaze as he took her. Swiftly, fiercely, his strokes deep and steady.

She moved against him, angling her body to take more of him, drawing her pleasure deep into herself.

He clutched her hips, the strong fingers digging into her soft flesh satisfying in a way no gentle loving ever could.

As they gazed into each other's eyes, their bodies joining together with desperate fervor, an incredible lightness filled her chest.

He was not immune to her.

And, more importantly, he would no longer try to be.

Suddenly anything seemed possible. Even love.

Chapter 26

Jane woke with a languorous stretch, the events of the night flooding back in deliciously vivid detail. Her hand drifted between the smooth valley of her breasts, the backs of her fingers curling down to the dip of her navel, her skin still sensitive and thrumming.

Rolling to her side, she expected to find Seth gone. As before. Bracing herself, she shoved a hank of hair from her eyes—and eyed the big body tangled in the sheets beside her. *Seth*.

He had not left her. Her gaze crawled over his ridged abdomen, the dark line of hair there that trailed into the nest of hair surrounding his manhood. Her eyes widened as that part of him grew before her very eyes. Her gaze flew to his face to find him awake and watching her with unnerving intensity.

"You're awake," she announced, the pulse at her neck hammering. Would he never cease to do that to her? Reduce her to a shaking mass?

One corner of his mouth quirked as he pushed himself up, moving toward her with the stealth of a jungle cat. "Clearly."

"You're still here," she breathed as he lowered himself over her, the warm, musky scent of him cloaking her.

He dipped his head until his mouth hovered a hairsbreadth from hers. "You have a bothersome habit of stating the obvious." His forearms rested on either side of her head, his fingers softly brushing her hairline.

Her heart clenched almost painfully in her chest. She smiled weakly, feeling suddenly shy. Always they came together at night. Never in the light of day. Never when he could see her clearly . . . see that she was not Madeline.

She swallowed, attempting to push free the awful thickness in her throat. The dark of night had always offered a measure of concealment, granting a sense of unreality to their intimacies.

His mouth covered hers in a kiss that was tender and thorough, melting her deeper into the bed . . . *deeper in love with him.*

He pulled back to murmur against her mouth,

his lips feathering hers as he spoke, "From now on, we'll have this."

Eyes wide, she nodded. "Yes," she breathed, heart swelling in her chest, understanding that while he was not promising love, or his heart for that matter, it was something. It was a beginning. Perhaps, in time, love could grow. They could be the friends they had once been.

They could be more.

Jane walked quickly toward the salon, where, according to the butler, Julianne worked on her needlepoint. She wrung her hands until they felt numb, bloodless. Determination burned in her chest. She could not keep Julianne's secret from Seth anymore. Not after last night. Not for a moment longer. Either Julianne told him or she would.

One of the tall double doors stood ajar. She pushed it open with her palm, stepping through the threshold. She stopped midstride, her jaw sagging at the sight of Mr. Knightly and Julianne locked in a passionate embrace on the sofa. Face flaming, she stepped back, hoping to save everyone the embarrassment of voicing her presence and wait until she found Julianne alone. With utmost care, she eased the door shut.

"Jane?"

Gasping, she spun around, one hand flying to her throat, the other pressing against the shut door behind her.

She must have revealed some of her panic, for Seth closed both hands over her arms, demanding, "What is it?"

She closed her eyes against the warm feel of his hands on her arms, both seductive and reassuring. With a small shake of her head, she opened her eyes, meeting the concern in his brown gaze directly.

She opened her mouth, but no sound emerged. His gaze flicked beyond her, over her shoulder. As though he could see through the door to the lovers beyond, his eyes narrowed, his concern for her diminishing as his focus shifted from her.

His hands dropped from her arms. Reaching around her, he turned the knob. She didn't budge as he pushed the door open. Shaking her head, she spun around, hoping Julianne and Mr. Knightly had ended their heated embrace and would not be caught—

Seth's breath escaped him in a loud hiss, fluttering her hair, winging through her heart like a bitter breeze.

The couple was still locked in embrace, oblivious to the world about to crash down upon them. The pins had come loose from Julianne's hair, and

Mr. Knightly took advantage, burying his fingers in the fiery mane.

Jane closed her eyes, regret rolling through her as Seth's enraged bellow filled the air. "Take your hands off her!"

Julianne and Knightly flew apart as if a bolt of lightning split them. Likely the same bolt Seth felt shoot through him at the sight of his valet ravishing his sister.

Shouldering past Jane, he stormed into the room, hands flexing at his sides, the urge to lay his hands on Knightly powerful and violent. He stopped short of actually succumbing to the impulse and clenched his hands behind his back.

Betrayal flayed his heart as he recalled all he and Knightly had endured together over the years. Certainly enough for the bastard to refrain from taking advantage of his sister. Her innocence, to say nothing of her disability, should have stayed his animal desires.

Julianne shook her head wildly, auburn hair tumbling over her shoulders, the very picture of wanton abandon.

"S—Seth," she began, panic tightening her expression. "Please. Don't be angry. It's not what it looks like. I love Gregory."

He glared at Knightly, suddenly convinced he had never seen the man before, until now. The libertine held himself stoically, solemn and unflinching beneath Seth's glare.

"How far has this gone?" he demanded, forcing a cool gust of wind through him, freezing his rage, his impulse to tear Knightly apart. "Have you compromised her?"

"Seth!" Julianne cried, her voice high with indignation as she gathered her hair and pulled it over one shoulder.

Knightly squared his shoulders. "I would not dishonor Julianne . . . or you for—"

"Speak not of honor," he cut in, fuming at Knightly's familiar use of his sister's name. "Considering what I've witnessed, I don't put much faith in your honor."

"I hold your sister in the greatest esteem," Knightly said evenly. Swinging his gaze back to Julianne, he added in a softer voice, "I love her."

"Gregory," Julianne gasped, groping for his arm, her rapturous expression turning Seth's stomach. Knightly's hand clasped hers.

"Julianne, go to your room," Seth ordered, feeling as if his world were rapidly unraveling.

Julianne's chin shot up. "I'm not a child, Seth."

"Seth," Jane spoke beside him, but he silenced

her with a wave of his hand, too focused on his sister, on shattering whatever spell Knightly had woven over her.

Knightly tucked Julianne's hand in the crook of his arm. "My intentions are honorable." Inclining his head, he added, "I wish to marry her. With your blessing."

"Marry her?" A rough, broken laugh rose from his throat. "And how will you manage that? You cannot support her with the care that she requires. Can you hire a companion to see to her needs? A housekeeper? A cook? A maid? How exactly will you afford to keep her in the manner she requires?"

A shadow fell over Knightly's face and doubt flickered in his once steady gaze.

Splotches of color broke out over Julianne's face. "I'm not helpless!"

"You can't marry," Seth ground out, as if she had not spoken. "And you shall never have my blessing."

Tears pooled in Julianne's eyes. "Seth . . . don't do this," she whispered, lips trembling.

He shook his head, forcing her sad plea out of his head. Staring only at Knightly, the one to blame in this mess, the one to have so foolishly and selfishly given Julianne romantic notions, he continued, "Consider yourself dismissed. Pack your things." He wouldn't have Knightly remain another moment to toy further with his sister's affections.

"Seth," Jane broke in, her voice more insistent.

He swung his gaze on his wife, his anger mounting at the look of disappointment on her face—as if *he* had somehow failed her.

"See, Jane," Julianne cut in, her voice hard and hostile in a way he had never heard. "I told you he would not understand."

He stared hard at Jane, watching as guilty color swept high on her cheeks. Something ugly twisted inside of him.

"You knew?" he demanded, feeling as he did the day he learned she was Aurora. Again, she had withheld the truth from him. Only this time, pain accompanied the betrayal.

"Why don't we all sit down and discuss this calmly," Jane suggested, her eyes bright with appeal.

"No, Jane." The sound of her name fell like a stone from his lips, as hard as the bitterness encasing his heart. "This is a family matter. It's none of your concern."

The color drained from her face, and his heart squeezed. His hand twitched at his side. Weak fool he was, he felt inclined to smooth the wounded look from her face, to offer words of apology.

330

Before he could succumb to the impulse, she gave a jerky nod and quickly stepped back. Turning, she exited the room, her skirts barely stirring at her ankles. He watched her leave, saying nothing even as the urge to stop her coursed thickly in his veins.

"I'll pack my things," Knightly's voice pulled him back.

"Gregory, no!" Julianne cried, her fingers white where they clung to his arm. "I'm of age. We don't need Seth's blessing."

He flinched at his sister's words, never realizing how much her good opinion mattered, unprepared for the pain of losing it, losing her. The ache in his chest deepened as he realized Julianne would never understand, never see that he only sought to protect her.

To have lost the love of his one remaining family member filled him with impotent fury. Not a day passed that he did not blame himself for his sister's accident, for stealing her life, but he had been able to live with himself knowing that *she* never blamed him, that she loved him and respected him.

Now Knightly had robbed him of that.

"Get out," he growled.

"Seth, no!" She took a sudden step in his direction, lifting a fist as if she intended to attack him. "I love Gregory."

"What do you know of love?" he asked, gentling his voice in an attempt to soften the severity of the question. "You've spent your life sheltered, protected, devoid of male attention."

Julianne drew a deep breath, her chest rising with the effort. "I know a good deal more of love than you. I'm not the one so afraid of being hurt that I can't see what's staring me in the face." She released a pent-up breath, the sound harsh and angry. Words rushed from her lips in a torrent. "The only one blind here is you."

Knightly ran the backs of his fingers over Julianne's flushed cheek, murmuring soft unintelligible words to calm her. Julianne turned into his touch like a flower seeking the sun.

Seth watched, disgusted that the bastard had the power to soothe her. Gritting his teeth against the sight of their familiarity, he pretended her words did not affect him, pretended she had not hit a nerve.

Knightly pressed a kiss to Julianne's forehead, the gesture somehow final. "I must go now."

Julianne choked back a sob.

Seth looked away, hands knotted at his sides, furious with Knightly for putting her through this ordeal, for giving her hope that she could ever lead a life where courtship and marriage were the normal course of events for her.

Setting her from him, Knightly marched from the room with stoic restraint, never once looking back. Julianne stumbled to the sofa and collapsed upon it, her shoulders shaking with dry, silent sobs that wrung his heart dry. Seth approached and gently laid a hand on her shoulder.

She jerked as though burned. "Don't," she cried. "Don't comfort me as though you have no hand in my misery."

"Julianne—"

"No," she bit out, her voice a crack of gunfire. "I never blamed you, Seth." She lifted her face. Tears glistened on her cheeks. "What happened to me was an accident. I never blamed you. But this, today . . . I shall never forgive you. You may be too afraid to love, but that doesn't give you the right to steal my chance."

She dropped her face into her hands then and wept, the sound ripping through him like the slash of a sword.

Without another word, he slipped from the salon and stalked upstairs, refusing to mull over her words, to examine them for truth. She didn't know what she was saying. Right now, pain incited her words. But the pain would fade. Along with the memory of Knightly. And time would prove him right.

He was halfway down the corridor to his chamber when the sound of his name stopped him.

Turning, he faced Jane, the sight of her doing nothing to ease the betrayal stinging his heart. She knew how deeply he took his role as Julianne's guardian. She knew and had said nothing.

She approached, hands clenched before her. Moistening her lips, she drew a breath and spoke quickly, as if she feared losing the courage to speak, "I know you're angry, but if you interfere between Julianne and Mr. Knightly, you will live to regret it."

He crossed his arms over his chest. "Is that so?"

"Yes." She lifted that little chin of hers at a stubborn angle. "I believe she genuinely loves him."

"She hasn't a clue—"

"No. *You* haven't," she fired. "Don't underestimate her. She possesses a warm and loving heart."

"That is not what I hold in question," he snapped. "She cannot manage the responsibilities of marriage. Can you imagine her having children in her condition?" He shook his head. "And to a man with no prospects. Such a life would entail more than she could endure."

"What kind of life would you have her lead, then? One where she stays indoors and has someone read to her and prepare her tea? Dull and bored all of her days?"

"Yes," he boomed. "She'll be *safe*. Anything else carries too much risk for a woman like her."

"A woman like her?" Jane echoed, her expression one of bewildered frustration.

He dragged a hand through his hair in mutual frustration. "Am I the only one aware of my sister's limitations?"

"You're certainly the only one willing to have them define the sum of her. She's not as helpless as you would have her."

"And who are you to meddle? Marrying you does not automatically invite you into all matters of my life. You have been assigned two tasks. Provide an heir and protect my sister as I would." He raked her with a withering glare. "The latter you've proven yourself ill-equipped to accomplish."

She flinched and pulled back her shoulders, the blue fabric of her dress straining across her breasts, distracting him in a way he despised, evidence of his intolerable weakness for her. At a time like this, with the sting of her betrayal still fresh, he should look on her with utter apathy, his heart hard against her.

"Julianne is my friend, and although you may disagree, I have her best interest at heart."

He gestured to the salon where even now the sound of his sister's tears stabbed his ears. "You may wish to reevaluate the manner in which you treat your friends."

"I'm not the one responsible for her tears! You're the culprit on that score."

His eyes flicked downward, to the slight curve of her belly nearly undetectable beneath her gown. "You may carry my child, but do not mistake that you have the right to lecture me on matters involving my sister."

"Indeed." Scorn laced her voice. She gave a single, tight nod. "We're simply husband and wife. Nothing more."

Nothing more. They were becoming too damned much more. More than he had ever intended. More than he would acknowledge to her. More than he could acknowledge to himself. Shaking his head, he turned to leave. Her voice stopped him.

"Walk away," she goaded. "You're good at that. That and living in the past."

Tension knotting his neck and shoulders, he swung back around. "Explain that remark."

That slim nose of hers lifted, giving her the appearance of looking down on him. "If you permitted your sister to live her life, you might actually have to start living your own." Her furious gaze swept over him. "Instead of living in the past and pining for a woman who will never love anyone more than herself."

He grabbed her by the arms and gave her a small shake.

She still thought he loved Madeline? Did she know him so little? How could she think such a thing when all he thought about, all he craved, was her?

"I'm not pining after Madeline," he growled savagely. "You're the only woman . . ." He stopped himself just short of saying something truly regrettable. The sort of thing that gave a woman total control over a man.

"What?" she demanded.

Shaking his head, he released her and took a step back. Hands dropping limply to his sides, he stared at her, letting his silence speak for him.

"You don't love Madeline." She nodded as if only now realizing that fact, accepting it for the truth. "You don't know how. You're incapable of love."

"You're right, of course," he agreed, wondering at the dull ache her words caused. "I warned you of as much when I married you."

337

"Yes, you did." Her eyes took on a faraway look as she nodded again. "Although I didn't let that stop me from hoping. Foolish, I know." Her gaze snapped back to his, her eyes mysteriously moist. "But that's not good enough anymore. Not for me. I can't live like this."

"Like how?"

"In love with you," she confessed, her voice quick and desperate, harsh in the narrow corridor.

Seth stared.

She smiled mildly. An indulgent, mirthless smile that only added to his bewilderment.

Jane loved him? Panic and elation bubbled to life in his chest. He stomped down on the elation, cautioning himself to keep his head, to stay in control.

"Why do you think I became Aurora and followed you to Vauxhall? I wanted to be with you. Only you. *Always* you." Her smile slipped and her expression became one of infinite sadness. "I never stopped loving you. Not once all these years. But I see now you're not even remotely like the boy I once loved."

She dipped her head, her voice small and quiet, pulling at some forgotten part of himself that he refused to release. "I mourn him. That boy was not afraid to give his heart."

Afraid? He stiffened. Through hard lips, he reminded, "I told you when we married not to expect—"

"Yes, yes." She lifted her gaze, a smile that failed to reach her eyes curving her full lips. "I know. You were unfailingly honest with me." She drew a deep breath. "That's all very well. Only I can't live like this anymore. I thought I could. I thought . . ." Her voice faded and she sighed.

Rubbing her forehead, she looked suddenly tired. "I thought so many things. Mostly that *my* love could bring you around. But I was wrong. So wrong. Because not only can *you* not let yourself love—you forbid anyone around you to love either. Whether it's your sister . . . or me. I'm finished living my life at the whim of others, Seth."

"What are you saying, Jane?"

"I think I'm being fairly clear." Her gaze drilled into his steadily. "You can't love. And you won't let me love you." A small, tired laugh escaped her. "So what's the point of any of this?"

Before he could respond Rebecca arrived at his side, her words spilling forth in an agitated rush, "You need to attend to your sister, my lord. She is insisting on going after Mr. Knightly and wants me to help her pack."

Sighing, he nodded. Turning back to Jane, he said, "We'll finish this discussion when—"

"It's finished, Seth," she murmured, her words final in an oddly unsettling way. "Go. Do what you must."

She whirled around, her steps falling silent on the runner.

With that curious tightness constricting his chest, he watched her disappear inside her room, wondering why he felt as though something very important were disappearing from his life.

Something that he may never have a chance at again.

Chapter 27

"I don't know about this . . . don't know at all."

Jane gave Anna's hand a reassuring squeeze as she settled across from her in the carriage, a curious calm settling over her that made her exodus from Seth's life not nearly as difficult as she had feared. "It's for the best."

"Running away—"

"It's hardly that," Jane objected evenly. "Most *ton* marriages consist of the husband and wife living apart."

"But your husband—"

"Won't care," she finished, splaying a hand on the seat to steady her as the carriage lurched forward. She rather suspected Seth would be relieved to hear she had gone. His horrified expression when she had told him she loved him

341

had been all the incentive she needed to reach the decision.

"That man is not going to like you up and leaving like this. Pride alone will send him running after you."

"Perhaps," Jane allowed, resolve hardening her heart. "But pride won't keep me at his side." Only his love could do that. And love was the one thing he would never give her.

Jane had meant every word she'd said to Seth. She couldn't continue as she was. One day she would wake up and find her love for him gone, replaced with bitterness and resentment for a man incapable of loving her back. Leaving was her only option.

Anna sighed and shook her head in a way that told Jane she disagreed. "Where are we going, then?"

"To the cottage. Mr. and Mrs. Lowery will be happy to have us. We won't be in anyone's way there."

Most especially Seth's. He could go on ruining his sister's dreams for a life of love and happiness and live exactly as he pleased.

Without her. Without love.

"What do you mean she's gone?" Seth rose from his seat at the empty dining table. His sister had yet to emerge from her room, refusing to see or speak with him. Her absence at breakfast came as no surprise. Jane, however, he had hoped to find in her usual seat.

"She left yesterday, my lord."

"Why was I not informed?" he demanded, flinging his napkin on the table with unchecked violence.

The hapless butler darted a nervous look to a nearby footman. "We thought you knew, my lord."

That his wife had left him? No, he did not know. Apparently he was the last to know. His fists curled at his sides. Though he might have guessed. He knew when she walked away yesterday afternoon that something had changed.

"Where has she gone?"

"I'm not certain, my lord. Although I think I heard her mention the cottage to your sister."

"My sister knew she left?" It appeared he was in fact the last to know.

Nodding, he stalked from the dining room and up the stairs, determined to locate his errant wife and teach her that she could not run away from him simply because she disapproved of the way he handled matters with his sister. He would not stand for it. He wanted her back. In his bed. In his life. Regardless that she believed herself in love with him, they would go on as if she had never made that foolish declaration.

He stopped suddenly, one hand poised to knock on Julianne's door.

Dragging a hand over his face, he cursed. Haring off after Jane would show her precisely how much control she wielded over him. Too much. More than he had vowed to give any woman again.

Fine. Let her remain at the cottage. He would not go traipsing after her like some lovesick fool.

Suddenly the door opened. Julianne stood there, pale and expressionless.

"I thought I heard your footsteps." Leaving the door open, she turned and moved back inside her room.

Encouraged that she was at least speaking to him, he followed her into her room, watching as she took a seat on a chaise near the window.

"How are you feeling?" he asked.

She snorted, smiling humorlessly. "You expect me to tell you? When you discount my feelings as whims? When you bullied the man I want to marry out of my life?"

"That is not—"

"Save your denials. You're here about Jane, aren't you? Have you only just realized she left?"

"Yes," he admitted. "Did she speak with you before she left? Did she say she was going to the cottage?"

"Yes. She felt sorry for leaving me here. With you. But I told her you could do nothing more painful than you already have, and that she needed to do what was best for her."

"You make me sound like a monster."

"Do I?" She tilted her head thoughtfully. "You're no monster. Merely a man. Flawed, to be certain. It's a wonder Jane loves you."

His chest tightened at his sister's words. "She said that, did she?"

"She didn't have to. It's why she left, of course." She faced the window, staring out of it almost as if she could see. "I hope you'll leave her be."

"Of course I won't." He inhaled sharply. "She's my wife."

"But you don't love her. Or won't." Julianne shrugged. "Same difference. Why do you care if you live apart from her?"

He opened his mouth to explain, then shut it with a snap.

Why do you care if you live apart from her?

Why did he? Seth thought hard, trying to formulate a reason. One he could tolerate. And not the one pushing at his carefully erected barriers.

Julianne's smug voice interrupted his anxious musings. "I thought so."

"It's not right," he snapped, scowling. "A husband and wife should live beneath the same roof." Turning on his heel, he called over his shoulder. "I'm bringing her home."

"She won't come," Julianne retorted. "And who could blame her?"

She'll come, Seth vowed. He would not return without her. Resolve filled him. No matter what it took.

Jane pulled her shawl tighter about her shoulders at the sudden gust of wind that threatened to rip the warm chenille free. A glance to the heavens revealed dark skies rolling overhead. A storm was coming.

Turning, she headed back down the beach, intent on returning to the cottage. Her slippers sank into soft sand as she walked, disappointed that the coming storm had cut short her afternoon stroll.

The wind picked up, tearing strands of her hair free from its tidy coiffure and whipping the tendrils across her eyes. Scraping the loose hair back off her face, her vision narrowed on a figure emerging in the distance.

Her steps slowed as she watched the shape grow

and take shape into a man, dark cloak whipping about him in the wind.

"No," she whispered, a heaviness settling into her chest as his face came into focus.

Absurdly, she glanced left and right, as if she would take flight, as if there was somewhere to flee along the thin stretch of shore.

Deciding to hold her ground, she stopped, not taking another step as he advanced on her, the grim lines of his face becoming alarmingly visible.

At last, he was upon her. She noted her fingers had grown numb where they clutched her shawl around her.

Before she had any idea what she meant to say, she blurted, "Go away."

A muscle rippled along his jaw. One word escaped him, hard and biting. "Never."

"Why did you come? I don't want you here." She stared into his eyes, dark and unreadable in the graying light. "Please don't make this more difficult—"

"I'm afraid it's too late for that."

"Why? Why can't you let me be?" A desperate sob scalded the back of her throat. "Do you wish to punish me? To—"

"I *wish*," Seth began, stressing her own words, "to take my wife home. Where she belongs."

Jane shook her head, scooting back a step. Then another. The prospect of spending the rest of her days with him, living with his apathy and indifference as he took his pleasure in her body and left her with nothing in return, would slowly destroy her.

"No."

He followed, closing in like a stalking predator. "Yes."

"I don't belong with you," she insisted, continuing her retreat. Foolish, she supposed. But there was nothing rational about her need to flee. The very sight of him fed ambrosia to her starved heart, undermining her determination to be free.

"Stand still," he hissed, reaching for her.

"Why can't you let me go?" she pleaded, fingers loosening their hold on her shawl as she jerked her arm from his groping hand. The wind snatched hold of the blue chenille, carrying it away.

Stumbling, her foot caught on a bit of debris, and she went down in a graceless heap, a cloud of sand rising around her.

"Jane!" Seth dropped to his knees beside her. "Are you hurt?"

She shook her head, searching his face. "Why?" she whispered.

Eyes locking with hers, he grasped her by the arms, the strong feel of his hands deceptively reassuring. At the look in his eyes, her heart slowed and she felt as though she hovered along the edge of a great precipice.

Crouched over her, he warded off the worst of the wind but she could still not stop the chill that skated over her.

"You have me, Jane," he declared. Pausing, he moistened his lips. "I can't let you go because you're the reason I live. The reason I was born."

She dipped her head and dragged in a great lungful of air, his words too much, impossible to hear, impossible to believe.

Firm fingers forced her chin up. "I'm sorry I couldn't say it before. I've been a complete ass. About so many things."

"*What are you saying?*"

He brushed the loose hair back from her face. "If I can't have you with me, I'll cease to exist. Jane, it has always been you. You were my first friend, the only one who mattered. A part of me always knew it. I was mad to ever think I loved your sister. Even then, when I was too young and foolish to know any better, it was you. *I love you.*"

I love you.

"I was selfish," she confessed. "I should have spoken out the day my father tossed you out, but I didn't want you to marry Madeline."

He cupped her cheek, catching the trail of a wet tear with his thumb. "Thank you, Jane. Thank you for saving me for you."

She flung her arms around him then, burying her face in the warm wall of his chest. "I never stopped loving you."

His chest swelled on a breath beneath her cheek. "It will be you until the day I die."

"I never thought to hear such words from you."

His arms tightened around her. "Prepare yourself to hear them every day for the rest of your life."

Epilogue

Jane lifted her face to the breeze's cooling caress, basking in the kiss of spring on her skin.

"Momma, come on," her daughter urged, tugging insistently on her hand as they strolled between two perfectly symmetrical rows of apple trees. Ahead lay a blanket with several baskets. A veritable feast covered the cloth, leaving little room to sit. Evidently Seth had already unpacked their lunch. Her gaze roamed the waving grasses, searching for her husband as she readjusted their young son on her hip. A year old, James wiggled to be put down.

"Auntie Julianne, Uncle Gregory, hurry up!" Olivia called back to the remainder of their party.

Jane tightened her hold on her squirming son and reminded her daughter, "Your aunt cannot move quickly these days, Olivia." Jane glanced over her shoulder to smile at her sister-in-law, waddling to keep up. Even with her husband's arm supporting her, Julianne looked winded, one hand supporting the bulge of her belly as she walked.

Turning back around, Jane gasped when a cloud of apple blossoms showered her.

"It's raining flowers, Momma!" Olivia squealed, trying to catch the delicate white blossoms in tiny fists, her small features screwed tight with determination.

Jane looked up, knowing as she did whom she would find. Perched high in the branches, Seth grinned down at her as he shook a branch. The cheerful expression on his face—similar to the way he had looked as a boy, when she had first lost her heart to him—stole her breath.

"Come down from there before you break your neck," she admonished.

Deft as a monkey, he lowered himself to the lowest branch, dropping down to earth with a resounding thud. Olivia clapped her hands and pounced into Seth's arms with wild glee, nearly knocking him off his feet.

Seth hugged his daughter, eyes warm and tender on Jane as he sketched a bow. Stepping forward, he tucked a sprig of apple blossoms in her hair.

Her heart caught in her throat and she blinked

past the burn of tears in her eyes. The simple gesture, the look in his eyes . . . reminded her of a time long ago. Only today the love in his eyes was for her. And the blossoms twirling through the air no longer echoed bitter memories.

Seth nodded to the spread of food before them and lowered Olivia to the blanket. "Hungry?" he asked.

Jane nodded and deposited James beside his sister, smiling when the little boy plunged a finger into one of the custard pies.

Facing Seth again, she allowed him to pull her into his embrace. "Famished," she murmured, smiling coyly as his eyes darkened, the centers glowing with a familiar fire.

"Then I better feed you."

Apple blossoms swirled around them, fragrant on the air, wild as moths in the wind as he lowered his head to kiss her.

Closing her eyes, she let the wonder of the moment rush over her . . . the reality far better than any fantasy her heart had ever dreamed.

Next month, don't miss these exciting new love stories only from **Avon Books**

The Perils of Pleasure by Julie Anne Long

An Avon Romantic Treasure

When Madeleine Greenway saved Colin Eversea's life, she never imagined it might lead to her own death. Racing against time to uncover secrets hidden for years, Colin and Madeleine must confront a danger they never imagined—and a love they always hoped could be.

The Undead Next Door by Kerrelyn Sparks

An Avon Contemporary Romance

Jean-Luc must go into hiding, and where better than a small town? Getting to know the lovely Heather Westfield will certainly make the time fly, but when an old enemy resurfaces, they must risk everything to give this once-in-a-lifetime love a chance.

The Governess Wears Scarlet by Sari Robins

An Avon Romance

The Viscount Steele must hire a governess to protect his nephews as he struggles to uncover a dangerous plot. But when the secrets that he and the governess unexpectedly share come to light, will their passion survive?

The Night Before the Wedding by Debra Mullins

An Avon Romance

Gabriel MacBraedon is his clan's only hope—he must marry or fall to an ancient curse. Gabriel masquerades as a man of wealth to convince the lovely Catherine that he could make her a worthy husband. But will he be able to win her heart before she discovers the truth?

REL 0108